Exactly Where You Need to Be

Also by Amelia Diane Coombs

Between You, Me, and the Honeybees

Keep My Heart in San Francisco

Exactly Where You Need to Be

AMELIA DIANE COOMBS

SIMON & SCHUSTER BFYR
NEW YORK LONDON TORONTO SYDNEY NEW DELHI

An imprint of Simon & Schuster Children's Publishing Division
1230 Avenue of the Americas, New York, New York 10020
This book is a work of fiction. Any references to historical events, real people, or real places are used fictitiously. Other names, characters, places, and events are products of the author's imagination, and any resemblance to actual events or places or persons, living or dead, is entirely coincidental.

Interior design by Hilary Zarycky
The text for this book was set in New Baskerville.
Manufactured in the United States of America
First Edition
2 4 6 8 10 9 7 5 3 1
CIP data for this book is available from the Library of Congress.
ISBN 9781534493544
ISBN 9781534493568 (ebook)

For the murderinos,
the girls who were told they're too much,
and the girls who never felt like they were enough.
This one's for you.

Let's use our powers of anxiety for good and not evil.

—Georgia Hardstark

Get a job. Buy your own shit. Stay out of the forest.

—Karen Kilgariff

ONE

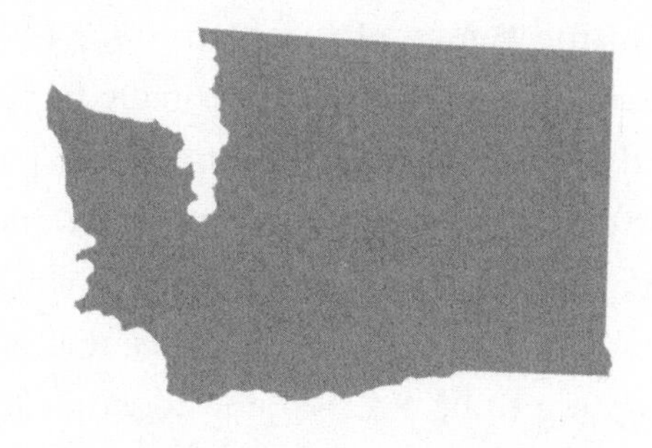

Barmouth, WA

WEDNESDAY, AUGUST 3

Everyone needs a "bury a dead body in the woods" best friend. I mean, it's the highest level of friendship possible. Someone you can trust, without question, to cover your ass when life goes sideways.

For me, that person is Kacey Hodge. Loyal to her core, my exact opposite in almost every way. If I ever had to bury a dead body in the woods? Kacey would be right beside me, shovel in hand, wiping sweat off her brow. She's my ride or die. However, I'd rather bury a dead body than help Kacey clean out her bedroom, which is how I'm spending my afternoon. Because I've never met someone who owns more clothing and random shit than my best friend.

"I can't believe my mom is making me do this," Kacey mutters from the depths of her closet, where she's pulling out her lesser worn items and tossing them into the cardboard box in the center of her bedroom. "I swear, Florie, she's using college as an excuse to finally purge my room. She's wanted this for *years*. It's so unnecessary."

I'd argue that it's very, very necessary. Rosemary also said that if Kacey doesn't clean her room, she can't go on the Hodges' family vacation next week. Since that trip is the last remotely exciting thing we're doing together before Kacey leaves for college, this cleaning spree isn't optional.

I hold up a Russian nesting doll from her knickknack shelf. "Really? Because there's literally no reason for you to bring a Russian nesting doll to college. None. Whatsoever."

"It's *vintage*," Kacey says, but, after a hesitation, nods. I place the doll into the box. "Hey, can you turn the speaker up?"

I grab the Bluetooth speaker, shaped like a retro radio, off Kacey's dresser and nudge the volume button on the side. We're listening to our favorite podcast hosts, Eleanor and Trish, cover the murder of Joan Dawley.

"The guy, this asshole," Trish is saying through the speaker, "hired two felons to kill his wife—"

"What a dick," Eleanor responds dryly, like she's not the least bit surprised.

Trish snorts. "You want to hear the worst part? The plan fell through—one of the hired men was arrested for parole violations—but *someone* still bludgeoned the wife to death."

Episodes drop every Wednesday, so Kacey and I get

together at her house for our weekly dose of Eleanor and Trish. *Murder Me Later* is more than a podcast to me—it's held a special place in my anxious heart for the last two years. Because their podcast is about murder, sure, but it's also about mental health and listening to your gut—one thing I'm often ashamed of, and the other I almost always ignore. Plus, it's the whole reason Kacey and I are even friends.

Even if they hadn't brought me together with my best friend, I'd still be a huge fan.

Maybe it's weird, but I love true crime. Learning about all the worst-case scenarios, the survival stories, the tragedies, is almost calming. Probably because my obsessive-compulsive disorder feeds off all the unknown bad in the world. For me, the monster you know is always better than the one you don't.

I've composed emails to Eleanor and Trish, trying to tell them how much their podcast means to me, but I never hit send. That fear, that doubt, always creeps up. I'll check the time and realize I've spent two hours writing one paragraph. I have dozens and dozens of emails I'll never send gathering electronic dust in my drafts folder.

I'm a coward—even on the internet.

"Okay," Kacey announces fifteen minutes later. She's surveying the pile of clothes and random crap inside the cardboard box. Her thick, dark brown curls escape wildly from a sloppy bun, and her brown eyes are scrutinizing. "Do you think my mom will notice if I don't go through my shoes?"

"Definitely." I join Kacey on the floor by her bed, beneath which she's stored dozens of shoeboxes. Even though I love a good cleaning session, the whole afternoon has left me feeling off balance. Messes are a part of who Kacey is, and this is another reminder that she won't be around for much longer.

When the podcast ends (the husband did it, but his mistress helped), Kacey groans and stretches out on her back. Despite the constant mess, I love Kacey's bedroom. The hexagonal green wallpaper, the four-poster bed and gauzy canopy. The small window overlooking the backyard. There's just something so *joyful* about her room. I stretch my legs out and lie down between the many piles of clothes.

"Do you have to be home for family dinner?" she asks, bundling a cable-knit sweater beneath her head like a pillow.

I stare at the vaulted ceiling. "Yep. My dad got home from Seattle a few hours ago."

"But you're still coming over tomorrow night for the livestream?" She tosses a pair of socks into the air and catches them.

"Wouldn't miss it." Eleanor and Trish are hosting their very first live Q&A tomorrow. I smack the socks out of the air when she throws them again, and they land on her dresser. "Seven, right?"

"Seven," Kacey confirms, then stretches her arms overhead with a sigh. After a moment, she says, "How have we done *nothing* this summer?"

"We've done . . . stuff," I say defensively, but she's right. All we've done the last two months is binge all fourteen seasons of the original *Unsolved Mysteries*, learn how to read tarot, and get sunburns at the lake on weekends.

Now summer's almost over. Soon Kacey's trading small-town life for Portland and college. And I'm staying in Barmouth,

whether I want to or not. Turns out, when you have a mental health disorder, what you want doesn't matter anymore. No, what matters is what everyone else—parents, therapists, counselors—thinks you're ready for.

When the guidance counselor, provided by my homeschooling program, chatted with my mom at the start of senior year, he suggested I take a gap year. Put college on hold until things—aka my OCD—were more settled and under control. Mom agreed with him, and last year, I agreed too. But it's hard to feel good about that decision when I'm helping my best friend pack her life away so she can leave me behind.

Kacey shifts onto her side, her hands folded beneath her cheek. "We're pathetic. This summer was totally unmemorable."

"Hey, it's not over yet. We still have the beach house next week," I point out, though I know the Hodges' annual family beach trip isn't what Kacey had in mind.

"I'm still pissed that Sam stayed in Idaho," she says with a pout.

"Um. Same," I say, even though I'm actually relieved that Sam, Kacey's older brother, decided to stay at his vocational school for the summer, where he's studying carpentry.

Before I found out that Sam had decided to stay in Idaho for a summer workshop, I spent weeks panicking over his return to Barmouth. Like, I gave myself actual stomachaches thinking about it. Worrying over what to do when I came face-to-face with him for the first time in eight months. Turns out, all that worrying was for nothing, and to say I'm relieved that Sam's in another state is the understatement of the century.

If only his lack of physical presence could erase him from my brain.

I shove aside all Sam-related thoughts and stare across the floor at my best friend. "You sure you have to go to college?" I joke. "What does Portland have that Barmouth doesn't, anyway?"

Kacey rolls her eyes. "Everything."

"That's rude."

"Everything but my best friend," she says with a small smile.

I try to smile back, but it's hard. Because what will happen when Kacey's in Portland? Our friendship might be solid, but it's still new. What if we grow apart? What if she finds way cooler, city friends to hang out with? I'm not saying the thought keeps me up at night, but . . .

My phone dings in my sundress pocket.

MOM: Dinner's at six. Do you need me to pick you up?

ME: Nope! See you in a bit

"I gotta head home." I stand up, trying not to cringe at how much messier we made Kacey's bedroom. But we successfully cleared out her closet, bookshelf, and shoes. Goodwill is going to be *very* pleased. Or horrified.

Kacey sits up. "Wanna sleep over after the livestream tomorrow?"

I step gingerly around the piles and grab my purse off her bed. "Yeah, for sure."

"Wait, don't forget the pictures." Kacey points to an envelope partially hidden beneath a jean jacket on her bed. She came across a stash of photos Rosemary printed out for her graduation party in June and wanted me to have the extras.

"Thanks." I stuff the envelope into my purse. "I'll see you later."

Kacey gives me a mock salute. "Bye, babe."

I wave before shutting her bedroom door behind me, and I head downstairs.

The walk from the Hodges' to my house takes ten minutes, tops. Handy, considering I don't drive. Our small town of Barmouth, Washington, is about an hour northeast of Seattle and two hours south of the Canadian border. To put it simply: the middle of nowhere. As a tourist town, Barmouth is usually pretty busy during summer and winter, but there's jack shit to do here if you're a local.

The upside to small towns, though, is most things are within walking or biking distance, and it's been great being able to walk to Kacey's whenever I feel like it. The Hodges are always welcoming; I even know where their Hide-A-Key is.

Kacey and I didn't become friends until the start of junior year, during those brief months before Mom decided homeschooling was the Answer. Junior year was a shit show. Back-to-back obsessions and panic attacks in bathroom stalls between classes. But at least one good thing came of it: befriending Kacey Hodge.

I was packing up after homeroom on the second day of school when I hit play on an old episode of *Murder Me Later*—and loudly broadcast Trish explaining how Lizzie Borden axed-up her dad. (Did you know Lizzie Borden was acquitted? Yeah, me neither.) My earbuds weren't plugged in like I thought, and everyone turned to stare at me. Mortifying.

That is, until a girl with wild curls and a mischievous smile walked over to me and said, "I *love* Eleanor and Trish. Did you listen to this week's episode yet?"

While I've had friends—casual friends, people to hang out with at school—I never had a best friend before Kacey Hodge. I never knew friends like Kacey existed. People who love you fiercely, who understand you, and stick by your side. Even though I was homeschooled for the second half of junior year and all of senior year due to my OCD, I still saw Kacey every day. The fact that she's leaving so soon feels like another one of the universe's cruel jokes.

I have no idea what our friendship will look like when she no longer lives down the street, just a ten-minute walk away.

Three weeks. I have Kacey for three more weeks, and I need to make every single moment count.

When things were really bad with my mental health, the only place I felt comfortable was my house. Not surprising because I was struggling with mild agoraphobia at the time, but it's always familiar, always comforting, and above all else: always the *same.* Tidy rooms, carpets with vacuum lines indented into the fibers, and vanilla-scented candles. A soundtrack of jazz humming in the background. Schedules, routines, and color-coded calendars.

Kacey thinks it's weird as hell, but I don't mind it.

For a few months after winter break, I went to this OCD group therapy Lauren, my therapist, runs. So many of those kids had parents who'd dismissed their diagnosis or outright didn't care. My mom doesn't work, and she devotes a lot of her free time to me. She cooks all my meals, picks up medications, and always prints out new articles she's found about exercise methods and breathing techniques for stress reduction. And even though my dad's only home a few times a month—he quit his local accounting gig when I was in elementary school and works at a tech startup in Seattle—he cares too.

Maybe my parents are a *little* much. But it's better than having parents who don't care.

After dumping my keys and shoes in my bedroom, I wander back downstairs to the dining room. Papers are strewn across the table, covering the lace-edged place mats, and Dad's laptop is open, the screen pulled up to some spreadsheets.

He looks up as I enter, and a wide smile breaks across his face. "There's my girl!" I lean down and loop my arms around his neck as he hugs me. "Did you just get back from Kacey's?"

I step out of the hug and claim the dining chair beside him. "Yup."

Mom bustles out of the kitchen and sets a big bowl of butternut squash pasta in the center of the table, and a smaller salad bowl beside it. "Hey, honey," she says, and sits across from me.

"So." Dad slides all the loose papers and his laptop into his briefcase before serving himself some pasta. "How's Kacey doing? She must be nervous about college, huh?"

I spear a ravioli with my fork and pop it into my mouth. "More excited than nervous, I think."

Last year, the thought of starting college made me want to curl up in a constant anxiety ball on my bedroom floor. That's why I agreed with my mom and the counselor about putting college on hold—until my mental health got better. But when I least expected it, I started to feel that itch for change. For something more and different and all my own.

And that itch keeps cropping up more and more lately.

"Maybe I should start looking at some schools," I say. "You know, for when I apply."

Dad's brow raises slightly, and he glances across the table at Mom. "That sounds—"

"You'll have plenty of time to research colleges later," Mom interrupts, sipping her seltzer. "One thing at a time, okay?"

I pop more raviolis in my mouth so I don't have to answer right away. Swallowing, I say, "You're right," and flash Mom a tight smile. "One thing at a time."

Except, I don't know what's next. What that next *thing* would be, if not college.

I barely touch the rest of my pasta, my stomach sour. Instead, I smush my food around with my fork and wonder what Dad was going to say. Did he think it was a good idea? But for the rest of dinner, we don't approach the topic of college or Kacey again.

As much as I love my parents, sometimes I wish I had parents like Kacey's. Every time Kacey has wanted to do or try something new or scary, Rosemary has never, ever doubted her. When Kacey decided to pursue 3D sculpture at the Pacific Northwest College of Art, Rosemary and Alec beamed with pride. Even when Sam decided to forgo the traditional route and went to vocational school, they were nothing short of supportive.

And sometimes I want that. The support and warmth and hugs and late-night cups of hot cocoa. Parents who believe their kids can do anything—be anything—and never doubt their dreams.

"Are you feeling okay?" Mom asks after dinner as I help carry the dirty dishes into the kitchen.

I set the plates in the sink. "Yeah, just . . . thinking about Kacey leaving."

Mom's expression softens as she slides on her pink kitchen gloves and fills the sink with hot, soapy water. Even though my mom isn't Kacey's biggest fan—she thinks she's too "wild"—she understands how much she means to me. "You still have the beach house next week. And maybe in the fall or winter, we can take the train into Portland. Do some shopping and visit her?"

I glance from the dinner plate in my hand to my mom. "Really?" My mom and I aren't close like Rosemary and Kacey, but when I was younger, we spent a lot of time together. Probably because I relied on her for, well, everything. But we've spent less and less time together since I befriended Kacey. Hopefully my mom's happy about that, but sometimes it makes me feel guilty.

"Sure! It'll be fun." Mom smiles, and all those fatigue lines on her face ease. She should smile more often—and I don't want to think why she doesn't. Part of me worries it's because of me and my constant battle with my brain chemistry.

I turn my attention back to the dirty dishes. "It's a date."

After the dishes are clean, I retreat to my bedroom. My room is small and tidy, the opposite of Kacey's. The walls are painted an ugly yellow that Mom promised we'd paint over when I brought it up a few years ago—but we never did. There are shoes lined up against one baseboard, stacks of books, and some custom true crime Funko Pop collectibles Kacey gave me for my eighteenth birthday in May. Nothing special, but it's my safe haven.

I swap my sundress for pajamas and a baggy sweater—it's still early, but I'm not going out again—and sit on my bed. I grab the envelope of photos Kacey gave me from my purse and slide them out. Leaning against my headboard, I flip through the thick stack. Even if Kacey and I have only been friends for two years, it's been the most important and defining relationship in my life. And the most photographed. There are dozens upon dozens of them.

We're not alone in all the pictures, though. Some feature our friends from school.

And a lot feature Sam.

Sam at the lake, captured mid-push as he topples Kacey off the dock and into the water. Sam in the Hodges' backyard by his workbench wearing safety goggles and a huge smile while Kacey and I pretend to fight in the background holding two-by-fours like swords. Sam on the Cherry Creek Falls trail last summer with Kacey and their parents straggling behind. Sam, Kacey, and me—plus our dates—at prom last year.

The photos chronicle my friendship with Kacey, but they

also chronicle my crush on Sam. Ever since our instant connection in homeroom, Kacey's considered me like a sister. But Sam's never been like a brother to me. Not even close. It would've been way easier if he had.

Sam was always way out of my league, but he was also off limits as Kacey's brother. Not like it mattered. Sam never expressed any interest in me and used his fruit-fly attention span to date his way through the female population of Barmouth High. But then the holiday party happened last December, and I thought, maybe, Sam realized I wasn't just his little sister's best friend. But now I know better. I made an epic mess that night, and if I never have to see Samson Hodge again, it'll be too soon.

After gathering up all the Sam photos, I walk over to my desk. The trash can is *right there*, tucked beside my chair, but I shove the photos into the very back of my junk drawer instead and slam it shut.

Maybe, if I'm being really honest with myself, I was sad when I found out Sam was staying in Idaho all summer. But it's what I need. My feelings for Samson Hodge have become ingrained in me, like a bad habit. One I'm finally on my way to quitting. Because of Kacey. Because of me. Because I don't get the guy or the happy ending.

I don't even get a love story.

At bedtime, I try to stop the cycle. Like I do every night.

After checking that the front door is locked, I climb into bed, beneath my comforter and weighted blanket. I force my eyes shut, even though my mind is spiraling. I know the door is locked. I jiggled the handle; I checked the latch. But . . . what if it's not?

What if I'm wrong? What if it's not locked and I fall asleep, and someone sneaks in and stabs me? Or my parents? What if something too terrible to even fathom happens, and it's all my fault? The panic grips, tightening my chest while heat burns between my shoulder blades.

Tears pushing at my eyelids, I throw the blankets off my body and, careful not to wake my parents, sneak into the front hall. Stare at the front door. Visually, I can see that it's locked, the dead bolt thrown. That should be enough. But who am I kidding? It never is.

I twist and pull on the knob nine times. Something about three sets of three makes sense, but there's no logic behind it. Nothing about OCD is logical, and after the ninth tug, a wash of calm rolls over me. *Relief.*

I'm too tired to feel ashamed of caving yet again, so I crawl back into bed and finally fall asleep.

TWO

Barmouth, WA

THURSDAY, AUGUST 4, EVENING

The Hodges technically live in a separate neighborhood—Kacey lives on Maple, and I'm on Spruce—but our streets are nearly identical. Both houses are 1950s two-story Craftsman, bordered by the same state-protected forest that wraps around the edges of Barmouth. Our house is painted in shades of blue; hers is white with red trim.

But the similarities end there. For example, the Hodges' front porch is littered with discarded shoes and a pile of broken-down cardboard ready for next week's recycling pickup. My mom won't even let us put our bins out the night before; she wakes up at five and rolls them out every Tuesday morning.

I sidestep the mess and let myself inside.

As I shut the front door behind me, Rosemary bustles down the hallway leading to their garage. She's dressed for work, in light-blue scrubs and white sneakers. She and Alec must be heading out for a shift. Her face lights up when she sees me. "Hey, sweet girl! Kacey's upstairs."

"Thanks," I say, but rather than rush upstairs, I linger beside Rosemary.

If my mom had a polar opposite, it'd be Rosemary Hodge. My mom is all straight, rigid lines, and Rosemary is soft curves. She's petite, while my mom is nearly six foot. And sometimes I feel really, really guilty for wishing Rosemary were my own mom. But you can't *not* like her. Rosemary's this magical combination of a badass who takes no shit and is also a walking hug, which makes sense considering she's an ER nurse.

"Excited for the beach house?" Rosemary sets her insulated lunch bag on the sideboard to tug a sweater on over her scrubs.

I lean against the banister. "Counting down the days."

"I won't lie—I'm disappointed Sam's skipping the trip this year," she says, braiding the curls Kacey inherited. "I wish we could have the whole family together, you know? One last hurrah before Kacey leaves for college."

I dig my thumbnail into the banister, feeling gross for celebrating Sam's absence while his family misses him. "Right, yeah."

"We'll still have fun," Rosemary promises, and hugs me before scooping up her lunch bag. "I gotta run; Alec's waiting in the car. I'll see you in the morning!"

Upstairs, I find Kacey in their gaming room. The loftlike room is funky with floral wallpaper, squishy furniture, gaming consoles, and a foosball table. Kacey's sprawled out on the couch, dressed in black denim overalls, and her hair is tamed into two buns on top of her head. She hits the mute button on the TV, and whatever reality show she was watching goes silent. "There you are! The livestream starts in five minutes."

"Sorry." I let my duffel bag slide off my shoulder and land with a thunk on the carpet. "Dinner took forever." Mom kept bringing out more dishes, as if she could stretch our last family dinner for the next week into an all-night event.

"You're forgiven if you brought dessert." She pats the square of couch beside her.

I grab the box of cookies from my purse and toss them her way. Rosemary and Alec are vegans and raised their children to view animals as friends, not food. But it didn't work, and Kacey jumps on any opportunity to eat "real food," which is her term for anything non-vegan.

While Kacey breaks into the box of cookies, I load the *Murder Me Later* livestream on the TV. Viewers tweet or email in questions, and Eleanor and Trish will answer in real time. Part of me wants to send in a question, but who am I kidding? I don't have the lady balls or social skills.

I grab a cookie from the sleeve and recline against the cushions. After a moment, the *MML LIVESTREAM Q&A* loading screen is replaced by Eleanor and Trish.

"Welcome to our very first live Q and A," Eleanor says, and Trish cheers, waving at the camera. They sit in a pair of fancy armchairs with a small side table between them, which is full of fan-made mementos. A fan-drawn print of a live show hangs on the wall behind them, depicting Eleanor and Trish holding court onstage.

Eleanor is Filipino with long, sleek black hair that she often wears loose down her back. Trish almost always has her blond hair in vintage-styled pin curls and is originally from Austin—she has the Texan twang to prove it. They're both almost painfully beautiful, former struggling actresses turned podcast sensations and mental health advocates. Eleanor talks openly about her eating-disorder recovery and depression, and Trish never shies away from conversations about her bipolar diagnosis.

"We're so excited for this," Trish says, grinning wide.

Eleanor holds up an iPad and slides on her cat-eye reading glasses. "Okay, let's dive right in. . . ."

Kacey nudges me excitedly with her elbow, and I nudge her right back. As we watch, we work our way through the cookies.

"Okay, our last question comes from Ashlee in Oklahoma," Eleanor says on the screen. "'When's your next tour? Not everyone can make it out to California!'" Eleanor laughs.

Trish shrugs in apology, both hands up in the air. "Hopefully this winter, but don't worry, we'll update our website with all the specifics!"

"As a reminder, we'll be in my hometown of San Francisco on Friday the twelfth for the last show of our summer tour," Eleanor says, sliding her glasses off and setting them on the side table. "As of this morning, tickets are sold out—which is amazing. But our sister podcast, *Cold Cases, Cold Bitches*, is giving away two VIP tickets! Check out their latest episode to get the deets."

"Thanks for tuning in," Eleanor says. "Murder me later . . ."

". . . because I have shit to do!" Trish giggles after delivering the last line of their slogan, and they both wave before the livestream ends.

Kacey turns and grabs my arm. "I just had a genius idea! You know what would make this summer memorable?" she asks, not bothering to wait for my reply. "Meeting Eleanor and Trish."

"Sure, but the show's in San Francisco." I laugh, shaking off her surprisingly strong grip. There's no doubt meeting Eleanor and Trish would be amazing—the thought alone makes me buzzy and excited-anxious—but there's also no way it's happening. "Not to mention, my mom would never let me go. We don't even have a car."

"So what?" Kacey shrugs. "Let's enter! I doubt we'll win, but they're free tickets, Flor. Free VIP *meet-and-greet* tickets. This is literally the definition of having nothing to lose."

I'm quiet for a moment, because, well . . . she's not wrong. And meeting Eleanor and Trish would make this painfully forgettable summer unforgettable. This winter—or whenever Eleanor and Trish tour next—might be too late. Because everything's going to be different once Kacey leaves for Portland. Kacey will change, and I will, of course, stay exactly the same. Who knows if Kacey would even care about *MML* once she widens her horizons in college, or if I'd be the friend she'd want to go with.

We might never have a chance like this again.

I search for *Cold Cases, Cold Bitches* on my phone and play their most recent episode, jumping ahead by thirty seconds until they mention *MML*.

"Fellow cold bitches, do you want to see Trish and Eleanor of *Murder Me Later* fame in San Francisco next Friday? I'm giving away two VIP tickets, and all you have to do is tweet me your favorite episode of *MML*! The winner will be chosen this Saturday, at seven p.m. Pacific!"

The room goes silent as I hit pause. Kacey lifts her brows, and I nod. She hops off the couch and hurries down the hall to her bedroom. A moment later, she returns with her laptop and sets it on the coffee table.

"I doubt we'll win," I say, because I've always been the more realistic and level-headed one in this friendship, but . . . what *if* we won?

"Probably not," she says, logging into her Twitter account, "but this is fun, right?"

"Definitely," I say, because Kacey's energy is infectious. "Can you imagine if we won?"

Kacey falls back dramatically on the couch, one hand to her forehead as if she's fainted. "I'd die."

Laughing, I nudge her. "Appropriate for a murder podcast."

Kacey giggles and sits up, pulling the laptop closer.

A huge part of me wants to reel in my hope before I get carried away. Because when I've gotten my hopes up in the past, I've failed spectacularly. My new life philosophy is, if you never hope, then you're never disappointed.

But, maybe this once, I *want* to get my hopes up.

Like Kacey said, I have nothing to lose.

"Okay." Kacey hands me her laptop. "I sent in a tweet about episode 103."

"Mary Vincent case?" Fifteen-year-old Mary Vincent survived her attacker—who raped her, cut off her arms, and left her to die—when she followed the highway, completely naked, her arms packed with mud to stanch the bleeding, until a couple picked her up and rushed her to a hospital. She's a badass, present tense.

"Of course. She's a badass," Kacey says, and I smile. She taps her laptop lid. "But you should tweet your favorite too. Two entries are better than one, right?"

"Right." I log into my neglected Twitter account and compose a tweet to the *Cold Cases* host. Episode 97, the Golden State Killer case, is my favorite. Joseph James DeAngelo was formally charged with thirteen counts of murder and burglary, *forty years* after his rape-and-murder spree across the entire length of California. I love that DeAngelo thought he'd gotten away with his crimes, only to be brought to justice. To live out the rest of his pathetic years in prison, while his victims and their families finally got closure.

My cursor hovers over the tweet button.

Except this time, I don't chicken out.

THREE

Barmouth, WA

FRIDAY, AUGUST 5

I wake up in Kacey's bed, tangled up in her pile of mismatched blankets. Rare Pacific Northwest sunlight slants between the gap in the blinds, and Kacey's snores wheeze from the other side of the queen-sized mattress. I stretch out and roll onto my back, staring at the ceiling.

If I had to guess, I slept *maybe* five hours last night. No matter how tired I am, how exhausted, I rarely get a full night's sleep. Rather, I toss and turn due to insomnia and restless legs and an even more restless mind. But sometimes I sleep better at Kacey's, the weight of her body beside mine calming and familiar.

I swing my legs over the side of the bed and scoop my

hair back into a bun. Rosemary and Alec are still working, and Kacey's currently dead to the world—she's never experienced insomnia in her life—so I'm the only one awake. I grab a sweatshirt from my bag and tug it on over my tank top before heading downstairs.

The kitchen, with its white-and-gray striped wallpaper, is bright with morning light, and I move within it as comfortably as in the kitchen at home. I prepare a pot of coffee, and as it brews, I lean my back against the counter and stare out the picture windows overlooking the damp front lawn.

Despite my lack of a full night's rest, my brain wakes up quickly. Like it's afraid of being offline for too long. I'm already thinking about the contest and tomorrow night's announcement. That itchy, fervent hope of wanting to win *something* is a lot. It's an almost dizzying need to save this boring, forgettable summer before it's over.

The odds of us winning are slim (or slim to none), but now that we've entered, I can't quite squash the hope. And I'm kind of okay with that. After all, it's harmless, right? But the tickets feel like a last chance for me. Maybe it's because I've been focused on Kacey leaving for college, or because this summer feels like an end, but I can't stop thinking about how small my life is—and how it won't be changing anytime soon. How *I* won't be changing anytime soon.

The coffee maker beeps, and I shove all the heavy stuff deep down. I fill up two big mugs—creamer in mine, none in Kacey's—planning to head back to Kacey's room, but footsteps pound downstairs before I'm done stirring in my creamer.

My best friend rounds the corner from the hallway, her socked feet sliding on the tile. Her wild curls are tangled from sleep and she's still in her pajamas, but her eyes are wide and awake. "Guess what?"

I narrow my gaze skeptically. Normally, I have to waft a mug of coffee beneath Kacey's nose to rouse her from sleep. But before I open my mouth and ask if she was body-swapped with a morning person, Samson Hodge walks around the corner and into the kitchen.

"Hey, Florie." Sam leans against the counter, his hands in the pockets of his jeans. He's no doubt taking in my sleep-crusted eyes, my yellow tie-dyed ANXIOUS STRESSED TRUE-CRIME OBSESSED sweatshirt, and my blond hair slipping from its bun down the side of my head. A tentative smile plays on his lips.

Don't look at his lips, don't look at his lips, do NOT look at his lips, I remind myself, struggling to find something safe to look at. Because everything about Sam is, well . . . let's just say it's hard not to notice everything about the boy standing in front of me. Sam's shoulders are wide beneath his hoodie, and I forgot how absurdly tall he is, how I barely reach his shoulder. He cut his hair—shorter on the sides with a flop of wavy curls hanging against his forehead—and wears glasses with thick frames.

No one should be this attractive before ten in the morning. This is plain unfair.

"Sam's home," Kacey announces, and grabs her mug.

Over the last eight months, I've had actual dreams about the moment I'd see Sam again. And in exactly none of those dreams was I wearing my weirdest sweatshirt and no makeup, and had coffee-tainted morning breath. Now that the shock is wearing off, reality is quickly replacing it.

I'm stuck between panic (Sam!) and attraction (Sam!) and am momentarily unable to form words. Unfortunately, when the power of speech returns, I blurt out, "Aren't you supposed to be in Idaho?"

Sam quirks an eyebrow. "Thought I'd surprise everyone." He walks around the kitchen table and chooses a Snoopy mug from the drying rack. "I got in late last night." His back is to me so I can't read his face, which is somehow both relieving and frustrating, a combination of emotions I didn't know was possible.

"Huh." I glance at Kacey to see if she's picking up on the super-weird vibes practically blasting off me. But she's drinking her coffee, yawning into the mug between sips, and checking her phone's notifications.

Gripping my mug with white knuckles, I shift to the other side of the kitchen.

"Mom's going to be so excited. She was seriously bummed about you missing the beach house." Kacey puts her phone away and perches on the kitchen table, her legs swinging over the edge. "What happened to your workshop?"

Sam turns around and smiles. It's a good smile, and I hate just how good it is. "Ended early. My teacher punctured his hand with a nail gun."

They continue talking about the beach house trip and freak carpentry injuries, but I'm no longer listening. Because I can't separate looking at Sam and thinking about what happened in December. That moment when his mouth was on mine, my fingers were knotted in his hair, and I made a huge, irreversible (albeit enjoyable) mistake.

I regret the kiss. But I regret not telling Kacey about it even more.

As I finish the cup of coffee that I've anxiety-chugged, I realize that the worst part is Sam's absolutely fine. He doesn't care that this is the first time we've seen each other since that night. Nope, he's all smiles and small talk as I slowly and messily unravel.

Sam's fine—but the longer I stand in the kitchen, the clearer it becomes that I'm not.

FOUR

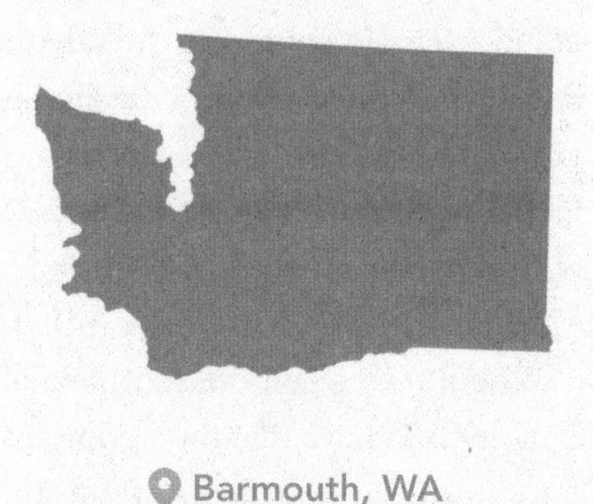

Barmouth, WA

SATURDAY, AUGUST 6, EARLY EVENING

Never before have I felt this much dread walking to my best friend's house. It feels plain wrong to walk *toward* the one person I've been trying to avoid—physically, mentally, and, let's be real, emotionally—for eight months.

Yesterday, Kacey was too busy catching up with Sam and didn't question me when I left immediately after breakfast. Normally I'd stay until dinner, but I had zero desire to hang around Samson Hodge while having an emotional meltdown. At least my spiral has shifted from panicky hurt into rage over the last twenty-four hours.

Because why did Sam have to come home right now?

When all I have left with Kacey is three weeks? We're supposed to spend every last second together between now and the end of the month, when she leaves for Portland. Sam's timing is terrible. I kick a loose pebble on the sidewalk a little too hard, and it ricochets off the mailbox of the Hodges' neighbor, Mrs. Miranda.

The Hodges' house comes into view, and I take a deep breath. Okay, I can't do anything about Sam being here, about him crashing my last few weeks with Kacey. But it doesn't have to be a *thing*. Sam doesn't have to be a thing. I'm not going to let him have that much power over me.

Hopefully we'll win these tickets tonight and resuscitate our summer, and Sam will be a nonissue. He won't be in town for long, and until he's gone, I'll avoid him. Yep, that's my grand plan on how to deal with my feelings for Sam. Good old-fashioned avoidance. I'm going to avoid the crap out of him until he's back in Idaho.

There's no sign of Sam as I approach the Hodges', but his Jeep is in the driveway. The rear is covered in bumper stickers—the newest one is for Craters of the Moon National Monument, stuck right beside a faded Olympic National Park logo. A decal of a rock climber clings to his back window, and mud is splashed along the sides, like he recently went off-roading.

Sam's an adrenaline junkie, and I wish I hated that about him. I mean, who willingly goes rock climbing and skydiving, off-roading on weekends, and backpacking into unknown mountains? Samson Hodge does, that's who. But I don't hate it. I love how much he loves adventuring, even though I'm better suited for the indoors. I'm basically the human equivalent of an indoor cat.

Sam's nowhere to be found when I shut the door behind me, and my heart rate calms. But I know not to let my guard down. Not after yesterday morning. I'm now 100 percent Team Hypervigilance. Apologies to my therapist.

Upstairs, Kacey's on the couch with her phone. Her curls are damped, twisted back with an alligator clip on the top of her head.

"Hey, Flor," she says, and locks her phone.

"Hey." I plop onto the cushion next to her. Kacey's hair is wet, and a red bathing suit strap peeks out beneath her black T-shirt. "Did you go to the lake?"

"Yeah, Sam and I got back an hour ago." Her eyes widen. "Shit, I'm the worst! I should've invited you."

"Don't worry about it," I rush to say, because a shirtless Sam? My cheeks warm at that particular mental image. I refocus before my brain goes off the deep end and add, "Three hours until the announcement!"

"You sound uncharacteristically excited."

"So what if I am?"

"What happened to 'I doubt we'll win'?" she asks in a very poor, dopey imitation of my voice.

"I can be realistic *and* hopeful, can't I?"

Let's say we do win. There's really no way for us to get to San Francisco. I don't drive, and Kacey has her license but no car. We're not the most mobile duo. But pretending is kind of fun.

"If we win, we're going," Kacey says. "Just so we're clear."

"How? My mom won't let me go. You know that." The only

way I can imagine getting to San Francisco would be by lying to my mom. And lying and I don't get along. Lying gives me massive anxiety, and usually I'll blurt out the truth and end up oversharing every small thing I've ever felt guilty about, like accidentally shoplifting a pack of gum when I was twelve.

Lies of omission—keeping something from someone—are just as bad as lying to their face. And I've only successfully lied once, but Kacey doesn't know that. Eight months is a record for me.

"I know, but you don't need her permission." Kacey pokes me in the shoulder. "Isn't it time for you to rebel a little? You're *eighteen*."

"If we win," I say slowly, "then sure. We'll lie our way to San Francisco."

My best friend grins. "Hell yeah, we will."

We decide to watch a true crime documentary until the announcement, and Kacey paints her toenails. But I zone out, unable to concentrate. There are too many thoughts and hopes and worries bouncing around inside my head.

Until I listened to *Murder Me Later*—and met Kacey, who shared my macabre interests—I thought I wasn't supposed to like the dark stuff. True crime and serial killers and survival stories. I felt like a freak. Now, I can't imagine my life without it. I don't have a ton of interests or passions, since it's kind of hard to think about the future when your future is on hold. But true crime is the one thing I never, ever tire of.

After an hour of true crime documentary, Kacey pauses the show.

"You want pizza?" she asks from her side of the couch,

brown curls spilling out of her clip as she leans over her feet with a bottle of red nail polish.

My stomach practically grumbles in response. "Always."

Since Rosemary and Alec are working, we order "real" pizza, and Kacey places a pickup order for the Ancient Pie. Then she says, "They'll be ready in forty-five minutes. Do you mind letting Sam know? He said he'd pick them up, but he's not replying to his texts."

"Can't you go tell him?" A spike of nerves flushes my body, and my palms start sweating.

She wiggles her toes, which are coated in a wet gloss of polish. "Do you really want me to ruin my pedicure?"

For a moment, I'm frozen. Kacey will get suspicious if I fight this too hard. I mean, a year ago I would've happily volunteered to help or talk with Sam. Even though she's clueless to my crush, she'll notice if I start actively avoiding her brother. Kacey can't know that things have changed.

"Okay, fine." I shove my flip-flops on and head downstairs.

In the hallway, I pause in front of the screen door and peer into the backyard. A small arbor with wisteria shades the patio, and the lawn slopes downward to a potting shed, workbench, and Sam. His body arches over the workbench, a blue-and-green flannel rolled up his forearms as he sands, curly waves hanging over his safety goggles.

If I walk out there, I'll be alone with Sam—like *truly* alone. The last time I was alone with Sam . . .

Nope!

I turn around and head the opposite direction. As I walk home for my bike, I text Kacey.

ME: Couldn't find Sam but I'll bike and get the

KACEY: Really? He's supposed to be outside.

ME: I'm nervous about the tickets and maybe exercise will help. I don't mind

KACEY: Whatevs. And don't be nervous! This is supposed to be exciting!

Luckily, my bike rests beside our garage. Even if a lift downtown would be faster, I don't want to run into my mom. I'm way too out of sorts about Sam, and I need some alone time. I mount the mint-green Schwinn and begin pedaling to downtown Barmouth. Unfortunately, when I got dressed earlier, I wasn't counting on riding my bike. I steer with one hand, the other holding down my sundress so I don't flash every car I pass.

Almost an hour later, I return to the Hodges' neighborhood with three small pizza boxes shoved in my bike basket. I was lying about the exercise thing to Kacey, but I do feel calmer. Not calm, not even close, but better.

Was the whole idea an overreaction? Probably. But I couldn't force myself through the screen door and toward the boy my heart refuses to let go.

I dump my bike in the grass and head inside with the pizzas, using my shoulder to wipe sweat from my forehead. Before I reach the stairs, Sam walks into the hallway from the kitchen. He's ditched the flannel, and the white tee he's wearing is unnecessarily tight.

Does he even *own* any properly fitting clothing?

Sam takes one long look at me, clutching the pizza boxes to my chest with my sweaty hair sticking to my cheeks. Then he glances out the window facing the front lawn. My Schwinn rests on its side in the grass, the front wheel still spinning. "Did you bike all the way to the Ancient Pie?"

"Yup." I try to remain casual, even though I'm slowly edging closer to the staircase.

Sam raises his brows and takes a sip from his glass of water. "I could've driven you."

"I wanted the exercise."

"You hate exercise," he says with a teasing grin, that lopsided one that makes every nerve in my body perk to attention. "You're out of breath."

And even worse than that—the heat in my flushed cheeks is spreading, splotching my neck and collarbone. "Exactly," I say. "Which is why I need to exercise more."

Thankfully, Kacey bounds down the stairs and saves me from myself.

"Thought I smelled pizza." She does grabby hands. "Gimme! I'm starving."

I hand her the stack of pizza boxes and head upstairs without another word to Sam. Kacey follows after giving her brother his pepperoni, which he thankfully chooses to eat in the kitchen.

Crowded around the coffee table, Kacey and I dig in. She opens her box of pizza with apparent glee over the pineapple-to-jalapeño ratio. I grab a piece of my plain cheese pizza and curl my feet beneath me on the couch. Kacey hits play on the documentary, and we settle in as we eat.

Even though we have alerts turned on for the *Cold Cases, Cold Bitches* account, I still check her feed for updates every few minutes.

At seven on the dot, our phones chirp with an alert.

"You wanna check, or should I?" she asks excitedly, and pauses the documentary.

Part of me doesn't want to look. Because then the fun of allowing myself to hope will be over. There's no way we won those tickets. Our last chance at a memorable summer was just a silly fantasy, and I want to live in this moment of possibilities for a few more seconds.

Kacey takes my hesitation as her green light, and she grabs her phone off the couch. "One sec!"

I wipe my pizza-greasy hands off on a napkin. "Well?"

"We won," Kacey says quietly.

My stomach lurches, and it's possible I stress-ate way too much pizza. "No way. We didn't win. Don't mess with me, Kace."

Kacey shoves her phone in my hand. "Look! That's my tweet. Right. There."

My hands are sweaty as I grip Kacey's phone. The account quoted her Mary Vincent tweet with the following:

@coldcasescoldbitches: Congrats! You've won two VIP tickets to the @murdermelater show next Friday in SF! DM me ASAP for details"

"We won." I look at Kacey, then back to the phone. Two tickets. Two VIP tickets. San Francisco. Next week. "We seriously won?"

Kacey tackles me with a hug, and we sink sideways into the couch cushions. "Yes! We're going to fucking San Francisco," she squeals, hugging me tight. "We're gonna meet Eleanor and Trish!"

Excitement bubbles inside me. Kacey starts laughing, and it's contagious, so I'm laughing too. Except it's not exactly funny—it's unreal.

Full of laughter and with a flushed face, I sit up. I'm still clutching Kacey's phone with the tweet like it's evidence, undoubtedly taking a dozen accidental screenshots. Evidence of somehow, we *won.* I never win anything. Never.

"We really won." I drop Kacey's phone onto the couch and drag my fingers through my hair.

But we *can't* go to San Francisco. Can we? I was humoring Kacey when I told her that, if we won, we'd find a way. The problem is, I never thought that was an actual possibility. I hoped and fantasized, but . . . I *never* got past the part where we won the tickets.

As Kacey does an excited shoulder shimmy, I take a moment to breathe. Because, as anxious as I feel, this is a sign. It has to be. The odds of us winning were almost nonexistent, but we won. There's no way Mom will let me go, so that means I'll just have to find a way, somehow, to San Francisco. Without telling either of my parents. That's . . . doable, right?

This is my last summer with Kacey. The last three weeks where we're *us.* I don't know what'll happen after she leaves for Portland. I don't know, and the not knowing scares the shit out of me.

I have to make the rest of our summer count.

"Okay," I say resolutely, and turn to Kacey. "How're we—two chronic pedestrians—getting to Northern California?"

Kacey breaks out into a huge smile. "Does that mean we're going?"

"We're going."

Sam chooses this very moment to come upstairs. But he doesn't linger, just passes through the game room to reach his bedroom. He only pauses to ruffle Kacey's hair, which pisses her off, and she throws a pillow at her brother's retreating figure. Sam laughs, and a second later, I hear his bedroom door close.

Turning back to Kacey, I swallow hard, trying to remember what I was going to say before Sam showed up. "Um. Right," I say, finding my brain again. "Strategies for getting to San Francisco."

With one hand, Kacey smooths her curls, and with the other, she pops a lone chunk of pineapple into her mouth. "There's Amtrak. Or the bus?"

I shake my head. "We are *not* taking public transportation. Remember the Greyhound Bus Murder? Do *you* want to be killed with a machete and eaten on public transportation?"

Kacey deflates, wrinkling her nose. "Right. And hitchhiking is out."

"Mary Vincent," I remind her. "This isn't 1970, Kace. Also, hitchhiking was never *in*." I worry my bottom lip between my teeth. Kacey has her license, but no car. She's also a pretty awful driver.

"We could ask my parents to use their car," Kacey suggests. "But they'd totally tell your parents."

I grunt in agreement. Our parents aren't exactly best buds, but they both adhere to their code: complete and utter parental transparency. Rosemary and Alec love me—but not enough to break the code.

Rather than wilt in defeat, this makes me want to find a way even more. Despite all odds, we won those tickets—and there's not a chance we won't be in San Francisco next Friday.

"Don't some car rental places rent to drivers under the age of twenty-five?" I reach for my phone to consult Google. Okay, I'm officially scraping the bottom of my ideas barrel.

"Maybe? But that'd be expensive." Kacey sighs and drops her head back against the cushions. *"Fuck."*

"We'll figure it out," I promise her.

Sam wanders back into the game room. He grabs the lone slice from the coffee table and takes a bite. "I'll drive you," he says, his mouth full of *my* last piece of pizza.

I choke on my spit. "Um—"

"Seriously?" Kacey sits up beside me.

"Sure. Why not?" He glances between us, unfazed by what a huge offer this is. Does he not know how far away San Francisco is? Do I need to pull up Google Maps for him?

"Because you literally just drove eight hours from Idaho," I say—way too loudly—and Sam's brows arch in surprise. I have no idea what my face looks like, but it can't be good. I've never been particularly talented at hiding my emotions. And I have a lot of emotions right now.

Kacey elbows me—*hard.* "I'm not complaining." She steeples her fingers. "But what's in it for you?"

Sam shoves the rest of the pizza into his mouth and chews. After swallowing, he says, "Why does there have to be something in it for me?"

Kacey stares at her brother, eyes narrowing. "Because you're doing that *thing.*"

"What thing?" He runs a hand through his hair. "I'm not doing anything."

"You're getting all defensive. And now you're blushing!"

Sam's nostrils flare, but she's right—he's blushing.

Kacey laughs gleefully, clearly enjoying this moment of Sam embarrassment. "This is about a girl, isn't it?"

"Can't I do a favor for my little sister out of the kindness of my heart?"

Kacey snorts. "Not a favor this big." Then she snaps her fingers. "Amanda's in San Francisco!"

Sam pauses. "Yeah. So?"

"Ooh, you two are talking again?" Kacey asks, then adds, "I always liked Amanda."

"Yeah," Sam says after a torturous moment. "I promised her I'd visit this summer. Lucky for you two nerds, huh?"

An uncomfortable heat—embarrassingly familiar—spreads across my chest, and I focus on my hands, picking at my yellow nail polish like it's the most interesting thing in the room. My stomach hurts, and it's not because of the pizza.

Amanda and Sam didn't exactly date. They were constantly on-again-off-again for all of Sam's senior year, seeing different people in between. But Sam was a serial dater, and Amanda was the closest thing to a serious girlfriend that he ever had.

Kacey nudges my shoulder with hers. "What do you think, Flor? Sam driving us is our best bet."

I meet Sam's gaze and force my voice steady. "Sure. Thanks, Sam." Then I make myself smile at him for the first time since he walked into the Hodges' kitchen yesterday morning.

"No problem." Sam scratches the side of his neck, then adds, "Lemme know the details when you have them." Then he disappears into his bedroom.

Kacey grabs my hands excitedly. "Sam's the best!"

I stare down the hallway toward his bedroom. "Yeah. The best."

FIVE

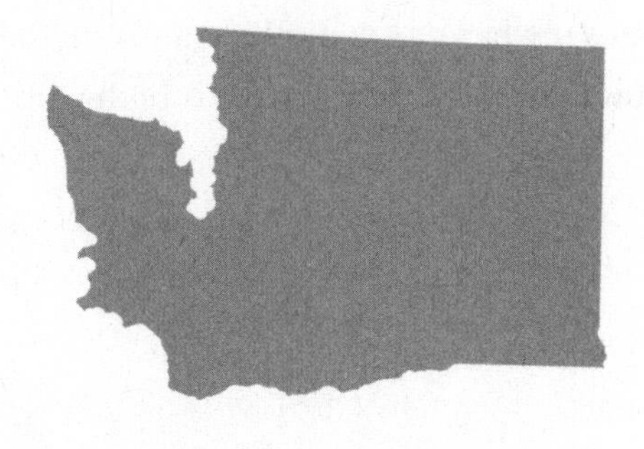

Barmouth, WA

TUESDAY, AUGUST 9

Normally, the universe likes to kick me in the shins and run. But, for whatever reason, everything is falling perfectly into place for this trip. Sam's offer—however emotionally devastating—set the plan into motion. As did a cover story to tell my parents. Something that, if we're being honest, I didn't think would happen. But the live show coincides with the Bainbridge Island trip, otherwise known as the one non-parental trip I'm preapproved for.

This literally happens *once* a year.

Kacey and I have convened at our favorite coffee place, Rise and Grind, to work on our plan. She didn't question my suggestion to hang out at the café instead of their house earlier. Considering I'll have to spend over seventy-two straight hours with Sam on our trip, I'm avoiding him as much as possible up until the point I can't avoid him anymore. Very healthy.

When Sam isn't around, it's easy to pretend I haven't lied to Kacey for eight months. But now that he's crashed my summer, the more I regret my decision to not tell her about the kiss. If I'd told Kacey eight months ago, maybe it wouldn't have turned into a big deal. But if I tell her *now*? Eight months after the fact? She might never forgive me.

But I did this for eight months. I can pull off another three weeks. Totally. It'll be easy.

Kacey's foot nudges mine beneath the table, and I glance up from my iced latte, weighty guilt tightening the space between my shoulder blades.

"Pay attention! I haven't even gotten to the best part," Kacey says excitedly, sipping her nitro cold brew. "My mom and dad are spending Thursday and Friday night at some fancy hotel in Seattle. They want to be alone on their anniversary." Her nose wrinkles in disgust.

I sip my iced chai, my ankles tucked around the legs of my chair. "Seriously? Thursday *and* Friday?"

"Yep. They're meeting some friends who were in their wedding on Thursday for a celebratory dinner—then Friday is their actual anniversary. Twenty years." She rolls her eyes at this, but there's love in her tone.

Twenty years. I can't even imagine being with someone for that long. Not because I don't want it—I probably want it too much, in a pathetic and lovelorn kind of way—but more like I can't imagine that future inside my head or align it with my reality. Can't imagine someone who'd be willing to take all my bad with my good. Messy, anxious girls don't get those happily-ever-afters, those love stories. We get the heartbreak. The boys who find us *too much* or *not enough.* That's just the way it is.

"So, if we leave Thursday," I say, and refocus on our plan, running it through my head, "they'll have no idea as long as we get back by Saturday?"

"Exactly." Kacey sets aside her nitro and rubs her palms together like a cartoon villain. "And worst-case scenario? They find out *after* we've left, but we'd still make the show."

"Sure," I say uneasily, "but my mom will kill me if she ever finds out."

"And you can die happy having seen Eleanor and Trish."

"You're not funny, you know that, right?"

"I'm hilarious," Kacey says. "But don't worry, babe. The plan is simple, which is a good thing since you're allergic to lying. I didn't want to complicate things too much."

"I'm not worrying. It's a good plan." I ignore her other comment. It's not Kacey's fault that she doesn't know I've successfully lied to *her* for eight months. Not like that's brag worthy. Every time I think about it, my stomach hurts.

"Sam agrees that leaving Thursday, stopping halfway for the night, and driving the last leg on Friday is our best bet." Kacey tips back the rest of her nitro. "The show's at eight, and with the meet and greet, we'll probably be there until ten."

I set my chai latte aside. The plan almost seems too good to be true. But considering Sam's driving us . . . okay, maybe it's not too good to be true. "Leave Thursday, stop overnight, and get to San Francisco Friday evening? That's doable."

"If we get back on the road right after the meet and greet, we can push until Oregon and be home Saturday afternoon. It's a lot of driving, but Sam doesn't mind. He's gonna hang with Amanda at her dorm during the show."

Picking at an old, peeling *Murder Me Later* logo sticker on the back of my phone, I will my face to remain neutral. "Perfect."

"I'm not sure when my parents are coming back Saturday, but if they arrive before us, we can say we were out at the beach or even in the city. They'll never know." Kacey gives me a big, excited grin. "The plan is fucking foolproof."

Despite my reservations, Kacey's right. It's a good plan. And if we get found out, I'll have to come clean and confront my parents—something I'd really love to avoid, if possible—but I'm eighteen. I technically won't be breaking any laws. I'll just be defying them. Which, now that I'm thinking about it, might be scarier than breaking the law.

"Even if our parents find out," Kacey continues, "we don't have to come back home. We don't have to turn back. We'll get in trouble regardless if we're caught. Might as well go the distance and do something worthy of getting grounded over. Right?"

I swallow the anxious lump in my throat. "Right."

"It'll be epic. I can't wait."

"Me either." Despite my lingering worries, I smile at my best friend and sink into the moment. Because this is exactly what I need this summer. We have the tickets, the ride, and the cover-up. Not even my anxiety can fault the perfection of our plan.

We direct-messaged the host of *Cold Cases, Cold Bitches* Saturday on Twitter and sent her our contact info. The host confirmed that the two VIP tickets—complete with a meet and greet—will be ready for pickup at the San Francisco Masonic's box office on Friday.

"If you start feeling anxious or are stressing out, let me know, okay?" Kacey adds softly from across our small bistro table. "But you've got this. This trip is going to be everything, Florie. *Everything*."

"Don't worry about me," I tell her. My mind is already three days in the future, when I'll get to tell my two heroines how much they mean to me. Even so, anxiety is a given with me. But I'm not going to let my worries ruin this.

Once I'm done with my iced latte, we head back out into the uncomfortably warm day. It's late afternoon, the sun shining bright in the sky, and the downtown is flooded with tourists.

"Wanna come over?" Kacey spins the combination on her bike lock and glances over her shoulder.

I keep my head turned away as I enter my bike lock combination to hide any emotions playing out on my face. Considering I go over to the Hodges' almost every day, it'll be suspicious if I *stop*. But I'm also not in the headspace to be around Sam after the other night. "Can't, sorry." I dump my purse in my bike's wicker basket. "My mom wants me around since we're leaving tomorrow, but you can come over, if you want."

"Sure," my best friend says, and hops on her bike. "We're

going out to dinner with Sam so I can't skip, but I'll head over after."

I pedal beside Kacey out of downtown Barmouth with conflicting emotions. We're headed to San Francisco in a matter of days. But Sam kissed me, and it very clearly meant nothing to him. His lack of feelings is proof that I made the right decision over winter break. So that's good, right? I never wanted that kiss to complicate things with Kacey, anyway.

This is better, for sure. Even if it stings a little. Or a lot.

I'll probably never know why Sam kissed me, but it's not like he led me on.

Samson Hodge isn't a bad guy. He's just not my guy.

Unlike the Hodges' house, mine isn't nearly as welcoming for Kacey. There's no Hide-A-Key for my best friend, no open-door policy. She has to ring the doorbell, like the UPS delivery person or the Jehovah's Witnesses. The doorbell chimes around eight that night, and Mom's reading out on the back deck, so I jog downstairs and unlock the front door.

"Hey." I step aside to widen the gap for Kacey.

Behind her, idling in my driveway, is Sam's Jeep.

He waves from the driver's seat, and, once again, I wonder what I did to anger the universe, because I'm wearing one of Dad's ratty old basketball jerseys and yoga pants. I raise a limp hand in response before ducking back into the house and shutting the door behind Kacey.

"Sam drove you?" I ask as she slides off her shoes.

Through the sidelights, I watch as Sam reverses out of my driveway.

"Yeah, we came from dinner." Kacey hobbles on one foot, kicking off her sandal. "Mom and Dad are going straight to work, so we took the Jeep."

"Oh, um, fun." I cross my arms and glance out the window until the Jeep's taillights disappear down my street. "My mom's outside, but let's go upstairs. I want to show you something."

Kacey raises a brow. "Intrigue."

We head upstairs to my bedroom. Kacey belly flops onto my bed, and I shut the door.

I walk over to my desk and open the bottom drawer, unearthing the project I've been working on since I got home from Rise and Grind earlier.

"Okay." I perch on the edge of my bed and flip open the purple binder, feeling like a nerd for being so excited about this. "I printed out some different routes to San Francisco, and I'm still researching motels at the halfway mark. I also found this app that lists and rates all nearby bathrooms—"

"Oh no, no, no. Sorry, babe." Kacey leans across the bed and yanks the binder from my hands. "But we're going out of your comfort zone for this trip. None of your weird binders allowed."

"It's not weird! It's practical," I point out and frown. Because my binders *are* practical, and I spent hours putting this one together. Kacey might want to go out of my comfort zone, but I'm not leaving anything up to chance if I can avoid it. "There's a map of the West Coast and all its major highways. What if one of our phones dies?"

Kacey gives me a blank stare, the binder still in hand. "If all *three* of our phones die and we somehow lose our chargers, then you can say *I told you so*, but this"—she waves the binder in the air—"isn't coming with us."

I sink back against my headboard and hug my knees. Kacey's right, and I know she's right, but my chest is going all hot and itchy.

Lauren, my therapist, would no doubt file this need for my binder under my hypervigilance tendencies, but I'd rather be hypervigilant than not vigilant at all. Especially on an eight-hundred-mile road trip. There are too many things that can go wrong. And everything *needs* to go right.

"Fine." I pout and rest my chin on my knees.

Kacey tosses the binder into my open closet and then grabs a notebook and pen off my desk. "Stop stressing." She uncaps the pen with her teeth. "We both want the rest of summer to be memorable, right? Then we need to focus on doing memorable things, not avoiding gross rest stop bathrooms."

"Can't we do both?"

Kacey sighs and opens the notebook, scribbling something across the top of a clean sheet.

I unravel myself from around my knees and lean over to read:

KACEY + FLORIE'S WILD AND SUPER-COOL
BFF ROAD-TRIP BUCKET LIST

"Meeting Eleanor and Trish will be, by default, memorable." Kacey taps her pen on the paper. "But who says we can't make even more memories along the way? It's a road trip, Flor. We're eighteen! No parents—and more specifically, no Helene. If we're going out of your comfort zone, let's go all the way. Okay?"

I shift beside Kacey, my shoulder pressing into hers. "Okay," I agree cautiously. "Like what, though?"

She leans over the notebook and writes:

1. Be spontaneous (yes, Florie, that means YOU)

2. Find bangin' outfits for the Eleanor and Trish meet and greet

Kacey hands me the notebook and pen. "Any ideas?"

I grin at the list because, okay, Kacey has a point. Taking the pen, I add a few more ideas, much tamer than my best friend's. But when I pass the notebook back to Kacey, she has a mischievous look on her face and scrawls the next item.

5. Kiss a random hottie

"Pass." I shake my head. "That one's all you."

"What?" Kacey balances the notebook on her lap, her curls bouncing around her face as she laughs. "Don't you want to find a random hottie to make out with?"

Heat flushes up my neck, because the last person I made out with was Sam. And I really shouldn't be thinking about kissing Sam right now. Or ever. "Fine, you can leave it on there. But no promises."

After fifteen minutes, Kacey and I finalize our list of ten, vague, not-really-bucket-list ideas. My additions are way, way more boring than Kacey's, but I like to think we balance each other out. The full list reads:

KACEY + FLORIE'S WILD AND SUPER-COOL BFF ROAD TRIP BUCKET LIST

1. Be spontaneous (yes, Florie, that means YOU)
2. Find bangin' outfits for the Eleanor and Trish meet and greet
3. Be embarrassing tourists
4. Buy a memento in each state
5. Kiss a random hottie
6. Break a traffic law
7. Say yes, no questions asked
8. Visit a roadside attraction
9. Anything that makes us ask "Is this a bad idea?"
10. HAVE THE BEST TIME OF OUR LIVES

Kacey carefully tears the sheet of paper out of my notebook and folds it in half. "By taking this piece of paper, you, Florence Cordray, hereby enter a legally binding contract with me, Kacey Hodge, to do your best to complete every item on this list. And I agree to do the same. Deal?"

"Deal." I take the list. Like most of Kacey's suggestions and ideas, the list kind of scares me. But in the best way possible. I've never been good at stepping outside my comfort zone, but luckily (or unluckily, depending on the situation) for me, it's Kacey's specialty. "Thank you," I say, and hug her.

"Anytime, anywhere." She squeezes me before letting me go.

I tuck the list into my suitcase. "We should really download that bathroom app, though."

Kacey groans, throwing herself back onto my bed. "You're a lost cause," she says, but she's already unlocking her phone and opening up the App Store.

"You'll thank me later."

SIX

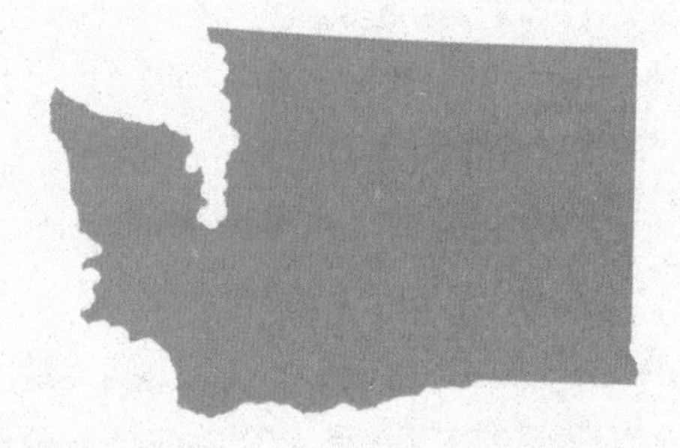

Barmouth, WA to Bainbridge Island, WA

WEDNESDAY, AUGUST 10

After Kacey left last night, my anxiety started to climb. Without her enthusiasm and list making to keep me focused on all the exciting parts of our trip, I nose-dived into anxiety. I barely slept, checked our front door three separate times, and gave up on sleep around 5:00 a.m. I've already pounded back two cups of coffee, which is making me more jittery, but I'm also exhausted. It's a bad combination.

"Are you sure you don't want a ride?" Mom asks, following me downstairs.

I fiddle with the strap of my duffel bag. "That's okay," I say as we reach the landing. "It's not a long walk." Normally I'd take her up on the offer, but I need the walk to clear my head.

Mom nods, and I can't tell if she's disappointed. Since she's not the emotional type, she'd never tell me if she *wanted* to drive me, or to see me off in person. "Well. You'll be home next Tuesday, right?"

"Next Tuesday." I force a smile to show her that I'm not an anxious mess.

"Sounds good. I'll see you next week, honey," she says, and reaches her arms out.

I hug my mom, inhaling a whiff of her floral perfume, and press my eyes shut. Mom's always been comforting, in her own unique way. Maybe I never got hot cocoa and heart-to-hearts like Kacey, but I have the support of always having someone on my side.

Even if I've begun wondering what it'd be like to go it alone lately.

"Bye, Mom." I lean up to kiss her on the cheek.

Mom's eyes are bright and assessing, as if she's checking me for cracks. "Be safe and text me when you all arrive, okay?"

"Of course." After I double-check that I have everything, I head outside.

The moment the front door shuts behind me, I manage to relax—a tiny bit.

Whenever I'm around my mom, it's like I can't escape my OCD. Maybe that's because it's the basis for what our relationship has become. At first, I liked focusing on my diagnosis. Learning as much about OCD as possible made the situation feel manageable—and Mom helped with that. But as much as my mom helps, she can't ever really understand.

Mom looks at me and just sees *anxiety*. She has no idea what goes on under the surface, no matter how many books and *Psychology Today* articles she reads. And OCD isn't what the media's made it out to be, especially purely obsessional OCD, which is what I struggle with. I enjoy cleaning and organizing as much as the next person, sure, but that's not what obsessive-compulsive disorder is about. More often than not, OCD is fighting against a monster that feasts on your worst fears. A monster that makes you doubt everything, from your actions to your thoughts to even your emotions. There's no upside to OCD. No superhero cleanliness. No extra sense of awareness. *Nothing.*

OCD doesn't make my life better, but at the same time, I'm not broken, which Mom sometimes makes me feel. I'm learning to cope with my disorder, and I think I'm doing better every day. I want to believe in myself and know that if I do fall, I'll be okay and pick myself back up. Because living in fear, living in constraints and rituals and obsessions, really isn't living at all.

As I enter the Hodges' neighborhood, I push my shoulders back. Try to ignore my rapid heart rate, my dry mouth, and the sweat dampening my bra even though it's a pleasant seventy degrees out. The minivan is parked in the driveway, the trunk popped with suitcases piled inside, and Sam's Jeep is in the open garage.

I walk up the driveway with my bag weighing down my shoulder. Before I can climb the porch steps, the front door opens and Rosemary Hodge bustles out.

"Oh hi, Florie," she says, and I scramble out of the way as she carries an ice chest to the minivan. "How're you doing, sweet girl?"

"Good!" I try to lean into my excitement, instead of dwelling on the anxiety over lying to my parents or Sam's overall existence. *Eleanor and Trish,* I remind myself. *Eleanor and Trish and a memorable summer.*

Rosemary lugs the chest into the minivan; ice sloshes against soda cans. "Go ahead and drop your bag by Sam's car. The kids are inside. We should be ready to go in maybe ten minutes?"

"Perfect." I backtrack to dump my duffel in the garage.

As I slide the bag off my shoulder, I pointedly *don't* look at the front seat of the Jeep. Because if I don't look at the front seat, I don't have to think about how it felt to sit there as Sam leaned closer and closer until his lips hovered over mine.

Knock it off, I tell my brain, and turn my back to Sam's car.

Inside, I glance around the entry hall and stare at the staircase, wondering if I should go find Kacey, when Alec Hodge rounds the corner. In his arms are a precarious pile of suitcases, but he's all smiles. Sam gets his height from his dad, who also tops out at six foot five. But neither of the kids inherited Alec's ghostly pale skin and shock of near-black hair.

"Florie!" He nudges my shoulder good-naturedly as he passes. He's in board shorts and an ancient Soundgarden T-shirt. "Ready for the beach house?"

Alec is from Toronto and has the best Canadian accent. I could listen to him say "house" for hours. "Yeah, can't wait. Thanks again for inviting me."

"Of course, kiddo. You're family," he says over his shoulder as he heads outside.

I smile, but I can't help but wonder—will I still be "family" when Kacey's in Portland? I've depended on the Hodges so much the past two years. Probably too much.

When I reach the second floor, Kacey isn't in the game room, so I head down the hall. Her bedroom door is partially open, and I knock.

"Hey." I nudge the door open farther, then wince. Kacey's suitcase is still on her bed, half-packed. And what clothes we didn't donate to Goodwill are currently carpeting the bedroom floor.

"Hey hey," Kacey says, digging through a pile of bathing suits. "The rainbow or the blue?" She holds two bathing suits up to her body.

I raise a brow. "We're not"—I lower my voice—"actually staying at the beach house. Why're you bringing a bathing suit?"

"We'll be there for a few days when we get back." She shrugs, tossing both suits in her bag. "Plus, keeping up appearances for my parents."

"Are you anticipating them going through your clothes?"

"You never know." She sticks her tongue out at me. "C'mon, help me with this."

At her request, I climb onto her bed and sit on the bulging suitcase while she zips it up. "Yeesh, why do you need so many clothes?" I mutter as she struggles with the zipper.

"It's not that much." She lugs the suitcase off the bed. I give her a pointed look, and she laughs. "Fine, it's way too much. But I couldn't make up my mind on what to wear for Eleanor and Trish."

"Uh-huh," I say disbelievingly, just to annoy her. But to show her I'm not serious, I help her lug the monstrous suitcase out of her bedroom.

Unlike Kacey, I only packed a handful of casual dresses, leggings, and a sweater. Nothing that would remotely be considered bangin' to wear when we meet Eleanor and Trish. Kacey and I aren't the same size—where she's curves, I'm straight, prepubescent lines. But maybe she'll let me borrow a cute jacket or something.

"Five-minute warning," Rosemary calls up to us.

Kacey frowns at her suitcase. "Lemme get this down to the car."

"You got it?" I ask. "I'm gonna pee real quick before we go."

Kacey waves me off.

As I reach the bathroom, the door across the hall opens.

"Oh, hey," Sam says, and swings his duffel bag over his shoulder. He steps out into the hallway. The khaki shorts show off his tanned calf muscles, and he wears a yellow-and-orange checkered flannel open over a snug white T-shirt. Add in the hiking boots and he looks like a hot trail guide. Or an REI model. Is that a thing?

I hesitate, staring at him *one* second too long, then say "Hi" and lock myself into the bathroom before he can reply.

Like every other time I've seen him since he returned to Barmouth, Sam is acting completely normal, and I'm either staring at him—my cheeks flushed like I'm a neon billboard for sexual repression—or ducking into the nearest room to get away from him.

The next few days are going to be a *blast.* Can't wait.

After using the bathroom, I wash my hands and inspect my reflection. My blond hair sticks to my forehead, and I try wiping the sweat-foundation mixture off with the back of my hand with little success. Gross. I dig through my purse for my makeup bag—*not* because of Sam—and try to freshen up.

Combing my fingers through my sweat-stringy hair, I sigh.

I don't look like a competent, fearless girl. I don't look like a girl who's about to lie to her mom in order to have one epic blast with her best friend before things change forever. I don't know *what* that girl would look like, but I doubt she'd look a thing like me.

But I'm here, aren't I? I'm doing it.

Florie from last summer would've never even entered the *Cold Cases, Cold Bitches* contest. She would've never put herself—or her hopes—on the line like that. Lauren the therapist always tells me that the only person I can compare myself to are the former versions of myself. And all the past versions of Florie would've *never* done this. No amount of cajoling from Kacey would've convinced me. Not even the promise of three solid days with Sam, which in the past would've been *very* appealing, could've brought me to this moment.

My fingers grip the edges of the bathroom counter as I lean my weight into my hands and stare at my reflection. Maybe that fearless girl wouldn't look a thing like me, but I have to acknowledge the changes happening beneath my skin, changes that are invisible and life altering all at the same time.

If one year brought this much change, what could next year look like?

Unlike Kacey, I love the smell of the ocean. That salty smell that's almost textured when you take a deep breath. Since Barmouth only has a lake and is hours from the coast, I rarely get to stand close enough to the Pacific to breathe it in. But the beach house is right on the water, two stories, painted baby blue, and it even has a widow's walk.

After we're all unpacked, I linger outside on the porch swing.

I still remember how excited I was when Kacey invited me along on my first Hodges' Annual Beach House trip last summer. We'd been friends for less than a year, but we'd gone from strangers to best friends during junior year, and I was sleeping over at least once a week. Maybe that doesn't seem like a big deal, but when I was younger, I used to panic during sleepovers and always ended up calling my mom. One time, I faked an asthma attack to get out of sleepover camp, and I don't even *have* asthma. But that Bainbridge Island trip ended up being one of my favorite memories.

So, yeah, I didn't even hesitate when Kacey invited me to Bainbridge Island again with her family. Because I have no idea what'll happen next summer, if Rosemary and Alec will rent the beach house like normal, or if Kacey will even come home for the summer. She promised she would . . . but people change. That's kind of the whole point of college, isn't it? To grow up?

I've never told Kacey how nervous I am about her leaving or what it'll mean for our friendship. Other than a few joking pouts about her leaving for Portland, I've done my best to play the role of the supportive best friend. To not be a downer. Besides, someone as brave and badass as Kacey Hodge wouldn't understand.

The front door bangs open, and Sam steps out onto the porch. He stops in his tracks when he spots me, spinning the Jeep's keys around his finger. "I'm going to the store. Uh, any chance you wanna come with?"

"That's okay." I cross my arms over my chest and stand up. "I was headed inside anyways."

I walk toward the front door, trying to move around Sam, at the exact moment he tries stepping out of my way, and we nearly collide. Flustered, I shift to my left—and Sam shifts to his right. *Again.* Like we're in the middle of the world's most awkward dance.

"Sorry." Sam laughs and steps to the side, holding out his hands in an *after you* gesture.

I shake my head and brush past him, letting myself inside.

The rest of the afternoon passes quickly, Alec roping Kacey and me into helping him make dinner. Sam returns maybe an hour later, and then we all crowd around the small circular table in the eat-in kitchen. It's a tight fit, elbow to elbow, but at least I'm squished between Kacey and Alec.

Sam's across from me, picking at his bowl while scrolling on his phone. Probably texting Amanda. Pushing aside a big leaf of kale with my fork, I stab a chunk of sweet potato with unnecessary force.

"Pass the salsa?" Kacey asks, and I slide the bowl toward her. Alec tricked us into cooking something called "the ultimate hippie bowl" for dinner, and all I know is there's a lot of kale. Too much kale. Pretty much the only way to make it edible is to load it with condiments until you can't taste any of the original ingredients.

"Kace, do you and Florie have any plans while you're on the island?" Rosemary asks, then pops a forkful of kale into her mouth.

I choke on my Jones Soda mid-sip, and Kacey thumps me on the back.

"Nothing much," she says smoothly, then gently pinches my arm beneath the table.

My nostrils still burning from the carbonation, I add, "Yeah, nothing planned. Just like last summer. There's nothing different—"

"You two should come with me later," Sam interrupts, and knocks his knee into mine beneath the table. The contact is brief—his bare knee against my bare leg—and it shuts me up fast. "I met some people when I was at the store. They're hanging out at Rockaway later."

Only Samson Hodge can make new friends during a grocery store run for fresh sprouts and pumpkin seeds.

"That sounds fun." Alec pushes up from the table. He walks over to the counter to load his bowl with seconds. I love Rosemary and Alec, but I truly don't understand how they eat this crap. "It's such a nice day. No rain."

When we drove off the ferry, it was sunnier on the island than it was in Barmouth. Not *sunny*, but maybe 50 percent less clouds. And at a high of seventy-six degrees, this is ice cream and shorts weather.

"I don't know." I say, and focus on my food. I spear a slice of sweet potato with my fork and try to scrape off a stubborn piece of kale stuck to it using the side of my bowl.

"Thanks for the invite, Sammy," Kacey says. "We're in."

"Cool." Even though I'm staring at my sweet potato, I can sense Sam looking at us. "We'll head out around eight."

I shoot my best friend a sideways glance. The quirk of Kacey's brows and the determined set of her lips all spell bad news for me. As we stare at one another, she lifts her brows even higher.

"Okay." I give up on my sweet potato situation, dropping my fork into the bowl with a loud clank.

"You done?" Sam asks, holding out his hand for my bowl, and when I finally force myself to look at him, he smiles. He took a shower after his grocery store run, and his waves are damp against his forehead.

In response, I hand him the bowl and scoot out from the table. Turning my back to Sam, I say, "Thanks for dinner, Alec. Can I help clean up?"

Alec waves me off and leans back in his chair. "Nah, kiddo. You're all good."

Kacey scurries after me as I book it for our shared bedroom. "What's wrong?" she asks as we head upstairs. Her fingers loop around my wrist, but I keep walking until we reach our room.

When Kacey shuts the door behind us, I turn to her. "Do we really have to go to the beach?"

Kacey crosses the room to our bunk beds and kneels on the floor, unzipping her twenty-pound suitcase. "No, we don't *have* to. But it'll be fun." She yanks out a yellow top and holds it up against her chest. "Cute?"

"Cute," I agree, but I'm irritated. I pace around the bedroom as Kacey changes. "I'm . . . really nervous about tomorrow. Hanging at the beach with a bunch of strangers isn't going to help. Let's just hang out here!"

Kacey tugs the shirt on. "You'll have me. And Sam." She walks over and grabs my hands, halting my anxious pacing. "Flor, I get it, okay? The San Francisco trip is huge and scary. We've never done something like this. Even *I'm* nervous. I can't imagine how you feel."

Something inside me softens. "Thank you."

"But if we hang out around the beach house all night," she says, and drops my hands, pausing by the vanity to fluff her curls, "I'm just going to worry. You're just going to worry. And *someone* might say something incriminating to my parents."

"I won't say anything!"

"You almost did at dinner."

"No, I was awkward. I'm *always* awkward. This is very normal for me!"

Kacey meets my gaze in the reflection of the mirror. "You almost choked on your soda and then started word vomiting."

"Fine." I cross my arms. "We can go to the beach."

Kacey grins. Then she flounces out of the bedroom, calling over her shoulder, "Meet you downstairs after you change."

Change? Into what? I glance down at my sundress and

bare feet, the flannel tied around my waist. It'll be chillier down by the water, so I grab tights from my duffel bag and yank them on underneath my dress. After ditching the flannel, I pull on a pink-and-blue striped sweater and figure it's good enough.

Yes, I'm aware that I'm dressed like a twelve-year-old.

Whatever. Not like I need to impress anybody.

SEVEN

Rockaway Beach, Bainbridge Island

AUGUST 10, EVENING

The walk to Rockaway Beach isn't a long one.

Hanging back behind Kacey and Sam, I shift my attention to my surroundings rather than feed into my anxious thoughts. The crunch of the asphalt beneath the soles of my shoes as we trek down the side of the road. The almost too-fresh air, the coolness stinging my nostrils. The occasional swish of a car driving by, snippets of music and laughter trailing the vehicles.

Sam slows down until his pace matches mine. "Earth to Florie." He bumps his shoulder against mine. "What do you think?"

"What?" I shift on the pathway, creating some much-needed distance between us. Because when Sam touches me, it's like my brain blacks out, and it's really inconvenient.

"Told you she wasn't listening," Kacey calls from ahead, and holds up her phone to take a video of the sunset.

"I was saying we should plan something fun before Kacey's going-away party, since I'm back in town," Sam recaps. "Maybe drive back into the city or something?"

"Um. Sure, sounds fun." And by fun, I mean *not a chance in hell.* Sam's not going to worm his way into any more of my time with Kacey. How long is he even planning on sticking around? My best-case scenario would be Sam leaving when we get back from Bainbridge. "When are you going back to Idaho?"

"C'mon, you're not that eager to get rid of me, are you?" he jokes beneath his breath. When I don't laugh or even reply, he adds, "Class picks back up in early September or something. Figured I'd play it by ear."

Of course he did. Of course he doesn't have a schedule or plan like a regular person.

We turn off the road and down a winding path to the rocky sand beach. The kids Sam met at the health food store are set up near the cliffs. The four of them are grouped around a small bonfire, sitting on beached logs and a few mismatched camping chairs. Music plays from a Bluetooth speaker, and an ice chest is tucked beneath one of the chairs, partially out of sight. As if the bottles they're holding aren't a tip-off that they brought beer.

"I thought fires weren't allowed here?" I say to Kacey, remembering what Alec said last summer when we visited Rockaway Beach together.

Kacey rolls her eyes. "Don't be a nerd." She loops her arm through mine, dragging me onto the beach and closer to the bonfire.

Sam lifts his hand in a wave once we reach the group, seamlessly in his element. "This is my sister, Kacey," he says, taking the beer he's offered, "and our friend Florie."

"Hi." I untangle myself from Kacey and tuck my hands into the pockets of my sundress.

The guy who handed Sam his beer is wiry and short, with a shock of red hair and freckles. He seems a few years older than us; probably how he got his hands on the beer. The other guy is closer to our age, his locs tied into a bun, and the two girls are pale brunettes. One girl has hair nearly to her butt, the other sporting a cute pixie cut.

"I'm Holden," the redhead says, and nods to his friend, "and that's Anthony."

"Hey," I say, feeling more and more like the problem every second. Everyone seems nice enough, but I'm the grump who can't even force a fake smile onto her face.

The girl with the horse's mane of hair stands up and walks over. "Hey, I'm Erica," she says, and then *hugs* me. I'm too weirded out to hug her back. Has she never heard of personal space? "And that's my sister, Hanna."

I nod at the girls, and I hope I come off as cool and aloof. Not like I'm currently wondering if I might have a panic attack and mentally calculating how long I have to stay here before I can return to the beach house, crawl into bed, and watch true crime documentaries on my phone until I fall asleep.

Anthony and his friends also brought camping lanterns, s'more supplies, and extra firewood. I perk up at the sight of the marshmallows, because a s'more might make staying here *slightly* worth it. Especially after that epic fail of a dinner.

Anthony leans over and drags the ice chest out from beneath his chair. "Want one?" he asks, but I shake my head. "We have soda, too, if that's more your style."

I hesitate then say, "Yeah, okay. Soda works."

Anthony roots around in the ice chest and hands me a can of cola. Then he hands Kacey a beer and opens one for himself.

"Thanks." I pop the tab and take a sip.

"No problem." He smiles, and walks over to the bonfire.

Kacey opens her beer and nudges me forcefully in the ribs. "Now that's a random hottie if I've ever seen one," she says under her breath.

I take a swig of my soda. "What is wrong with you?"

"Number five! Kiss a random hottie." She suggestively pumps her eyebrows, glancing between me and Anthony.

"Not happening." I'm really going to regret making that list, aren't I?

Luckily, Kacey drops it, and we perch on the ice chest while Sam sets up an extra camping chair and stretches his legs out in the most ridiculous display of manspreading that I've ever seen. Erica scoots her chair closer to him, and they fall into conversation. I try to not notice, to not care, just how close Erica sits, laughing at every other thing that he says.

Okay, Sam's funny sometimes, but no one is *that* funny.

I prepare a marshmallow on a skewer and angle it close to the hot coals while Kacey launches into a conversation with Holden and Anthony about some reality show they all watch. I will never understand how both Kacey and Sam find conversing with strangers so easy.

"Oh, no way," Sam says after a few minutes, as I'm sliding my gooey marshmallow onto some graham crackers. "Kace, guess what?"

Kacey looks across the flames at her brother. "Huh?"

"Hanna's going to PNCA too." Sam nods his head toward Erica's sister.

Kacey turns to Hanna, who's sitting on a recliner beach chair, scrolling on her phone. "Really?"

"Yeah!" Hanna pockets her phone and walks over to us. Ignoring me completely, she grins at my best friend. "Hey," she says shyly.

Kacey might not notice, but I definitely notice how Hanna checks her out.

Rather than awkwardly third-wheel Kacey and Hanna's conversation, I stand up and motion for the girl to take my seat on the ice chest. Then I plop into Hanna's abandoned chair and bite into my s'more.

Kacey's always been ten times more social than me, and I'm not worried about her next fall. She'll form new relationships—platonic and romantic—without a problem. And even though I'll still be Kacey's best friend when she's in Portland, I can't help but worry again like I'm being left behind. Like everyone is moving forward, and I can't keep up.

I check my phone. It's officially nine. Maybe I can convince Kacey to leave in the next thirty minutes or so. I can survive another thirty minutes.

As I take a big, messy bite of my s'more, Anthony wanders over to my chair. "Florie, right?"

"Yeah." I casually try wiping off the marshmallow on my bottom lip. Anthony's not bad-looking. Okay, he's legitimately hot and somehow rocking that man bun. But I have exactly zero energy to have a conversation with a stranger right now, let alone make out with one like Kacey wants me to.

"Where are you headed next year?" He sips his beer and shifts his weight from one foot to another.

"For what? College?" I chase my s'more down with soda, and the carbonation fizzes in my chest.

Anthony laughs like it was obvious. "Yeah, college."

"I'm not," I tell him, and almost wince at how harsh my voice is. How *end of the conversation* I sound. But I don't want to make small talk about my nonexistent future.

Anthony takes the hint and wanders to the other side of the bonfire. I almost want to call him back and apologize, but I'm too tired. Socializing is exhausting. And anyway, he shouldn't waste his time flirting with someone like me. A girl who can't get over her pathetic crush, go to college, or even sleep through the night without checking her door nine times.

Wiping my hands off, I stand up and walk over to Kacey. She's still chatting with Hanna, and I crouch down to poke her in the arm. "Hey, you good if I go down to the water?"

"What?" Kacey turns, her cheeks flushed and rosy. "Oh, sure."

After dumping my soda can in a nearby recycling bin, I walk down the rocky beach. The bonfire was near the cliffs, and the closer I get to the water, the more the sounds of the group and music fade.

I pick my way carefully along the rocks and shallow tide until I come across a beached log and sit down. The breeze is colder this close to the water, and I pull the sleeves of my sweater over my hands. Some times are easier than others to ignore my stagnant life. But seeing Kacey move toward her future makes me ache.

I dig the toe of my shoe into the damp sand and watch seagulls dip into the waves before shooting back into the sky. At least nature always reminds me that me and my problems are small, even if they feel huge sometimes.

"Florence Nightingale," a voice calls out in greeting from behind me.

Only one person calls me that ridiculous nickname. I take a deep breath; then I exhale and call over my shoulder, "That nickname isn't as clever as you think it is."

Sam walks across the rocks, one hand tucked into his jacket pocket—the sherpa-lined denim one he's had for as long as I've known him—the other loosely gripping the neck of his beer. "Nah, it's pretty clever."

What am I supposed to do? Sam's nearly at my driftwood bench. It's dark without the light of the bonfire, and if I get up and run in the opposite direction—which is the most appealing option—I'll probably trip on a rock and break my ankle. And I really don't want to meet Eleanor and Trish in a cast.

Before I figure out my next move, Sam reaches me. "Is it okay if I . . ." He gestures to the log with his beer bottle. Apparently I nod, because he sits beside me.

I sneak a glance at Sam, tracing his profile in the fading light. He put on his jacket, but he's still wearing shorts, and a burst of goose bumps trails his shins and calves.

"What're you doing over here?" he asks after getting settled.

I force my attention from Sam back to the water, my heart thrumming in my ears. Sam and I are alone. Like, *alone* alone.

"Nothing," I say, aiming for nonchalance. "Just wandering around."

"All by yourself?"

"Kacey looked kinda busy."

"Yeah. She already has anime-heart eyes."

"Some things never change." I shrug, because like her brother, Kacey is a flirtaholic.

After a beat, Sam asks, "Did you do something different with your hair?"

"What? No." Self-conscious, I smooth my palm down my shoulder-length dirty-blond hair.

"Oh." His gaze shifts from mine as he looks down, tearing at the label on his beer bottle.

Maybe I'm not the only one finding this painfully awkward.

"My bad. I thought it looked different." Sam glances up, but there's nothing pained or uncomfortable about his expression anymore. Maybe I imagined it. Or maybe I'm that forgettable to Samson Hodge. "Not that it looked bad before," he adds with an easy grin.

"Um. Thanks." I'm torn between wanting this conversation to end and for him to stay here, talking to me. Even if it's all meaningless. That's what being around Sam does.

"So, how was the rest of senior year?" he asks, tapping his beer bottle against the side of his leg. *Tap tap tap* pause *tap tap tap.*

I chew on the inside of my cheek. "Oh, you know, fine."

"Just fine?" Sam shoots me a concerned look. "Okay, what about graduation?"

I tuck my hands under my thighs because I'm turning fidgety fast. "Homeschooled, remember?"

"You didn't have a graduation ceremony?"

I shift on the log to face Sam. The outline of his body is blurring with the moonlight, and the shadows make his jaw and cheeks even sharper. "Some homeschooling programs have ceremonies, but since mine was all online, there wasn't one. Barmouth High offered to let me walk, though. Since I'd been a student until halfway through junior year."

The salt air gusts up, wreaking havoc with his hair, and I pretend not to like it.

"And you didn't go?"

"No." I shrug. "Well, I went to cheer on Kacey, but I didn't walk."

"Why not?"

Originally, I wanted to walk. Senior year hadn't turned out anything like I'd hoped, and an actual graduation ceremony would've been fun. More importantly, it would have been *normal* when the rest of my high school experience had been anything but. The cap and gown, a clichéd lei around my neck. Huddling with Kacey and my former classmates for photos. I hadn't had any college fairs or senior prank days or senior prom. I just wanted one cheesy high school memory.

But my mom wasn't thrilled when I mentioned it—instead she asked me if I really felt comfortable walking onstage, in front of so many people. Because if not, we could do a small family dinner at my favorite fancy restaurant in downtown Barmouth. Sure, the idea of walking had filled me with major anxiety, but it was the kind of anxiety that might've been worth it. Mom had a point, though. The more I thought about walking, the more I panicked. In the end, I didn't walk, and we went out to dinner after I cheered Kacey on from the crowd. I don't tell Sam any of this, though.

I wiggle my hand free from beneath my thigh and push my hair back, the wind blowing strands into my face. "No reason, really."

Sam nods once, but from the quirk of his lips, it's clear he doesn't believe me. Rather than press, he sips his beer, then cracks his neck. Constant movement, like he doesn't like standing still.

I'm not sure what else to say. I'm terrible at small talk, and every time I look at Sam, all I can think about is making out with him. But there's no way I'm bringing up the kiss. It clearly meant nothing to him, and what would I even say? It happened, and now it's behind us. So I keep my mouth shut and stare out at the ocean.

The silence stretches on for a bit too long, and I'm about to take my chances with the rocks and run away from this conversation when he clears his throat.

"You stoked for Friday?" He sets his beer bottle into the sand, wipes his palms off on his thighs.

I dig my thumbnail into the log. "Yep. The drive is going to suck, though."

"I think it'll be great," Sam says confidently.

"You do?"

"Oh yeah. I *love* a good eight-hundred-mile road trip."

"No one loves eight-hundred-mile road trips."

"The junk food? Delicious. The tourist traps? Hokey. The company? Awesome." Sam grins teasingly. When I don't respond, he nudges me with his elbow and goads, "C'mon, Florence Nightingale. Admit it. It'll be eight hundred miles of *fun*."

I snort, finally cracking. "Eight hundred miles of fun? That sounds like a bad billboard slogan."

Sam picks up his beer and tips it toward me in acknowledgement. "There it is."

"There's what?"

"You're smiling! Up until now, I would've thought sitting here with me was pure torture, based off your facial expressions."

I roll my eyes, but my cheeks are burning hot. "Yeah, well, don't let it go to your head."

"Too late." Using the knuckle of his pointer finger, Sam pushes his glasses up the bridge of his nose. A move that would be dorky on anyone else, but on him? It makes my heart stammer. Glasses adjusted, he jumps to his feet. "C'mon."

"Where?"

Sam nods his chin toward the bonfire. "Let's head back to the group."

"Oh, that's okay." I shoo him away. "This log is very comfortable."

"We won't stay for much longer." Sam checks his watch, a clunky, waterproof thing with a compass for hiking. "And I might need your help prying Kacey away from Hanna."

This makes me smile, but thanks to Sam, I'm now overly aware of my lips. "We'll leave soon?"

Sam nods. "Promise."

"Okay," I agree, and stand up, brushing splinters off the back of my dress. The moonlight fades in and out behind clouds, casting the rocky beach in deep shadows, the air salty and wet, and I carefully pick my way forward among the rocks.

"Flor, wait." Sam's fingers curl around my elbow, and I turn around. He shifts his weight back on his heels, then drags his teeth along his bottom lip. And after a pause that my head fills with a million possibilities, he says, "We're good, right?"

The million possibilities burst and vanish, like a light bulb burning out. I glance toward the darkened ocean, seriously conflicted. Isn't this what I wanted? To be "good" with Sam? But if that's the case, why can't I breathe? It's like someone's just kicked me in the stomach.

After a moment, I turn back to him. "Of course we're good," I say, way too enthusiastically. "Why wouldn't we be?"

Sam takes a swig of his beer, then looks at me with this big, relieved smile on his face. "Awesome," he says, and gives me a brotherly pat on the shoulder. "Let's head back—it's freezing over here."

I trail behind Sam and think, *Fuck my life.*

EIGHT

The Beach House, Bainbridge Island

THURSDAY, AUGUST 11, MORNING

I've barely sipped my morning coffee before everything kicks into gear at the beach house.

"Now," Rosemary says to her kids from the kitchen counter as she peruses her checklist—a woman after my own heart. "I emailed you both our hotel info just in case you can't get ahold of us on our cells. We'll be back on Saturday, probably midday or in the evening."

"Don't call unless someone is seriously injured or something is on fire." Alec removes the vegan-egg omelets from the stove. After a thoughtful pause, he adds, "Or both."

Rosemary laughs. "Don't listen to your dad. Call or text whenever."

Alec slides a plate of omelets onto the kitchen table. Kacey digs into her omelet, and I poke at the fake egg (fegg?) on my plate with my fork. I frown as it jiggles like Jell-O.

Sam fills up his coffee mug and slouches into the seat across from me, yawning into his fist. True to his word, we left the beach not long after we returned to the bonfire. Kacey, significantly more drunk than Sam, left with Hanna's phone number and passed out the second after I helped hoist her into the top bunk. But I wasn't able to sleep. I tossed and turned, replaying that moment on the beach like a bad movie. I feel foolish, remembering how much I enjoyed sitting there with Sam. Because that question—*"We're good, right?"*—and that pat on the shoulder tell me everything I need to know.

Alec loads the dishwasher. "Rose, it's our anniversary. They'll be *fine*."

"Yeah," Kacey pipes up between bites of omelet. "We're competent. And adults now."

Rosemary raises an eyebrow. "One of those statements is true," she murmurs, and walks over to Sam to kiss him on the cheek. "You're in charge, okay?"

Sam shoots his mom a smile. "No calling or texting unless someone's on fire. Got it."

Rosemary sighs, and gives her husband an exasperated look.

I love Rosemary and Alec's love, the way they can practically read each other's minds, have conversations without words. When I first met them, their connection was both fascinating and enviable. As much as I want that, my brain isn't a happy place, and I'm not eager to share it with others. Everyone has intrusive thoughts, sure, but a brain like mine doesn't know which thoughts have value and which are designed to destroy me from the inside out.

I'm *not* my thoughts, but that doesn't mean I'm ready to share them with another person.

"Okay, we're going now," Alec announces, and guides his wife by the shoulders out of the kitchen and into the hallway.

Kacey pops up from the table to hug her parents goodbye, and I wave as they carry their weekend bags from the master bedroom. Then Alec and Rosemary shut the front door behind them, leaving the three of us all alone in the beach house.

Sam finishes off his breakfast, then gets up to dump his plate in the sink. He claps his hands together. "Okay! You two ready to hit the road?"

"Tone down the cruise director energy, please." Kacey wanders back into the kitchen, massaging her temples.

"Never," he says, and tosses a wink my direction.

I shouldn't smile. So naturally, I smile. Then I shove more fegg omelet into my mouth as a punishment because *what is wrong with me?* Last night was more proof that I made the right decision in December. Sam's not into me. He was never into me. These are the facts.

Upstairs, Kacey and I take turns showering. Then we repack our bags. I try to focus on the big picture rather than my tangled emotions. Today, we're headed to San Francisco. Tomorrow, we meet Eleanor and Trish. Sam is just our transportation.

A glorified, long-distance rideshare that looks freakishly good in a pair of jeans.

Kacey and I funnel downstairs, where Sam's waiting for us with his bag. After he taps in the beach house's alarm code and locks the front door, we head to the Jeep. Kacey lags behind with her ridiculous luggage, so Sam and I walk down the driveway to where the Jeep's parked along the street beneath some maple trees.

"Leave your bag and I can pack it," Sam offers as he pops open the Jeep's back doors, and I place my bag at his feet. The cargo area is crammed full of junk: an ice chest, a fire extinguisher, a bag of tools, two and a half pairs of hiking boots, a stack of two-by-fours.

I lift my brows. "You sure there's enough room?"

Sam shrugs, then picks up the lone hiking boot with a frown. "I'll figure it out."

Kacey reaches us and dumps her suitcase on the ground, then she leans against the side of the Jeep and sips from her water bottle. "Last night was a bad idea," she moans.

"Told you so," I say without an ounce of sympathy.

"Can I sit in the back?" She gives me manipulative puppy dog eyes. "I'm gonna nap."

Sorry, *what*? There's no way I'm sitting up in the front with Sam! Those front seats are way too close to each other. There's barely any elbow room, let alone the three-foot bubble of personal space I'd ideally like to have whenever Sam's around. I need to ease into things.

"Nap? What if I need a nap? I'm the one who barely slept last night," I say, sweat quickly dampening my armpits.

"You don't nap," Kacey points out, which is true. Sleeping during the day is even worse than at night for me. "Don't you want me fully rested if I drive later?"

"You're not driving my Jeep," Sam tells his sister, shoving the ice chest aside to make room for our bags.

Defeated, I slump against the side of the car. "Fine. Whatever. Take the back seat, Kace."

Kacey blows me a kiss before crawling into the back of the Jeep. After getting comfy, she dramatically drapes a sweater over her eyes to block out the light.

Sam nudges Kacey's suitcase with the toe of his shoe, but it doesn't budge. "What the hell did she pack in there? That's twenty pounds, easy."

I glance down at the hot-pink suitcase, the stitching on the sides bulging. The trip has barely begun. I need to keep my shit together. I can't let myself be so easily affected by Sam. Avoiding him will be impossible over the next few days.

I'm going to act normal. Like I totally believed what I said last night. We're good. We are *so* good. Because if you can't beat 'em, join 'em.

"Free weights. An encyclopedia set. All of Mrs. Miranda's lawn gnomes," I try to joke, mentioning their neighbor who has a concerning number of gnomes in her yard.

"Hey," Kacey protests weakly from inside the Jeep, but we ignore her.

Before leaving for Idaho, Sam used to regularly prank Mrs. Miranda by moving her lawn gnomes around in the middle of the night. An innocent crime that made us double over in laughter as a flustered Mrs. Miranda would run around her yard every morning in her robe, trying to put them back in their right places.

Sam chuckles and leans down to hoist Kacey's suitcase into the Jeep. "I miss Mrs. Miranda," he says fondly. "Maybe I'll have to pay her a visit before I head back to Idaho." The back of his black tee rides up, exposing a stretch of his bare skin and the waistband of his boxers.

Face hot, I climb into the Jeep's passenger's seat. A moment later, Sam slides in beside me. Yep. Way too close. The car may be bulky, but this front seat is almost claustrophobic. I can smell his body wash and pine deodorant, and it smells *good.* Ugh. I'm the most pathetic person on earth.

Sam fits the key into the ignition, then looks my way. He holds my gaze for one unnerving moment that makes me wonder what he's thinking. Is he trying to forget about what happened the last time we were in the front seat of this car like I am?

Sam's hand on the back of my neck as he drew me closer. The way his lips brushed mine, almost like it'd been a mistake, like he expected me to change my mind and push him away. Then that second kiss, which was definitely no mistake . . .

Then Sam clears his throat, and the Jeep revs to life. Thankfully, he looks away as he shifts the car into gear, and we're off. Good. I have enough to worry about. Like officially lying to my parents. I am no longer where I said I was going to be. This is really happening.

Eleanor and Trish, and an unforgettable summer.

That's why I'm doing this.

But I'm also doing this for *me,* and all the past versions of myself who never chased after something they wanted. And it's scary because there's no backing out now, no changing my mind. I'm doing this. Even if it means being trapped in a car with Sam Hodge and my confusing, cockroach feelings that refuse to die for eight hundred miles. Even if it means lying to my mom and dad. Even if it means I might leave and fracture so bad, I'll stop leaving the house again.

I exhale and will myself to calm down. I pretend like I'm leaving all my baseless anxieties behind as we roll away from the beach house and toward the ferry dock. Every concern, every fear, every little thing that holds me back.

I tell myself I'm leaving it all behind.

I don't know if I believe those words, not yet, but I think them all the same.

NINE

Bainbridge Island Ferry to Tacoma, WA

THURSDAY AFTERNOON

My chill lasts all of thirty minutes.

Thirty measly minutes.

By the time Sam maneuvers the Jeep off the ferry and into the thick of downtown Seattle traffic, my panic skyrockets from a steady, manageable five to an alarming nine. The reality of the situation—the lies, the road trip, *Sam*—become impossible to ignore. Because we're zipping through Seattle traffic with Sufjan Stevens blasting through the speakers, officially on our way.

I'm not sure if I should throw up or give myself a pat on the back.

When my phone buzzes with a text from my mom, I'm

heavily leaning toward throwing up. Because what if she found out already? What if I can't even leave the city without setting off some internal Helene Cordray alarm alerting her to my location?

I unlock the phone and read.

MOM: Found your medicine in the bathroom. Did you forget it?

First, relief. Then, annoyance. I don't know why I'm annoyed, but I am.

I sigh at the screen, then tap my phone to my forehead.

"Everything good?" Kacey sits forward to peer over my shoulder. She woke up when we were on the ferry and Sam bought her coffee from the café. Fully hydrated and semi-caffeinated, she's slightly more alive to the world now. Yet I'm somehow still stuck in the front seat next to her brother.

"Yeah, yeah," I say, well aware Sam's listening. And I'd rather die than talk about my anxiety meds in front of him. "Just my mom."

ME: Nope, I brought ten days' worth in my meds case. Thanks!

Maybe I shouldn't be irritated—Mom's looking out for me—but all those little comments make me feel like someone who can't be trusted to take care of themselves.

MOM: Oh good! How's the beach house?

My stomach turns.

ME: It's nice! [smiley]

The beach house *is* nice. We're just not there to appreciate its niceness.

I stuff my phone back into my purse. Out of sight, but never out of mind.

"Can we pull over soon?" Kacey asks, and leans forward

between our seats. "I need more coffee. Lots of coffee. All the coffee."

"Sure." Sam glances at Google Maps. "We actually need gas. I meant to fill up last night. Florie, can you look up some gas stations and change the destination?"

Sam and I both reach to unlatch his phone from its holder at the exact same time.

Flustered, I pull my hand back. "Sorry." The spot where his hand brushed mine is hot, the warmth moving up my wrist to my arm and throughout my entire body. The fact that my body responds like this—to something as tame as his hand touching mine—is beyond embarrassing.

Clearing his throat, Sam says, "Here," and holds the phone out, his eyes never leaving the road.

I take the phone without any more accidental hand contact and find a Shell station down the street from a Starbucks in Tacoma. Twenty minutes later, we're off the freeway and driving through the city. When Sam approaches the Starbucks, Kacey heaves a sigh from the back seat.

"Starbucks? *Really?*"

"Don't be a snob." Sam surveys the busy street and its lack of parking. Since we're arriving right around ten, the streets are crowded, and every one of the angled parking stalls in front of the coffee chain are taken.

After another lap around the block, Kacey says, "Just drop me off. I'll grab the coffees while you fill up. Then circle back and pick me up."

Sam doesn't hesitate and says, "Sure," and pulls alongside the curb.

"Good idea, I'll come with you," I hurry to say, already reaching for my seat belt.

"I've got it." Kacey slides out of the back seat. "Besides, I need you to pick out the road trip snacks at the gas station. I don't trust Sam; he'll end up buying six bags of Sour Patch Kids. *Again.*"

Before I can formulate an argument, she slams the car door shut and jogs into the Starbucks.

I glance beside me, and Sam smiles. "Shall we?"

"Sure." I lean against the passenger's-side door. He eases off the brake and drives forward, following the directions to the gas station.

Sam parks beside a pump at the Shell station and turns the Jeep off. As he unbuckles his seat belt, he says, "I'll start filling up then meet you inside?"

"Yeah, okay." After shaking my shoulders, as if it can dissipate my anxious energy, I grab my purse and head into the attached mini-mart.

The bell jangles as I step inside. Gas station mini-marts are strange. They're all exactly the same. The same aroma—like Icees and disinfectant and cigarettes. Those big dispensers of crappy coffee by a hot dog grill and the attendant behind the counter who is clearly checked out. No judgment. I would be too.

I wander over to the snack aisle. We'll have to stop for lunch and dinner, but we definitely need snacks. And considering the only food Rosemary and Alec brought to the beach house could qualify as squirrel food, we didn't bother packing any. I mean, who likes kale chips?

Tilting my head back, I assess my options. Then I grab a bag of BBQ potato chips for Kacey and a tube of Pringles for myself, tucking them both beneath my arms.

"What? No sea salt and vinegar?"

I glance over my shoulder at Sam, who has joined me by the chips. He's frowning at my selection with both hands shoved into the front pockets of his jeans. "Nope. They'll stink up the car," I tell him, then move on to the candy section.

"Sure, but it's *my* car." Sam grabs a gigantic bag of sea salt and vinegar chips off the stand and follows me. He shakes the blue-and-white bag for emphasis, saying, "I've never understood why you hate these. They're delicious."

I flick my gaze from the bag to Sam's face. He lifts his brows, and the corner of my mouth curls. "I hate vinegar," I tell him, not focusing on the fact he's remembered my chip preferences. "Therefore, I hate sea salt and vinegar chips. They're Satan's chips."

Sam laughs. "Satan's chips?"

"Yep." I shrug. "They're disgusting."

"You're missing out, weirdo." He clucks his tongue then turns to the candy display.

My heart thrums from its closeness to Sam, and I force my mind back to last night. His relief when I told him we were okay, the way he patted me on the shoulder like I was a little kid. Right now I'm feeling ten different emotions all at once, but mostly, I feel like a sucker who keeps falling into the same flirtation trap, over and over and over again.

Meanwhile, an oblivious Sam grabs three bags of Sour Patch Kids off the shelf, plus several other sour candy variations,

humming along to the pop song playing on the gas station speakers. Glancing sideways at me, he says, "Okay, you think my taste in snack food is gross? You're buying Good and Plenty."

I clutch the pink-and-white box to my chest. "Excuse me? What's wrong with Good and Plenty?"

"Black licorice is gross enough. Covering it in candy doesn't make it taste any better."

"Black licorice is *way* better than red. Stop judging my snack food." In defiance, I grab a second box of Good & Plenty and add it to my pile. "At least these won't stink up the car."

"Hypocrite." He chuckles, his shoulder bumping into mine as he reaches for a pack of gum on the shelf.

"If you're hungry later, I'm not letting you eat any of these. Consider them off limits."

"Right." Sam draws the word out. He scoots past me to bring his goods to the cashier, our bodies far too close for one brief, torturous second. "Like that's ever stopped either of us before."

My mouth drops open. I follow him to the check-out counter and dump my snacks beside his. "Are you seriously flirting with me right now?"

Sam glances sideways at me, one hand digging into the back pocket of those tight jeans for his wallet. "I don't know what you mean." Debit card in hand, he pays for his snacks. "What do you think?" he asks the cashier with a wink. "Am I flirting with her?"

The cashier, a woman in her mid-sixties with big hair,

watches us as she scans a tube of Pringles. Her face is far from amused. "Keep me out of your lover's quarrel."

I die a little inside. No, a lot. I die a lot inside. "We're not—" Flustered, I turn to Sam. "I get it. You flirt with any- and everything. You're an equal opportunist flirter! *Whatever.* But just because we're good doesn't mean you can flirt with me, okay?"

Sam takes his bag of road trip snacks and leans one hip to the counter. His expression is bemused. "What, exactly, is an equal opportunist flirter?"

"I mean it, Sam," I say, rooting around in my purse for my wallet. The cashier finishes scanning my items, shamelessly rolling her eyes. "If we're going to survive the next three days, you need to tone it down."

"Oh, I'm just having some fun," he says, and thanks the cashier as she slides over my bag. He scoops it up and leads the way out of the mini-mart. Once we're outside, he pauses and holds the bag out for me. "I don't mean anything by it, you know."

"Yeah." I swipe my bag of snacks from his hand. "I know."

That's kind of the problem.

TEN

Centralia, WA

THURSDAY AFTERNOON

I watch Sam demolish not one, not two, but *three* cheeseburgers for lunch. Sure, he's six foot five and probably needs thousands of calories just to roll out of bed in the morning, but how on earth can someone eat three cheeseburgers in one sitting? I should find the whole display revolting, but I don't. Because I like everything Sam does, and it's incredibly annoying. Thanks, hormones.

Meanwhile, I could barely choke down half of my burger due to my nerves.

As Kacey and Sam finish eating, I push my barely touched plate aside and set my phone on the table, opening Google Maps. Studying our route beats watching Sam demolish another cheeseburger. If we keep up our current pace, we can probably make it to the Oregon border before eight or nine tonight. Then, tomorrow, we'll only have six or seven hours to cover to reach San Francisco.

The waitress drops off our bill, and we all chip in to pay for the burgers, shakes, and fries.

Once we're outside, I ask, "Think we can make it to the Oregon-California border tonight? I mapped it out and it seems doable."

"Lemme see." I hand Sam my phone with the loaded Google Maps route as we head toward the car. Since the mini-mart, he's been perfectly polite to me. But we've been around Kacey this entire time, so it's hard to tell if anything has sunk into his thick skull yet. Peering down at my phone, he says, "That's slightly more than halfway, but if we can make it, I'm game. What time did you two want to be on the road by tomorrow?"

"Earlier the better." I punch the crosswalk button with my elbow, and we wait for the light to turn. "I don't want to push our luck." A stream of cars chugs along the road, and the streets are busy with kids taking advantage of the last weeks of summer vacation, tourists exploring the historic Centralia downtown.

The light turns, and we cross the street. The car's parked to our right, but Kacey veers off toward the left once we reach the sidewalk. She comes to a stop in front of a storefront called Cheeky Monkey Vintage and Thrift.

"Is that, or is that not, the coolest jumpsuit you've seen in your entire life?" Kacey asks once I catch up with her, pointing to the window display. A mannequin is posed with arms akimbo, dressed in a blue polka-dotted jumpsuit with wide legs.

I tilt my head. "I haven't seen many jumpsuits in my life, but sure. Let's go, Kace—"

"The list, Flor. Bangin' outfits! This is it, I know it." Kacey presses her palm to the glass in longing. "This jumpsuit would be *perfect* for tomorrow night."

The rigid part of me wants to stay on schedule—and hit the road—but I remember what Kacey said when we made our list. How we should make even more memories along the way, tick off items, and have *fun*. "Yeah, okay. Maybe I can find something too."

Sam crosses his arms, watching us with a wrinkled brow. "What list?"

We both ignore him. That list is about me and Kacey. Sam's intruded on way too much this summer already.

Kacey hooks her arm through mine and drags me into Cheeky Monkey. It's a dusty, crowded place, full of yellowing books with cracked spines, patina-dulled silverware, and creepy porcelain dolls. The air has that boxed-in smell of dust—like a grandmother's house. But there are also racks and racks of clothes spread throughout the store.

Sam trails us, letting loose a low whistle when he steps inside. "Hey, Flor, does this place remind you of Kacey's room?" he asks, wandering over to a shelf of used books.

I mentally give Sam brownie points for effort because he's trying to act normal. What I said must've gotten through to him, because any jovial or flirty undertones to his voice are gone. Maybe he's actually *trying*.

"Nah, this place is cleaner than Kacey's," I say, and do my best to loosen up.

Kacey shoots us both dirty looks, but luckily, she hasn't picked up on the weird energy between me and her brother. She releases my arm and beelines for the register, asking to see the jumpsuit on display. As Kacey waits, the sales associate begins the super-awkward job of undressing the mannequin.

"I'm gonna browse," I tell Kacey.

"Go find something that's not a shapeless sundress," she says, and waves me off.

Sam's still perusing the books, so I meander deeper into the eclectic store by myself, my fingers trailing over the edges and seams of vintage and used clothes. On a rack in the far corner is a simple shirtdress, white with red, navy, and yellow piping. After lifting the hanger off the rack, I search out the tag and check the size. Close enough.

I collide with Kacey on the way to the dressing rooms. The coveted jumpsuit is draped over her arm.

"Okay, what do you think?" I lift the dress to my body. "Bangin' enough?"

My best friend nods her approval. "Definitely. Try it on!"

The store has two small dressing rooms, and we each duck into one. I pull the flimsy curtain closed, and, after checking there aren't any gaps, I tug off my clothes and pile them on the chair in the corner.

On the other side of the plywood divider, Kacey struggles into the jumpsuit. I can hear her hobbling around on one foot, swearing as she bangs her elbow into the divider. For whatever reason, she loves jumpsuits. No one should have to completely undress down to their bra and underwear to use the bathroom—but maybe that's just me.

I unzip the back of the dress, then slide it on over my head. The mirror on the back wall is warped, cloudy and old, but the dress fits. Tighter around my hips than I would've expected, but not in a bad way. I'm not Kacey; puberty didn't treat me well. Or at all. A late bloomer, I didn't get my period until I was fifteen, and any development stopped there. My chest is flat, my hips narrow. In this dress, though, all the parts of me I dislike almost look good.

"You done?" I ask Kacey. "I need a zip-up."

"One sec!"

I pull the curtain back and, on socked feet, pad out to the full-length mirror stationed near the dress racks in the back of the store. Sam wanders my direction, staring down at his phone, a brown bag stamped with *Cheeky Monkey Vintage and Thrift* in his other hand. I try—and fail—to grasp the zipper before he reaches the mirror, all too aware of the bare skin and the band of my bra strap currently on display. In my reflection, I catch sight of my rapidly reddening cheeks.

"Need help?" he offers, and lifts his gaze from his phone to mine in the mirror.

I shake my head. "Kacey'll be out in a sec."

Sam sighs and tucks his phone into his pocket. "Don't be weird."

"How am I being weird?" I ask, totally aware of how weird I'm acting. "I'm not being weird."

"You're definitely being weird." His voice is low even

though we're far enough from the dressing room and Kacey's prying ears. "And if your weirdness is because of the mini-mart, chill out. I heard you loud and clear, okay?"

Flustered, I drop my hand from the back of my dress. "Okay, fine." Cool air brushes my bare skin and goose bumps ripple up my arms.

"Besides," Sam continues, setting his bag on a nearby chair, "I've zipped Kacey up dozens of times. It's not rocket science."

When he stands behind me, I don't breathe. Just study my pug-patterned socks as his fingers brush the back of my neck as he moves my hair out of the way. Then he rests one hand on my waist to create tension as he uses the other to tug the zipper upward. It's a slow, agonizing movement that has me mentally kicking myself because this was such a bad idea.

I'm glad that my embarrassing outburst in the mini-mart amounted to something—Sam no longer acting so Sam-like will help me cope during this trip—but it's not just the accidental flirting that sends my heart rate skyrocketing. No, it's *everything* about him, and the fact his hand is still on my waist is slowly killing me. I should've waited for Kacey, because even if my brain is determined to move on from this pathetic crush, my heart will undoubtedly betray me.

Clearing his throat, Sam steps back. "Consider yourself zipped."

"Um. Thanks." I readjust the dress around my hips. There's not a chance in hell I'm making eye contact with Sam, so I keep staring at my socks.

"You look good in white, you know," he says, so conversationally we could be talking about the weather. "Not flirting, just an observation."

I lift my gaze from the floor—but Sam's already turning away. He's back scrolling on his phone, no longer looking my direction. Before I can gather my thoughts and say something, *anything*, in response, Kacey yanks back the curtain to her dressing room.

"Well? Was I right, or was I right?" Kacey skips over to us and does a twirl, becoming a whirlwind of blue polka dots.

I turn away from Sam and force a laugh. "You look amazing."

"You do too!" Kacey shuffles over beside me to check herself out in the full-length mirror. "You buy that dress, I'll buy this jumpsuit, and we'll wear them tomorrow night. Can you *imagine* our meet-and-greet photos with Eleanor and Trish? They'll be so beautiful, we'll have to frame them."

"I'm gonna wait outside," Sam says. In the mirror, I watch as he grabs his bag off the chair; then he disappears between the circular clothing racks and towering hat stands.

"Flor?" Kacey nudges me.

"Sorry, what?"

"You good to go? We should buy these then hit the road."

"Yep!" I step into my changing room and resist the urge to scream my frustrations into the decorative pillow on the chair in the corner.

I was wearing white the night Sam and I kissed. A silver skirt and white top to my parents' holiday party, to be exact; I'd felt like snow and miracles. When I took off my coat after arriving at the venue, Sam said I looked nice. A throw-away compliment, but at the time, it'd felt like *everything*.

But this? This is a coincidence. A lot has happened since that moment, and I doubt Sam even remembers what I was wearing. I doubt that night was even that memorable to Sam at all.

I change out of the dress and pull my clothes back on. Then I hurry out of the dressing room and head straight to the register, where Kacey's buying her jumpsuit. Through the window display—which is now home to a naked mannequin with perky plastic breasts—Sam's leaning against a parking meter.

Armed with our thrift store finds, Kacey and I meet Sam outside.

As we walk back to the Jeep, Kacey motions to Sam's Cheeky Monkey bag and asks, "What'd you buy?"

"Oh, just picked up a gift." He tucks the bag beneath his arm as he searches for his keys.

"For Amanda?" Kacey teases, and pokes her brother in the ribs.

Sam flips his sister off in response.

The Jeep's parked in a small lot beneath an apple tree; the ground is covered in smashed fruit. Now that Kacey's not napping, she takes the front, and I slide into the back. We follow the GPS directions to the highway and put Centralia in the rearview mirror.

We turn on another true crime podcast, and then we're driving down I-5. I lean my cheek against the window. Surprise surprise, I can't get Sam out of my mind. He lives up there, rent free. Where does he get off complimenting me? Sam must not realize what he's saying. How those words sound to me, a girl who's pined after him for nearly two years. Not like he knows about the extent of my pining. But still.

I should be mad. Except . . . I like it way too much to be angry. I like it *so much.*

I press my eyes shut.

You build things up, I remind myself, *and you daydream.*

KACEY + FLORIE'S WILD AND SUPER-COOL
BFF ROAD TRIP BUCKET LIST

1. Be spontaneous (yes, Florie, that means YOU)
~~2. Find bangin' outfits for the Eleanor and Trish meet and greet~~

We're going to look amazing. AMAZING!

Maybe your self-confidence is rubbing off on me because we totally will!

3. Be embarrassing tourists
4. Buy a memento in each state
5. Kiss a random hottie

Hannah ♡ 206-555-1978

6. Break a traffic law
7. Say yes, no questions asked
8. Visit a roadside attraction
9. Anything that makes us ask "Is this a bad idea?"
10. HAVE THE BEST TIME OF OUR LIVES

ELEVEN

Portland, Oregon

THURSDAY, LATE AFTERNOON

Seated at a purple picnic bench outside Voodoo Doughnut, Kacey and I study our list.

Earlier this morning, before we left Bainbridge Island, Kacey initialed beside number five: kiss a random hottie. Guess she got more than Hanna's phone number. But other than number two—bangin' outfits—we haven't made much progress. We decided to make a brief stop in Portland to do something touristy and knock out number three. Sam suggested Voodoo Doughnut, which is indeed touristy, but he was way more focused on finding a way to get us to stop for doughnuts than anything else.

"Are the doughnuts enough, though? Should we find

KACEY + FLORIE'S WILD AND SUPER-COOL
BFF ROAD TRIP BUCKET LIST

1. Be spontaneous (yes, Florie, that means YOU)
~~2. Find bangin' outfits for the Eleanor and Trish meet and greet~~

We're going to look amazing. AMAZING!

Maybe your self-confidence is rubbing off on me because we totally will!

3. *Be embarrassing tourists*
4. *Buy a memento in each state*
5. Kiss a random hottie

Hannah ♡ 206-555-1978

6. Break a traffic law
7. Say yes, no questions asked
8. *Visit a roadside attraction*
9. Anything that makes us ask "Is this a bad idea?"
10. *HAVE THE BEST TIME OF OUR LIVES*

ELEVEN

Portland, Oregon

THURSDAY, LATE AFTERNOON

Seated at a purple picnic bench outside Voodoo Doughnut, Kacey and I study our list.

Earlier this morning, before we left Bainbridge Island, Kacey initialed beside number five: kiss a random hottie. Guess she got more than Hanna's phone number. But other than number two—bangin' outfits—we haven't made much progress. We decided to make a brief stop in Portland to do something touristy and knock out number three. Sam suggested Voodoo Doughnut, which is indeed touristy, but he was way more focused on finding a way to get us to stop for doughnuts than anything else.

"Are the doughnuts enough, though? Should we find

something even more touristy ?" I use a napkin to clean off my sticky fingers. Unlike Kacey and Sam, I couldn't bring myself to order one of the over-the-top doughnuts and went with a boring glazed. But it was delicious.

Kacey considers this, then takes a bite of her Old Dirty Bastard, bits of Oreo crumbling onto the picnic table. "Well, we're not in a rush, right? We're making great time."

I glance through the store window to my left, catching sight of Sam waiting in line for his second doughnut order. The storefront is just as funky as you'd imagine—stained glass windows, an elaborate chandelier, and art covering the brightly colored walls. He shuffles forward in line, looking down at his phone with his free hand tucked into the back pocket of his jeans. A pair of college-aged girls behind him in line shamelessly check him out, and I swivel from the window, cheeks warming.

Every time my pathetic, lovelorn brain wanders in Sam's direction, I have to remind myself that Sam's only here because he's driving to San Francisco to hook up with a girl.

A girl that is not me.

I mean, Sam's essentially on an eight-hundred-mile sex pilgrimage for Amanda.

"Ooh, this isn't list related, but we should totally hit up PNCA." Kacey pulls her phone out of her purse and opens Google Maps. A few taps later and she adds, "Yeah, it's like half a mile from here! We could walk?"

I drop my gaze to my napkin and nod. "Sure, yeah." My stomach twists, and I wish it were due to the doughnut and the excessive amount of sugar I just consumed. But I know it's because visiting the Pacific Northwest College of Art is the last thing I want to do right now. And maybe that's selfish.

Ever since we crossed into Oregon, this weird and panicky feeling has been tightening my chest. Maybe it's being in Portland, the city about to steal my best friend, that's making me feel so funky. But for once on this trip, how I'm feeling has nothing to do with Sam. Kind of refreshing, honestly.

When I look on a map, the route from Barmouth to Portland isn't very far or dangerous. When I look at a map, I can pretend like it's within my ability to bridge that distance between us. But having driven it—even if the route from the ferry dock in downtown Seattle to Portland isn't the exact same as the one from Barmouth—I can't escape the facts.

There's no way I can drive that stretch solo to visit Kacey this fall. Every time I try to imagine it, my mind stops. Because how would that work? I don't have a license, and I'm afraid of public transportation. Kacey will be in Portland, and I'll be stuck in our middle-of-nowhere town for the foreseeable future.

Kacey bumps my knee beneath the table. The warm afternoon breeze picks up and blows her curls every direction. She's wearing these Lucky Charms earrings that constantly get tangled up in her hair. "I can't wait for you to see the campus! It's so freaking cool."

I force a smile, but Kace isn't buying it. Her brow puckers, and she asks, "What's going on in Florie Land?"

"Nothing." Florie Land is Kacey's somewhat endearing term for the hellscape that is my mind. I grab a tiny leftover chunk of doughnut off my napkin and pop it into my mouth.

"Psh. Something's always going on in Florie Land." She pushes her sunglasses onto the top of her head and leans her elbows on the table. "Tell me."

I give an exaggerated shrug. "Nothing we need to talk about, okay? I'm fine."

"You need to be more than fine on this trip," she says resolutely. "Number ten, babe—have the best time of our lives. Not the most *fine* time of our lives."

I worry my bottom lip between my teeth. Someone like Kacey Hodge can never understand how it feels to be left behind. But she's staring at me with those big brown eyes, so I say, "Sometimes it's depressing, feeling like everyone's moving on without you."

Kacey's face falls, and she reaches out across the table for my hands. "I'm not moving on without you, Flor."

"You are," I say, and try to keep my tone light. "And that's okay! Like, I haven't wanted to bring it up because you're so excited about school and Portland. But it's been hard. Staying in Barmouth . . ."

"I thought that's what you wanted."

I shrug one shoulder, watching as a pigeon picks at some smushed doughnut on the sidewalk. "I mean, yeah. College and moving and everything is pretty terrifying, and I didn't want to deal with it. And I look at you and you're just so—"

"Terrified," Kacey interrupts, and squeezes both of my hands in hers. "I'm fucking terrified."

I turn from the pigeon back to my best friend. "No, you're not."

"Yeah, I am. College is scary, Flor. That's normal."

Maybe Kacey's humoring me, but she sounds so sincere. "Really?"

"Oh yeah. My IBS flared for a solid month when I accepted my spot."

I snort-laugh. "Gross."

"I know." She grins and gives my hands another squeeze before letting go. Picking up her Old Dirty Bastard, she says, "While I appreciate your image of me—so fearless and badass—you have to know that I'm still scared, right? About being homesick and leaving my family. About living in a different state. Shit, living in a town with more than fifteen thousand people."

"Oh come on. You're going to rule this city by winter break," I tell her.

"Probably," she admits, but rolls her eyes. "You know what I'm really afraid of? That I'm only this cool *because* our town has fifteen thousand people. I'm going to be *such* a loser in college."

I laugh so loud, the pigeon takes flight, abandoning its doughnut. "There's only room for one loser in this friendship, and it's me."

Kacey kicks my shin under the table. "Oh shut up. You're way cooler than you realize. I mean, you're on a secret road trip to meet Eleanor and Trish. Can't get much cooler than that."

"You say that now. But you're going to make a ton of new friends and . . ."

"And what?" She grabs a chunk of Oreo off her doughnut and throws it at me; it hits bull's-eye, right in the center of my forehead. "Florence Cordray, you're the best friend I've ever had. You're my person, okay? Things'll change when I'm at PNCA, but we're not changing. Got it?"

That twisty stomachache and tightening around my chest vanish at Kacey's words. I slide off my bench and onto Kacey's, wrapping myself around her. Her arms encircle my waist and she hugs me back. I'm still going to worry about Kacey changing—about our friendship changing—but maybe it'll be okay. Maybe we'll change together.

"Can I tell you something I haven't told anyone except Lauren?" As I talk, I try not to get a mouthful of her hair.

Kacey leans her head to mine. "Duh."

"I'm exhausted, Kace. I've spent so much time and energy being afraid of falling down, of being vulnerable and failing." I untangle myself from her and shift on the bench. "Lately, part of me . . . I think part of me wants to fall, to mess up? Does that make any sense?"

My best friend smiles so wide, I see the cookie crumbles stuck in her teeth. "It makes a ton of sense. But I'm guessing messing up isn't really in Helene's vocabulary, huh?"

I shrug both shoulders. "Not really."

"I'm here for you, whatever you need. That doesn't change in two weeks." Then Kacey reaches over and hooks her pinky with mine. "Pinky promise."

Relief softens some of my anxious edges, and I grin. "Pinky promise."

Finding the novelty T-shirts—our Oregon mementos—wasn't difficult at all. And around the corner from Voodoo Doughnuts is the infamous Keep Portland Weird sign. The sign's painted on the back of a small theater called Dante's, and it's *just* touristy enough for us to feel like we can successfully check off number three. We're making some serious list progress.

In Dante's parking lot, Kacey and I pull the novelty T-shirts on over our clothes. They're identical—baby blue with a rainbow arching over PORTLAND, OREGON—and comically large. But perfect.

"Here." Kacey shoves her phone into Sam's chest. "Take a bunch, okay?"

Sam flips Kacey's phone around in his hands. "Okay. But what exactly are you two doing?"

"Being tourists." I smooth my palms down the oversized shirt.

When Sam came back out of Voodoo Doughnut, Kacey told him we had a few more things we wanted to do around Portland. But she didn't tell him about the list, and he's confused—but he's also been a good sport about following us around. Honestly, I think he's in a sugar coma. He ate, like, four doughnuts.

Sam huffs a laugh. "I can see that. Those shirts are—"

"Glorious," Kacey interrupts, and wraps her arm around my waist. "C'mon, Sammy! Take the photos."

"Everyone say 'weirdo' on three . . ."

Laughing, I lean into Kacey and smile into the camera.

I'm glad we'll have photos, but I won't need them to remember this moment.

This trip is already unforgettable.

KACEY + FLORIE'S WILD AND SUPER-COOL
BFF ROAD TRIP BUCKET LIST

1. Be spontaneous (yes, Florie, that means YOU)
~~2. Find bangin' outfits for the Eleanor and Trish meet and greet~~

We're going to look amazing. AMAZING!

Maybe your self-confidence is rubbing off on me because we totally will!

~~3. Be embarrassing tourists~~

SAY WEIRDOS

WEIRDOS!!!

It's official: I love Portland

And Portland loves you!

4. Buy a memento in each state

Oregon: Portland touristy T-shirts

5. Kiss a random hottie

Hannah ♡ 206-555-1978

6. Break a traffic law
7. Say yes, no questions asked
8. Visit a roadside attraction
9. Anything that makes us ask "Is this a bad idea?"
10. HAVE THE BEST TIME OF OUR LIVES

TWELVE

I-5 South, Wolf Creek, OR

THURSDAY NIGHT

The Jeep smells like cold french fries, coffee, and exhaustion. We barely made it out of Portland before rush hour descended upon the city, but the stop was totally worth it. Another list item checked off, plus I feel so much better now that I've talked to Kacey. And even though I wasn't jazzed about visiting PNCA at first, it was really nice seeing where my best friend will be living in a matter of weeks.

"Pull over up ahead," Kacey says when we pass a rest stop sign. There's shuffling in the back seat as she sits up, then sticks her head between the front seats. "I gotta pee."

Sam hits his blinker and pulls off the highway and into a parking spot at the rest stop. Towering trees serve as a backdrop to the small, cement building. It's past nine, the sky inky and star filled. Some big rigs are parked in the lot, and the streetlights flicker.

When I don't make any move to follow Kacey, she whines, "There's not a chance in hell I'm going in there alone. Not after that last chapter."

Sam takes off his glasses and rubs the bridge of his nose. "You two are going to give me nightmares with all this crap," he mutters, because we've listened to roughly four hours of a true crime audiobook about Robert Ben Rhoades, the Truck Stop Killer, since Portland. Kind of a poor choice in hindsight.

I don't have to pee, but I unclick my seat belt and climb out of the Jeep. Even though I'm tired and my shins are sore from walking around Portland, I'd rather chance my mortality in a rest stop bathroom than sit in the dark with Sam in the front seat of his Jeep.

Tugging on my flannel, I follow Kacey into the bathroom. We enter the women's, and Kacey ducks, checking the bottom of the stalls to make sure we're alone. "I hate rest stops," she says, and locks herself in the closest stall.

I step into a stall. Don't want to waste a pit stop.

"I think I found somewhere for us to stay the night," Kacey says in the stall beside mine, and metal creaks as she unspools some toilet paper. "I did some googling. But I don't know what you're going to think when I show you."

I frown and push down the toilet lever with my foot. "You're scaring me."

Kacey laughs, and I join her at the tiny row of sinks.

"Promise you'll say yes." She meets my gaze in the smeared, warped mirror. When I open my mouth to protest, she says, "Number seven. Trust me, you'll like it."

I dry off my hands on my dress since there aren't any paper towels or hand dryers. "I'm going to regret this, aren't I?" I tie my hair back, then fix my smudged eye shadow.

Kacey hip-checks me. "You saying yes?"

"Fine. Yes."

She pulls her phone out of her back pocket. "Awesome! I'm going to call them and see if there are any availabilities."

What place doesn't have an online booking system?

As we head out of the rest stop, she taps her phone, grinning ear to ear.

"One sec," she says to me, and steps off to the side beneath the only working streetlight.

I walk back to Sam's Jeep; he's standing outside, leaning against the driver's-side door with his head tipped back. Hearing the crunch of my shoes on the gravel, he glances over.

"What's Kacey doing?"

I hover near the grille of the Jeep and stretch my legs. "Booking our rooms for tonight."

Sam yawns, then takes off his glasses and rubs his eyes. "Where? I'm not sure how much more driving I have in me."

I stretch my arms overhead. "Not a clue." The vague anxiety in my chest multiplies. I'm already doubting my decision to say yes to Kacey without any details. That's the whole point—*say yes, no questions asked*—but my mind is already spinning away with possibilities.

"Really?" He sounds doubtful, probably because it's no secret I'm the control freak in our friendship.

"Really. I'm letting Kacey take the reins on this one." I try to smile, but my brain is forlornly thinking of my binder and all those motel options I preselected. All relatively cheap, with four-star reviews, high cleanliness ratings, and easy freeway access.

Kacey rushes over to us, an actual skip in her step. I have no idea how she still has energy after today.

"Okay," she announces, standing in front of us. "I booked the very last tree house at Out 'n' About."

"Sorry, what?" I ask. "Did you just say tree house?"

"Seriously? Awesome," Sam says, because of course he likes this idea.

"Give me your phone," Kacey demands, and I reluctantly pass her my phone. She pulls something up and hands it back. "That's their site." Then to Sam: "It's in Cave Junction, less than an hour from here. We'll have to get off the 5 and onto 199, though. Sound good?"

"I can do another hour." He grabs his to-go cup of coffee off the hood of the Jeep, swigging it back. "Especially if it means sleeping in a tree house. Nice idea, Kace."

As they talk, I thumb through the pictures. Big tree houses, small tree houses, zip lines, natural pools, and firepits. The images are almost magical. But there's nothing my brain hates more than a change in plans—even if the plans were only in my mind. When I pictured tonight, sleeping somewhere unknown with neither of my parents knowing where I am, I pictured some roadside motel. Mini soaps, a vending machine, and those really stiff, cheap towels in the bathroom.

A tree house, though? I didn't even know there were such things as tree house hotels. And we'll have to leave I-5, which was our straight shot into California. What if we get lost and end up missing the live show tomorrow? What if I can't sleep suspended, like, thirty feet in the air and am too tired to enjoy the show? What if our car breaks down, and, if we're off the main highway, we can't get a tow? *What if, what if, what if.*

I can usually spot an OCD spiral by these what-if thoughts. But what if my what-if thoughts are here to warn me? What then?

Fuck my what-ifs, I decide.

Because when am I ever going to get the chance to sleep in a tree house again?

Kacey arranged a late check-in for our tree house, the Peacock Perch. According to the woman who checked us in, it's their oldest tree house. And as we head up the wooden stairs, I can't remember what I was so nervous about. Every little chance I've taken on this trip so far hasn't led to any regrets or disasters. I'm never going to have a moment like this again, and I'm determined to enjoy it.

The door is carved with a peacock design, and the windows have colorful stained glass in turquoise and blues. We funnel inside, and Kacey, sweaty from hauling her suitcase up the flights of stairs, belly flops onto the mattress with a sigh. A double bed is in the center of the room, with a small cot built into the wall.

Sam tosses his bag on the cot, and my stomach swoops with the motion.

Maybe it's because I'm kind of exhausted, but for whatever reason, it doesn't register until this very moment that the tree house is one room. That there won't be a wall separating me from Sam tonight. Narrowing my eyes, I size up the space between the cot and the bed I'm sharing with Kacey. *Maybe* two feet? I'd ask Kacey to switch sides, but we've always slept this way: her on the left side of the bed, me on the right.

I dump my duffel on the floor and sit beside Kace, the tree house rocking gently with our movement.

There's no chance in hell I'm getting much sleep tonight, is there?

I tuck my hands beneath my thighs and glance around. Lack of personal space aside, the tree house is cozy, with working electricity, a small sink, and windows that overlook the treesort's campus.

Sam stretches out on the cot, his long legs dangling over the edge. "Today was so fucking long," he groans, dragging both hands over his face. "How many miles did we drive?"

"Almost five hundred, according to Google Maps," says Kacey, who kneels on the bed to look out one of the windows. She folds her arms along the sill, practically pressing her nose to the glass.

Even though there's a sink up here, there's no bathroom, so I grab my toiletry bag from my duffel. "I'm going to wash up," I say, and head outside, using the battery-operated lantern left on the windowsill to guide me. Carefully I work my way down the stairs and find the bathroom.

After peeing, I wash my hands, scrubbing my palms, cleaning beneath my fingernails. Then I brush my teeth and use a makeup-removing wipe to clean off my face. After I'm done, I study my reflection, my frizzed hair and tired eyes and chapped lips. And I smile.

For a moment, I let myself feel this one, small victory. The first day of our trip is behind us, and I'm still whole. Tomorrow. I just have to make it through tomorrow. *I've got this.*

Back inside the Peacock Perch, Kacey and I change into our pajamas while Sam's down using the bathroom, then we climb onto our bed. Sam returns and sits on the edge of his cot. And here I thought sitting beside him in the front seat of the Jeep was too cozy for comfort. I pull my legs up to my chest and lean against the wall. At least the part of the cot closest to me is the foot of the bed.

"Look what I stole from Mom," Kacey says, and tosses a baggie from her suitcase onto our bed. I do a double take, because inside the recycled sandwich bag are weed gummies. They're orange and in the shape of a marijuana leaf. Guess they're not going for discretion.

Sam leans over to our bed without getting up—they're *that* close—and inspects the baggie. "Mom's going to kill you." He holds the bag up to the light. "Mango Wango is her favorite."

Kacey gives an indignant scoff. "Like she'll notice. She buys them in bulk. Besides, us lying and driving to San Francisco will be Mom's motive. Not petty edible theft."

Sam considers this for a second before shrugging and helping himself. Kacey knows I usually stay away from all forms of illicit activities. Recreational weed is legal in both Washington and Oregon, but you still have to be over twenty-one.

Even if all I want is an escape from this brain, I've always been afraid of how off the rails it could go under the influence. For some people, THC makes anxiety worse, and my OCD is a one-stop shop for all things anxiety. I definitely don't need any help in that department.

Sensing my hesitation, Kacey says, "They're part CBD."

The Florie from a week ago would turn the gummy down. But isn't this trip all about pushing myself and all my rules? Isn't this trip about making memories with Kacey?

This is probably a bad idea, so I grab a gummy and pop it into my mouth. "Go ahead and check off number nine," I tell her, wrinkling my nose as the aftertaste hits.

"That's the spirit." Kacey leans over the side of the bed, pulling out the tub of board games our treesort oh-so-helpfully provided. "Anyone up for some Scrabble?"

We set up the board on our bed and pick tiles. Over the next thirty minutes, I manage to take the lead, but Sam's gaining on me, and Kacey's way too behind to catch up. I'm pretty confident I can win, and, when it's my turn again, I study my tiles. Try to make something out of them so I can knock Sam out of the running and bring home the victory.

I spell out the only word possible from my tiles to hit an open triple-word score. "Smooching. Fifty-four points with the triple."

Smooching?

I snort, covering my mouth with my hands. Of course I

had to go and spell "smooching" with Samson Hodge sitting two feet away from me! Okay, maybe there was more THC in those gummies than Kacey claimed, because now I'm laughing, really hard, and I can't stop.

Oh no. Am I high?

"Yep," Sam says from his cot, and I realize that I said that out loud. Oops.

I start laughing harder, and maybe it's contagious—or maybe "smooching" is an objectively hilarious word—because now Kacey's laughing too. She nudges me in the ribs and asks, "What is wrong with you?"

"Sorry," I wheeze. "Just. Smooching."

"Holy shit, you two are serious lightweights." When my watery eyes meet Sam's, he gives me this *look*. Some weird mixture of amusement and confusion.

"Whatever," Kacey says, giggling. "Not all of us spent senior year smoking our way through every hybrid strain in the tri-county area."

"You say that like it's a bad thing."

I wipe my eyes with my forearm, but I'm still all floaty. *Smooching*. The irony!

Kacey rolls onto her back, nearly knocking over the Scrabble board with her elbow. "Speaking of *smooching*"—I snort when she says it, and yeah, this was a bad idea because I'm kind of high—"can you please change your mind about kissing a random hottie? I wrote that one down for you, Flor!"

I might be high, but not high enough to agree to number five. "No way."

"Oh, come on," she groans, and flicks a rogue Scrabble

tile at me. "The last person you kissed was Evan Whitmore, and that was *last* summer."

Heat whooshes up my neck, and I turn away from Kacey, which is a mistake because Sam glances up from his tiles at the exact same moment, his gaze finding mine. He lifts one brow but doesn't say anything.

The heat intensifies. *Don't laugh,* I tell myself.

After a beat, Sam says, "Hey, uh, I forfeit. Florie wins."

"Fine with me." Kacey rolls upright, her hair everywhere, and yawns. "The only letters I have left are consonants. This game is rigged, I tell you. Rigged!"

I force myself to stop giggling so I can concentrate on putting the game away. I swipe "smooching" off the board first, dumping the tiles into the velvet storage bag. Ugh. Did I really need to win at Scrabble that badly? Why didn't I put down "mooching" or something and skip the triple-word score?

Kace yawns, her elbow knocking into me as she stretches. "What *time* is it?"

"Almost midnight." I'm finally calm enough to speak without dissolving into laughter, and I secure the lid on the Scrabble box. "I'm ready to call it a night."

"I'll set an alarm for six." Kacey puts the board game away and crawls beneath the comforter. "Sound good, Sammy?"

"Yep. See you nerds in the morning." He stretches out on the cot and flicks off the lantern. The small tree house is drenched in absolute middle-of-the-wilderness darkness.

"Night," I say, and Kacey grunts her sentiments.

I pull the comforter and an extra blanket up around my

shoulders while Kacey snuggles into the pillows beside me. I think the gummy's beginning to wear off, and I'm suddenly no longer tired.

Sam shifts around in the other bed, and I can vaguely make out the shape of his body in the darkness.

It doesn't take long for Kacey to fall asleep, her breathing evening out, punctuated by the lightest of snores. Despite the late hour and the gummy, sleep evades me as I lie curled up on my side.

The longer I lie there, sleepless, the more awake I feel. Almost like I never ate the gummy in the first place. No matter how I adjust, I can't get comfortable. Isn't weed supposed to calm you down and make you sleepy?

With Kacey beside me, though, I can't toss and turn; I don't want to disrupt her. So I keep curled on my side, facing Sam's bed.

Two feet might sound like a decent amount of space, but it's really not.

My eyes are closed, and I can't stop replaying that look on Sam's face when Kacey mentioned Evan Whitmore. That curious cock of his eyebrow. But Sam must've known before now that I hadn't told Kacey—after all, he didn't tell Kacey either—right? Why the surprise?

After punching my pillow, I roll onto my stomach and lean over the side of the bed. My phone's on the floor, plugged into the outlet, and I tap the screen for the clock. Half past midnight. Ugh. If I fall asleep right now, I'll only get five and a half hours of sleep.

I pillow my arm beneath my head and stare into the inky

I perch on the edge of the bed with my hands braced on my knees. Waiting for the tightness, the claws of anxiety, to release me from its grasp. *Just wait it out,* I urge myself.

"Florie?" Sam whispers from the cot, but we could yell and it's unlikely Kacey would wake up.

"Sorry, I didn't mean to wake you." Hopefully he can't sense the anxiety oozing off my body. "I'm having trouble falling asleep."

"Too excited about tomorrow?" Sam asks.

"Something like that."

There's a shuffling of blankets, and Sam's shadowy figure appears. Rather than sit on the edge, he shifts toward the foot so our knees press against one another in the very small gap between our beds. The warmth of his leg against mine almost pulls me out of my thoughts. Almost.

"You wanna go on a walk or something?"

"No, that's okay."

Sam's quiet, then says softly, "Come on, Flor. Fresh air will help."

I hesitate, but Sam's right. After glancing over my shoulder at Kacey's comatose body, I nod. "Sure."

Silently we slip out of our beds, stuff on our shoes, and escape into the night.

darkness. Obviously, I don't know what it sounds like when Sam's asleep, but there's no movement on the cot. No fluffing of pillows or tugging of blankets. It's just me, sleepless like always.

Deep breaths, I remind myself. *Clear mind.* Rather than focus on the thoughts spinning inside my mind, I focus on my breathing. And slowly my body and mind calm. Then a thought slips in.

Is the chain lock secured?

Kacey latched it before we had the gummies, but of course, I don't trust my memory.

I lie there, on my stomach, and will the thought to go away. To leave me alone.

But I've already lost enough sleep, and it's not like tonight's the night I'm finally going to kick my checking compulsion. I roll out of bed and quietly walk to the door. The chain is in place, but I unlatch and latch it again. There. It's locked. I'm safe. We're all okay.

As I try to turn away, something hot and tight grips my chest. *What if I didn't see the latch correctly? What if it isn't fully locked? What if I unlocked it when I was checking?* The claws of anxiety pierce my skin, sinking into my heart until it hurts to breathe. We're in a forest, which is, historically, rife with murderers! I can't be careless. I need to check it again. I need to be sure.

Teeth digging into my bottom lip, I step back from the door. Rather than argue logically with myself, I try to accept the uncertainty. Maybe I locked the door, maybe I didn't. Checking once isn't great, but if I do it again . . .

shoulders while Kacey snuggles into the pillows beside me. I think the gummy's beginning to wear off, and I'm suddenly no longer tired.

Sam shifts around in the other bed, and I can vaguely make out the shape of his body in the darkness.

It doesn't take long for Kacey to fall asleep, her breathing evening out, punctuated by the lightest of snores. Despite the late hour and the gummy, sleep evades me as I lie curled up on my side.

The longer I lie there, sleepless, the more awake I feel. Almost like I never ate the gummy in the first place. No matter how I adjust, I can't get comfortable. Isn't weed supposed to calm you down and make you sleepy?

With Kacey beside me, though, I can't toss and turn; I don't want to disrupt her. So I keep curled on my side, facing Sam's bed.

Two feet might sound like a decent amount of space, but it's really not.

My eyes are closed, and I can't stop replaying that look on Sam's face when Kacey mentioned Evan Whitmore. That curious cock of his eyebrow. But Sam must've known before now that I hadn't told Kacey—after all, he didn't tell Kacey either—right? Why the surprise?

After punching my pillow, I roll onto my stomach and lean over the side of the bed. My phone's on the floor, plugged into the outlet, and I tap the screen for the clock. Half past midnight. Ugh. If I fall asleep right now, I'll only get five and a half hours of sleep.

I pillow my arm beneath my head and stare into the inky

tile at me. "The last person you kissed was Evan Whitmore, and that was *last* summer."

Heat whooshes up my neck, and I turn away from Kacey, which is a mistake because Sam glances up from his tiles at the exact same moment, his gaze finding mine. He lifts one brow but doesn't say anything.

The heat intensifies. *Don't laugh,* I tell myself.

After a beat, Sam says, "Hey, uh, I forfeit. Florie wins."

"Fine with me." Kacey rolls upright, her hair everywhere, and yawns. "The only letters I have left are consonants. This game is rigged, I tell you. Rigged!"

I force myself to stop giggling so I can concentrate on putting the game away. I swipe "smooching" off the board first, dumping the tiles into the velvet storage bag. Ugh. Did I really need to win at Scrabble that badly? Why didn't I put down "mooching" or something and skip the triple-word score?

Kace yawns, her elbow knocking into me as she stretches. "What *time* is it?"

"Almost midnight." I'm finally calm enough to speak without dissolving into laughter, and I secure the lid on the Scrabble box. "I'm ready to call it a night."

"I'll set an alarm for six." Kacey puts the board game away and crawls beneath the comforter. "Sound good, Sammy?"

"Yep. See you nerds in the morning." He stretches out on the cot and flicks off the lantern. The small tree house is drenched in absolute middle-of-the-wilderness darkness.

"Night," I say, and Kacey grunts her sentiments.

I pull the comforter and an extra blanket up around my

KACEY + FLORIE'S WILD AND ~~SUPER-COOL~~
BFF ROAD TRIP BUCKET LIST

1. Be spontaneous (yes, Florie, that means YOU)

~~2. Find bangin' outfits for the Eleanor and Trish meet and greet~~

We're going to look amazing. AMAZING!

Maybe your self-confidence is rubbing off on me because we totally will!

~~3. Be embarrassing tourists~~

SAY WEIRDOS

WEIRDOS!!!

It's official: I love Portland

And Portland loves you!

4. Buy a memento in each state

Oregon: Portland touristy T-shirts

5. Kiss a random hottie

Hannah ♡ 206-555-1978

6. Break a traffic law

~~7. Say yes, no questions asked~~

Guess I should be glad it was tree houses and not matching tattoos . . . ?

FUCK missed opportunity! Can I take it back? Let's get tattoos!

8. Visit a roadside attraction

~~9. Anything that makes us ask "Is this a bad idea?"~~

I'm never getting high again

Yes, yes you are

10. HAVE THE BEST TIME OF OUR LIVES

THIRTEEN

Cave Junction, OR

THURSDAY, MIDNIGHT

If Eleanor and Trish were to narrate my life, they'd be yelling at me not to disappear from my tree house into the woods with some guy without telling anyone where I went. But I trust Sam. Way more than I should. In my junior year psych class, we read an article about the halo effect and how, when someone is attractive, we attribute more positive traits to them, like trustworthiness. So I guess this tracks.

Sam grabbed the lantern before we left, and we wander around the campus. The woman who checked us in gave us a brief tour and told us that quiet time is after ten; no one lingers by the communal firepit. Encircling the campus is a thick forest blanketing rolling hills. The air buzzes with mosquitoes, chirps with frogs and crickets.

Summer's practically over, but the past few days have been the most *summer* I've felt since I was a kid. I miss that feeling all the time. My earlier memories are hazy, but in them, I remember afternoons at the lake, Popsicles turning my hands sticky, and running down the rocky beach in my water wings. Barely—but just enough—I remember what it was like to live without obsessive-compulsive disorder.

As we walk, I keep glancing at Sam. I'm not entirely sure if he also couldn't sleep, or if I woke him and he's just trying to help me in my insomnia, and I don't ask.

Sam smells like the citronella bug spray from the bathroom, and his wavy curls are mussed from sleep. He must've left his glasses upstairs, and he seems younger without them. Sometimes it seems like Sam's so much older, so much *cooler*, than I am. He's barely a year older than me, but always out of reach. Always.

I'm never getting over Sam, am I? This is my life now. Constantly falling for the same guy who doesn't want me, over and over again. Until I die.

"What are you thinking about?"

Sam's question startles me, and I nearly trip over a tree root. But, luckily for me, it's not like he can read my mind. "Oh, nothing. Um, thanks for walking with me."

"Anytime." He smiles. "Why can't you sleep?"

I shrug, crossing my arms. "Chronic insomnia."

"I get that." Sam kicks one of the pine cones littering the path. "Sometimes . . . your brain gets too loud."

"Yeah," I say, even though I doubt he really understands. "Sometimes, all the time, whatever."

We reach the Peacock Perch after our loop, but rather than climb the stairs, Sam lowers himself down onto the bottom step, fiddling with the handle on the battery-operated lantern. I sit one step above him, tucking my knees close to my chest.

"You must be excited about tomorrow." He sets the lantern aside and stretches his long legs out in front of him. "I've never really listened to *MML* before this trip . . . I'm not sure if I get it."

"Get what?" I tug the sleeves of my sweater down over my fists.

Sam tilts his head toward me. "Doesn't listening give you nightmares?" he asks, then adds teasingly, "Hey, maybe *that's* why you can't sleep!"

I roll my eyes. "Nice try. No, I don't know. It's hard to explain."

"Try me."

I hesitate, because how ridiculous will this sound? Especially to a guy, to someone like Sam. I'm not sure if he *can* get it.

OCD and anxiety—they're monsters. I'm constantly on edge, worrying about every little threat around me. And being a girl means you're already at risk, just for existing. So many bad things happen to us *because.* Maybe it doesn't make sense, but learning about all the bad things that can happen helps take away some of the fear. The knowledge is like a weapon, the tiniest bit of protection.

I don't know how to explain that to Sam, how to have that

make sense. But he's staring at me, waiting for me to continue, so I take a deep breath and ready myself for embarrassment.

"The podcast helps, I guess. Like it's a really small way to take back some control. Most violent crimes happen to women, to *young* women, and it's just . . . expected, you know? No one's shocked when they hear about a rape or a man killing his ex. But on the news, or on true crime docs and podcasts, they ask *why did that woman walk home alone,* when they should really be asking *why did that man attack her?* They victim-blame.

"Eleanor and Trish are helping to change that narrative," I continue, and lean into my excitement. Who cares if Sam thinks I'm a morbid freak? "Like, until recently, most true crime storytelling has been done by men, and almost always centers around the perpetrator. Can you name a single one of Ted Bundy's victims? Probably not. And that's why Eleanor and Trish are different. They talk about the victims and try to inspire empathy. Because those women could be any of us. And, so, yeah. I think that's awesome. . . ." I trail off, chewing on my bottom lip.

Sam's silent beside me. Then he says, "I've never thought of it that way."

"You've never had to," I point out, relieved he's not laughing or rolling his eyes.

"We're kind of terrible, aren't we? Men?"

"You're not too bad." I grin because *of course* Sam understands. Because he's perfect and annoyingly unattainable, so naturally, he gets it.

Maybe it'd be better if he were rolling his eyes.

"Phew." Sam jokingly dabs at his brow with his sweatshirt sleeve.

My chest is warm and a million times lighter than it was earlier until I remember that while tomorrow is Eleanor and Trish, it's also *Amanda.* The warmth fades, and I hate that I couldn't stay present, in this moment. Hopefully I won't have to see them together.

I tilt my head back and stare up at the sky. If I were ever to see a shooting star, now would be an excellent moment. Because what I need—what I'd wish for in this very moment—would be to wake up tomorrow with zero feelings for Samson Hodge.

But the sky is too cloudy for shooting stars, so I turn back to Sam.

This might be my last moment to talk to him alone for the rest of this trip. Maybe if I stop running from what happened over winter break, I can move on. That, or the fading THC in my system is still messing with my brain. Before I change my mind, I say, "Hey, I wanted to say I'm sorry."

"What for?"

"Winter break. I shouldn't have, um, ignored you after . . . um, you know."

In the faint lantern light, Sam studies me. "After I kissed you."

The heat of shame works its way up my body. "Yeah. That." And while I'm doing the whole apologizing thing, I add, "And I'm sorry for snapping at you in the mini-mart. Not my finest moment."

He drops his gaze to the steps, his brow still furrowed. "What happened?"

"At the mini-mart?" I ask hopefully, because I'm not ready for this conversation. Nope. I want to take the apology back. Because I can barely think about that night and our kiss, let alone talk about it.

"After I kissed you."

I really, really wish he would stop saying that! Sweat breaks out on the back of my neck. "Oh, um, we don't have to talk about it."

"Did it have anything to do with me?" Sam asks, and the question is surprisingly vulnerable. "Was the kiss *that* bad? I mean, you didn't even tell Kacey. And you two tell each other everything."

"You didn't tell Kacey either," I point out, and dodge the question I don't want to answer. Because no, the kiss wasn't bad. Not even close. The kiss had been intense and perfect, two years of unrequited feelings explaining themselves against his lips. A kiss so good it makes me doubt if I'll ever have another kiss like it again.

That's how good of a kiss it was.

But there's no way I'm telling Sam any of that.

"Believe it or not, I don't usually tell my sister about the girls I kiss," he says lightly. "But you didn't answer my questions."

"It didn't have anything to do with you," I tell him, and shake my head. "And the kiss was . . . it was a very nice kiss."

"Then what happened?"

I exhale heavily. "Can we not talk about it? The past is in the past, right?"

"C'mon, do you really think it's in the past, Flor?" Sam stares across the steps at me—his hazel eyes are bright, almost golden, without his glasses. "Because I feel like . . . I feel like a lot of shit is unresolved between us, and I don't know how to make it right."

"You really think talking about it will help?"

"Ignoring it isn't really helping either of us, so . . ." Sam shrugs as his words trail off.

I wrap my arms around my legs, resting my chin on my kneecaps. "Okay. Um. Fine. What do you want to know?"

On the step below me, Sam shifts. Drags his hand through his hair. "You wanted me to kiss you, right? You said yes in the moment, but I want to make sure I didn't, um, make you do something you didn't want to do."

"I wanted it," I whisper, my face heating up, and I mentally cross my fingers that that was his only question. Because this is so embarrassing.

"Okay," Sam says, relieved. "And after? When we were driving back?"

Shit. I stare straight ahead into the pooling darkness and dig my thumbnail into the side of my thigh. This huge part of me wants to run for it. To never, ever speak of that night with anyone, and especially not with Sam. But the other part—the sort-of-logical part—of me knows I need to get this over with.

I close my eyes and take a deep breath, feeling a little sick to my stomach as I let myself relive the full awfulness of that night. Sam and I had been bored at my parents' annual holiday party, and, since I'd gotten my learner's permit, he offered to give me an impromptu driving lesson. Kacey was off talking with the owner of a local art gallery, and I was, of course, so into Sam that I said yes. We drove to look at the Christmas lights in a nearby neighborhood, and, somehow, Sam's mouth ended up on mine.

No, not somehow—I remember it so clearly.

Sam and I were parked outside a house with so many Christmas lights, it was like the Griswolds'. They even had a blow-up Santa that played "Jingle Bell Rock" on a loop and an animatronic Rudolph. The snow was slushy and icy outside, but the inside of the Jeep was hot, the heater on high. All night, the energy between Sam and me had been different . . . like, for the very first time, Samson Hodge saw me—actually saw me, not just his little sister's best friend—and liked what he saw.

We were talking, until we weren't. Until Sam reached across the Jeep and brushed the hair back from my cheek, his palm cradling my jaw. Until he unbuckled his seat belt and leaned over the Jeep's center console, his hand sliding from my jaw and curling around the back of my neck. Until his mouth opened against mine, and my fingers knotted in his hair.

It was perfect.

If I don't think of what happened next.

After I pulled away from Sam, I saw a text from Kacey asking where we were. I drove the Jeep back in a panic, the reality of what I'd done beginning to suffocate me. Kacey's brother *wasn't* an option. And what did the kiss even mean? Did Sam like me, or did he go around casually kissing girls who had secret crushes on him all the time? Maybe it didn't mean anything to him. And when a cat darted across the snowy road, I hit the brakes, causing the car to fishtail to a screeching stop.

I told myself I didn't hit the cat.

I knew I didn't hit the cat.

But my brain kept asking *what if.*

What if the cat was bleeding out under a bush? What if I caused that suffering?

"I thought," I begin, but I have to clear my throat to continue. "I thought I hit the cat." I press my eyes shut so hard little starbursts form beneath my eyelids. "I knew I hadn't, but the thought wouldn't let me go. I . . . panicked." And oh boy, did I panic.

I jumped out of the Jeep because I couldn't drive away, not unless I'd checked. Even though I couldn't find the cat or any signs of an accident—no blood, nothing—I told Sam to leave so I could keep looking. Kind of yelled at him, actually. And I kept looking once he was gone, until my fingers turned blue, and my mom showed up to take me, hysterical with tears streaming down my face, home. Sam must've told her where to find me.

I haven't driven since.

And until last week, that was the last time I saw Sam.

"Does this have to do with your anxiety and stuff?"

"Yeah, um, I have—" A rush of shame washes over me, and I don't dare open my eyes. "I have OCD. Did Kacey tell you?"

Sam's voice is careful as he says, "My roommate in Idaho has an anxiety disorder, and I kind of picked up on a few things. . . ."

More shame rolls over me, and I press my eyes shut even

tighter. Who did I think I was kidding? Before winter break, I tried my hardest to appear like any other girl, normal and functional around Sam. And I failed.

"OCD is different than just having anxiety." The words come out harsher than I intended.

"You can tell me more about it, if you want," he says. "I'd like to understand."

I hesitate, but I have nothing left to lose with Sam. But explaining OCD is hard—so much of it is internal. "I can try. . . . Um. We all have anxiety, right? Some worse than others. But OCD is like anxiety gone wild. My brain doesn't really know what thoughts or worries have value, but it'll latch onto something that causes me distress." My eyes are still closed, but they're damp. "And then I'll find something—anything—to ease the anxiety caused by the distressing thought or worry. But by easing the anxiety, it only worsens it. Because it's like I'm telling my brain, 'Hey, this worry has value. We should pay attention to it!' In reality, it's just some random, irrational fear my OCD is tormenting me with. It's a cycle. An exhausting cycle."

Sam doesn't say anything. When I finally open my eyes, I'm too nervous to stare straight at him. He's a blurry Sam-shaped blob in the corner of my vision.

Then he finally says, "I had no idea. That must fucking suck."

I almost laugh because, *yeah,* it fucking sucks. "Things are . . . kind of better now. But yeah. That's what happened. Any chance we can never talk about it again?"

"One more question, then we don't have to ever talk about it again."

I nod and push back the hair that's fallen against my cheeks. "Sure."

Sam taps his foot against the bottom step. "That's all it was? Why you panicked and ignored me?"

Ignored is harsh. Sam texted twice afterward. Once immediately after, to see if I'd made it home okay. Another before he went back to Idaho, and he asked if we could get breakfast. I didn't reply to either text. I couldn't, deleting them as soon as they landed in my inbox. When you're deep in an obsession, even when it's the only thing you can think about, any reminder cuts to the core.

"That's it," I tell him, and shift to look at Sam. He's leaning with his back against the railing, legs still sprawled out. "I mean, other than the fact I was worried Kacey would freak if I told her."

"That's why you never told her? You really think she would've cared?"

I resist the urge to point out that we're not supposed to be talking about this anymore.

Kacey never expressly said I couldn't date her brother, but she never knew about my feelings either. When we became friends, she mentioned how much it annoyed her when her friends crushed on Sam or tried to date him. *A conflict of friendship interest,* she said. And Kacey matters more than anything. But I don't tell Sam that. I tell him the truth: "I didn't want to find out. I should've told her months ago. Now it's too late."

Sam nods, then lifts his hand to his face as if to push back his glasses. He drops his hand when he remembers he's not

wearing them. "Thank you for finally telling me."

"Oh, don't mention it," I say, going for casual again. And really, really hope he never does. *Ever.*

The corner of Sam's mouth tugs with the hint of a smile like he's reading my thoughts, and his gaze is locked onto mine. Then the space between his brows creases. "Hey, um, so about tomorrow . . ." He trails off.

"Yeah?"

Sam hesitates, then says, "I hope you have the best time, Flor. You deserve it."

I swallow hard, then nod. "Thanks. For driving us and everything."

"My pleasure." Sam pushes to his feet, then holds his hand down. "C'mon, let's get you to sleep. You have a big day tomorrow."

Before I overthink it, I place my hand in Sam's. I don't think I've ever held Sam's hand before; his skin is rough with calluses from woodworking, and his skin is hot against my cold fingers. He hauls me upright, and after squeezing my hand, lets go.

Grabbing the lantern, Sam begins up the stairs, and I follow.

Kacey's still asleep when we tiptoe inside, and I'm equally relieved as I am guilty. For eight months, I avoided talking about that night, never acknowledging out loud that it'd even happened. And there's a certain amount of relief now that we've talked about it. I've spilled all my unattractive secrets to Sam. All the weird tension between us can vanish, and maybe I can finally, *finally* get over Samson Hodge.

Sam and I crawl back into our beds. Beds that are ridiculously close to each other. I tug the blankets up around my shoulders, my vision already adjusted to the dark. On the cot, Sam lies, facing me, with one arm pillowed beneath his head.

One more sleep until Eleanor and Trish, I remind myself.

And I put the boy on the cot opposite me out of my head as I shut my eyes.

FOURTEEN

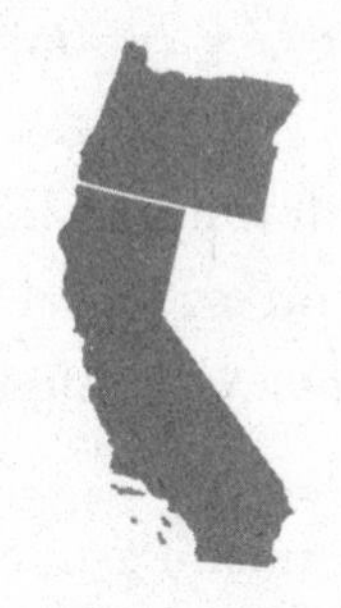

Cave Junction, OR to Crescent City, CA

FRIDAY, AUGUST 12, MORNING

Tonight I meet Eleanor and Trish.

After facing Sam last night—truly facing him and our kiss after eight months of meticulous avoidance—I'm able to focus on the whole point of this trip. I'm even able to appreciate how far I've come, both geographically and emotionally. Who cares if Sam will peel off from our little road trip trio to hang out with another girl? Not me! Because none of that will matter when I'm hugging Eleanor and Trish in San Francisco.

Kacey lugs her massive suitcase off the bed, and the entire tree house shakes as it hits the floor. She's half-awake and grumpy but determined to hit the road. "Let's get a move on. We have, like, seven hours of driving left, but that's not counting bathroom breaks and stuff."

"Lay off the caffeine," Sam says, nodding to the complimentary coffee we scored by the kitchens, "and we won't have to get a move on."

"I refuse to apologize for my small bladder."

I roll my eyes as I zip up my duffel bag. "Sometimes I forget that you two dummies are siblings. Then you go arguing about shit like this."

Sam laughs, his gaze catching mine briefly. Rather than avoid his attention, I smile. Because it's fine, everything's fine. Things are okay with Sam. After last night, I'm almost hopeful we can start over and be friends. Not like we were ever really friends to begin with, but maybe we could be.

Sam will probably be a good friend too. He's kind, as shown last night when I told him about my OCD. He said all the right things, and they helped. Part of me thought I'd wake up and seriously regret telling Sam last night, but I feel good this morning. Lighter. Like I'm finally able to move forward.

After we're packed, we climb down the staircase from our tree house. The southern Oregon sun is bright, basking us all in early-morning warmth. The treesort is bustling with families playing games and couples sipping big thermoses of coffee by the fire.

While Sam checks out in the front office, Kacey and I do our best to tidy the Jeep after yesterday's drive. As I clean, I eye Kacey for any signs that she knows about my late-night walk with Sam, but she's her usual not-morning-person self.

Between nursing her coffee and cleaning up trash, she barely speaks, let alone quizzes me about where I disappeared off to at midnight. We stuff chip bags, empty coffee cups, and clumps of wrapped-up used gum into an empty plastic bag, then dump everything in an outdoor trash can.

Sam jogs down the steps from the office toward the small dirt lot. He's bright-eyed despite our late night. He's also in a really good mood, and I try not to think too hard about why, because it must be Amanda related. He showered earlier, now dressed in tight-fitting jeans, hiking boots, and a short-sleeved white tee with his denim jacket on top. He's way more put together than Kacey and me. Since we're dressing up in our bangin' outfits for the live show, we decided to wait and change in a Starbucks bathroom or something when we arrive in San Francisco.

"Are we good to go?" Sam asks as he reaches us, and takes a bite of the doughnut he must've snagged from the office. It leaves little bits of powder residue in his scruff.

I resist the super-inappropriate urge to reach out and brush the powder from his face. "Think so. Kace?"

Kacey lugs her suitcase into the back of the Jeep, then gives us a thumbs-up. "Let's hit the road."

Sam winks at me—which is unsettling when I'm fully awake and downright confusing at seven in the morning—and climbs into the driver's seat. Kacey claims the back seat, leaving me up front with Sam. The closeness to him means way less than it did yesterday, when we first set out, and it's a little bittersweet. I slide off my shoes and tuck my feet beneath me, pulling my flannel around me like a blanket.

Sam and I roll down the windows as he drives, and summer air whips into the car. We don't talk; he focuses on the road, and I lean my forearm against the window and rest my head, my hair tangling with the breeze. We wind down the highway and cross over the Oregon-California line, where we're waved forward through an agricultural inspection station.

For the first time since embarking on this trip, I'm completely present. Light and present and *excited.* No bad thoughts, no worries. Just the happy tug of my heart that I'm finally getting something I desperately want.

About an hour into our drive, I sit upright and stretch. When I peer into the back seat, Kacey's comatose with a sweater draped over her face.

"How're you doing?" Sam asks, glancing briefly from the road at me.

I lean back in my seat and prop my feet on the glove compartment. "Good. Excited."

"Kacey still out?" He readjusts his hands on the steering wheel, eyes lifting to the rearview mirror.

"Yep. What I'd give for her circadian rhythm."

Sam laughs, and my stomach warms at the noise. "She's always been like this, ever since we were kids."

"Some people get all the luck." I sigh, and watch the roadside blur past us. For the past few miles, there have been these signs advertising wood carvings, fruit stands, and fresh honey. Another one flashes by, but this one advertises strawberries beneath the lettering.

"Fresh strawberries?" Sam must've caught the latest addition to the roadway sign like I had.

"Doesn't that sound so good?" I barely had any breakfast, just a protein bar. Sam begins to slow down. "Wait, what're you doing?"

He gestures up the highway. "The fruit stand is right there. Let's stop."

"Oh, no. That's okay." I hitch a thumb over my shoulder. "We don't want to wake up Kacey or anything. And we need to stay on schedule."

"Hey, Kacey," Sam says loudly, "want to stop and get a snack?" She snores louder in response. "Yeah, Kacey doesn't care. Plus, we're ahead of schedule."

I look at Sam's phone in the holder, where he has Google Maps pulled up. He's right. We're definitely ahead of schedule. At this rate, we'll arrive in San Francisco at three in the afternoon, and the show's not until eight.

Sam flicks on his blinker and slows the Jeep down, guiding it off the highway and onto the shoulder. The fruit stand is actually a small storefront with an outdoor ordering window, picnic tables, and a porta-potty. A few dirt parking stalls are on the left-hand side, and he eases the Jeep into one of the spots.

After rolling down the windows for Kacey and giving her one last, mildly guilty glance, I hop out of the Jeep and follow Sam. Redwoods and eucalyptus trees arch into the sky; the highway feels like a woodsy corridor. Sam steps up to the ordering window and taps his palm against the bell. A moment later, an older woman appears.

"One box of strawberries, please." Sam nods his head toward the shaded stand to our right.

I reach for my wallet, but Sam shakes his head. "I don't mind, as long as you promise to share."

I fight my smile. Friends share food all the time. This is good. Normal. "Yeah, okay."

Sam pays, then we pick out one of the cardboard boxes overflowing with berries.

"There's no way we're eating all of those." I laugh, because I'm pretty sure Sam just bought two pounds of strawberries. "I think we'd overdose on vitamin C."

Sam sits on the top of the shaded picnic bench and sets down the berries. "We'll save some for Kacey." When he sees me hesitating, glancing toward the car, he says, "C'mon, Florence Nightingale, a ten-minute detour won't kill you. I promise."

I pretend to consider this, but really, I'm basking in Sam's Sam-ness. Now that the air's been cleared, I'm not dissecting every word, every sentence, for a deeper meaning. It's refreshing.

"Ten minutes max," I tell him, and Sam makes a big show of setting the timer on his clunky wristwatch.

I hoist myself onto the table and grab one of the strawberries from the box between us. They're gigantic, fat and juicy. One bite and red juice runs down my wrist.

"Worth it?" Sam asks, and I nod.

"Oh yeah." I wipe the juice off my forearm with a napkin I find in my purse. "Thanks."

Sam's jean-clad shoulder brushes mine as he reaches for a strawberry. "No problemo."

I look him up and down; he's still wearing his jacket.

"How're you still wearing that thing? It's, like, eighty degrees out here." I ditched my flannel before we got out of the car, and I can't imagine how hot a sherpa-lined denim jacket is in this weather.

Unlike Sam, I can't make a casual outfit attractive, but in the harsh light of day, I wish I'd put in a *little* more effort this morning. The wrinkled sundress, the slip-on sneakers. My hair sliding out of its ponytail and my only makeup mascara and sunscreen. Good thing I no longer care about looking nice in front of Sam; not like I was ever very successful.

Sam pops the strawberry into his mouth, shrugs off the jacket, and tosses it onto the bench where we're resting our feet. The white T-shirt underneath is *tight.* Like, I-can-easily-make-out-the-muscles-in-his-arms tight. Like, it-hugs-every-inch-of-his-torso tight.

"You okay?" Sam asks, and reaches for another berry.

"Do you own any clothes that fit?" I joke. Not gonna lie, I'm genuinely curious if he's oblivious or if this is a very intentional fashion choice. But that doesn't mean I don't wish I'd kept my freaking mouth shut.

His brow raises. "I happen to think this shirt fits perfectly. But if you'd rather I take it off, I'll gladly—"

I nearly choke on my strawberry. "No! Please keep your clothes on."

Sam laughs, hanging his head back. "You made a good point, though. It's hot out here." He reaches for the hem of his shirt, and I slap his hand away.

"Oh my god!" I point to a sign hanging off the storefront: NO SHIRT NO SHOES NO SERVICE. He laughs even harder, and the sound is contagious. Sam is . . . actually a lot of fun. Sure, the thought of him shirtless makes my heart race, but he doesn't have to know about that.

Sam wipes his fingers off on a napkin and sighs. "If you feel that strongly, I'll keep my clothes on. Even if that means me dying of heatstroke."

"Drama queen." My cheeks ache from laughter and smiling. It feels good. Like really, really good. I inspect the box of strawberries and grab another. He watches me as I bite into it, and I cover my mouth. "Can I help you?" I ask through a mouthful of berry.

Sam smiles, the tiniest tug of his lips. But he's still looking at me, and the longer he does, the harder it is to remember why he's even sitting here on his picnic table with me. He's here because of Amanda—*the sex pilgrimage,* I remind myself with a wince—and I'm fine with that. I have to be fine with that.

Eventually, Sam says, "You're a mess. Seriously. There's juice everywhere."

I swallow and grab a napkin, wiping my lips. "It's part of the experience."

"Apparently." He laughs, and points to a red juice stain on his white tee. "Ready to head back?"

"Soon, yeah." I reach across the table and wrap my fingers around his wrist, angling his watch face in my direction. His skin is warm, the hair along his forearm dark, and my stomach does an annoying little flip. Dropping his wrist, I say, "We still have five minutes."

While I can't wait to get to San Francisco, I'm so sick of

sitting in that Jeep, and the break is nice. I glance toward the car, and I can barely make out Kacey in the back. "How is she still sleeping? It'd be impressive if I weren't so jealous."

"That gives me an idea." Sam's grin turns mischievous. "Have you ever played While You Were Sleeping?"

"Isn't that the Sandra Bullock and Bill Pullman movie?"

"Is it?" he asks quizzically, as if he didn't totally watch rom-coms with Kacey when they were growing up. He digs his prescription sunglasses from his jacket pocket and slides them on.

"Think so," I tell him.

"Whatever. *This* While You Were Sleeping is a road trip game. We take turns coming up with a story—something fictional that *could've* happened—and when she wakes up, we have to convince Kacey it really happened. You get one point if she says 'no way' and two if she says 'are you sure,' but we both win if we convince her."

"I'm game." I shift on the tabletop, tucking my legs beneath me. "Where do we begin?"

Sam chews on his bottom lip. "Okay, I have an idea. While you were sleeping, we drove through the border station into California." He nods for me to continue the story.

I think back to when we crossed the state border. "We had to stop and roll down the window for the border patrol. They asked us if we had any firearms, drugs, or non-native plants we were trying to bring into California."

"And . . ." He pushes his sunglasses up the bridge of his nose. "And that's when Florie made a joke about the gummies we ate last night."

I scowl at him for throwing me under the imaginary bus. "Yeah, um . . . I joked that we should've eaten them all so we wouldn't get arrested. But the officer overheard."

Sam laughs and nods enthusiastically. "Oh, she'll totally go for this. Okay! So! The officer overheard and I tried to explain, and they asked us to pull off to the side."

I'm starting to giggle now. After a moment of brainstorming, I continue. "Sam *lied* to the officers and said they were medical gummies and we *had* eaten them all. He even said they could check the Jeep."

"And this is when Florence began to panic and told them it was all a misunderstanding. Maybe she even started to cry?"

"I definitely *did not* start crying! No, I was very composed and cooperative. I told them that the Jeep was Sam's car, so if they found anything, it belonged to him and him alone."

His mouth drops open. "Traitor!"

I hold up my hands. "What? Every woman for herself."

Sam's smiling, cheeks flush with laughter. "And . . . because I'm extremely chivalrous, I agreed with what you said. I offered to let them search me, ready to take the fall. But before they could, the officer was buzzed on his walkie—there was an emergency—and he let us go. *Fin.*" He mock bows.

"Yeah? Think she'll fall for it?"

"Definitely. Also, Kacey is extra gullible when she's sleepy." Sam lifts his hand, and we high-five.

"This'll show her," I say jokingly, "for flaunting her REM sleep in our faces."

Sam shakes his head. "You're weird." Seeing my facial

expression, he hastens to add, "In a good way. The best way."

"Thanks. I think." I slide off the picnic table and gather the box of strawberries in my arms. We made a dent, but there's still more than half remaining.

Sam heads toward the Jeep. "Let's go prank my sister," he says, stretching his arms overhead. The move makes his shirt rise up a few inches, and I sigh inside. "I haven't pranked anyone in *weeks*. I'm jonesing."

Laughing, I put the strawberries in the cooler in the back of the Jeep to keep them fresh, then join Sam in the front seat.

"Good detour?" he asks, and turns on the Jeep.

"Best detour." I grin at him. "Thanks for the strawberries."

"Anytime, Florence Nightingale," Sam says, and he steers us back onto the highway.

When Kacey wakes up about thirty minutes later, I look at Sam, and he winks at me.

"Hey." She yawns and rests her chin on the back of my seat. "Where are we?"

"Outside of Crescent City," I say, studying Google Maps.

My best friend yawns again and wipes at the corners of her eyes. "What'd I miss?"

Sam glances my way, one brow hitched over the rim of his sunglasses. "Kind of a lot, actually. While you were sleeping . . ."

Back and forth, Sam and I spin our ridiculous border station drug story to Kacey, who hangs onto our every word.

Like Sam predicted, Kacey falls for it. *Hard.* Embarrassingly hard.

I earn five points (three "no ways" and one "are you sure?") and Sam only has four.

"I can't believe I slept through that." Kacey ties her hair back from her face. "Like, I'm a deep sleeper but *that*?"

Sam snorts, and he shoots me a dirty look as I start to laugh. But I can't help it. I've been stuck in this car for way too long. The harder I laugh, the harder Sam laughs, and we're totally screwed.

"What?" Kacey glances uneasily between us. "What the fuck? Why are you two laughing?"

"Sorry," Sam says between laughs, "but we made that up."

Kacey's mouth drops open, and she tugs my hair. "Flor? Is he serious?"

I press my hand to my stomach, which cramps from laughter and way too many strawberries. "We were playing While You Were Sleeping."

"That Sandra Bullock movie?" Kacey asks, confused for so many different reasons.

"Told you," I tell Sam, my eyes watering. "All you *actually* missed was a quick fruit stand stop. There are strawberries in the cooler if you're hungry."

"You two," Kacey says, "are the absolute worst."

"Oh come on." Sam takes a deep breath to calm down. He removes his sunglasses for a second to wipe his eyes, which are also watering. "You're just salty that you fell for it."

"Not my fault my family bingo card has you getting busted for drug charges," Kacey mutters, but she's smiling now. "It totally tracked. But you, Florie? You never lie. I feel so betrayed right now."

My laughter fades, and I try to ignore the acidic reaction in my gut. Because I do lie. I've lied to Kacey. And not the pranking kind of lie. A lie that could cause actual hurt to my best friend.

Sam, sensing my thoughts—or maybe he has naturally good timing—says, "Hey, if either of us fall asleep, feel free to do the same. We can tally up points when we arrive back in Barmouth. Flor has five points and I have four. Loser buys pizza from the Ancient Pie?"

This appeases Kacey, who grins. "You're on."

Sam offers me a small smile, and it's comforting. Like maybe he understands now, after last night, how hard it is for me to keep what happened between us from Kacey.

The corner of my lips curve in a smile mirroring his own. Because the tiny ache in my chest, the *guilt*, might be worth the memory. The strawberries and late morning heat and Sam's shirt and laughing until my cheeks hurt.

One perfect moment.

FIFTEEN

Highway 101, Piercy, CA

FRIDAY, EARLY AFTERNOON

"Nicole Kidman," Kacey says as she props her bare feet onto the glove compartment.

"Kristen Bell," I reply. Our Celebrity Alphabet game has been going strong for ten minutes. We're currently competing for the last candy bar.

"Betty White." Sam hits the blinker and merges into the slow lane as a red sports car zips past us.

Kacey is quiet in the back seat, then says, "Will Smith."

I bite my lip, trying to think of a celebrity whose name starts with an *S* when my phone buzzes from the depths of my purse. Kacey counts down on her fingers. "Wait, hold on—"

But my five seconds are up, and Kacey whoops. "You're out, Flor!"

"Oh come on," I say, and finally find my phone. "That's not fair. If it's my mom calling, I have to answer."

Kacey shakes her head. "Nope, thanks for playing. Good game. Better luck next time."

With a scowl, I flip my phone around: *Mom calling.* Ugh. "Be quiet, it's my mom."

"Don't answer it," Kacey says quickly, but I've already hit accept.

"Hey, Mom!" I cringe internally at how over-the-top and fake I sound.

"Hi, honey!" There's the low buzz of a TV show in the background, but I can hear her walking around. My mom's a pacer when she's on the phone. "How's everything going?"

"Good, yeah, we're driving to grab some late lunch." I motion for Kacey and Sam to be quiet. "What's up?"

"Just checking in," she replies cheerfully. "The house is so quiet with both you and your dad gone. I can't remember the last time you were both gone. Last summer, maybe?"

Leaning my head back, I press my eyes shut. Over the past twenty-four hours, it's been easy to nudge my mom out of my mind. Between Kacey and Sam and San Francisco, my mind has had little room for feeling guilty about lying to my parents. "Yeah, I bet . . . Hey, Mom, we're pulling up to the restaurant so I gotta go?" I hear the question in my voice and wilt.

Am I this bad at lying?

Mom's pacing stops. "No problem. Talk soon, okay?"

"Sounds good. Bye!" I hang up before my nerves get the better of me. I toss my phone in my purse. "Was I believable?"

Kacey meets my gaze in the rearview. "Totally. Plus, your mom isn't suspicious—she shouldn't have any reason to suspect you of lying. Only *you* know you're lying. You're overthinking it, babe."

Not a bad point. But still, I feel weird. Weird for lying and even weirder for getting away with it. I think that's the weirdest part—that I don't feel worse for lying to my mom. Maybe it's because everything today has been going flawlessly, and I'm having fun. I'm making memories even without that list to guide me, and if the only payment is me lying to my mom, then it's totally worth it.

"Overthinking it," I repeat, and grin a little. "Who, me? Never."

Mentally I push back against the worry, and I'm surprised that I'm successful. Because we've made so much progress—we're *finally* in California, on the 101, and on a straight shot into San Francisco. Kacey is amped and randomly keeps saying how excited she is to meet Eleanor and Trish, like she has to keep reminding herself that it's actually happening. And Sam . . . well, his infectious energy has helped keep me from sliding off into Anxiety Land.

I roll down my window and let the warm breeze whip my hair around. With our game of Celebrity Alphabet on hold, Sam turns on some music, and I stare out at the trees lining the highway.

Even if I'm feeling guilty over not feeling more guilty about lying to my mom, my mind isn't fretting or obsessing.

If only she could see me now. Usually, when I sit still, my brain glues itself to the worst, most cognitive-dissonant fear. But right now I feel the seat beneath my thighs, the sun on my skin, and I'm . . . happy.

Maybe, when I'm back in Washington, I'll tell Mom about the trip. About how well I did with the unknown. With all the triggers she tries to shield me from. Because, with each tiny victory, my fears aren't so scary anymore. I'm pushing and moving forward, rather than being pushed back into place.

"When are we stopping for lunch?" Kacey asks not long after my mom calls, and leans between the front seats. Her hair is wrangled into a bun on the crown of her head, and she smells like bug spray and coffee.

Sam checks the time on the dashboard's clock. "Whenever. Flor, wanna look at what's nearby?"

"Sure." I unlatch his phone from the holder and zoom in on the map. We're on Highway 101 all the way into San Francisco, and currently we're still in the middle of nowhere, surrounded by small towns and trees. I pinch the screen and zoom in closer along our route. "Ooh!" I say. "Think we have time for a detour?"

Sam grins over at me. "What were you thinking?"

"Confusion Hill! It's not out of the way at all." The tourist attraction is along our route, and a quick visit to their website confirms that they have a snack bar that sells a bunch of options, including hot dogs and ice cream.

"For number eight?" Kacey asks, mentioning the list: visit a roadside attraction.

Sure, it checks off number eight, but that's not why I want

to go. "I've actually driven down this way before, like, ten years ago. We were on our way to a family reunion, in Monterey. We drove, made a thing out of it."

Kacey's face twists into something unpleasant. "A road trip with Helene? Yikes."

I laugh, but she kind of has a point. Unlike our trip, there were no unscheduled stops, minimal bathroom breaks, and history and biography audiobooks instead of music and podcasts. "I remember seeing a billboard for Confusion Hill and asking my parents to stop. But they said we didn't have time. I doubt it'll be as cool as it would've been when I was eight but . . ." I trail off with a casual shrug, but I *really* want to stop.

Sam glances over at me. He's still in his tight T-shirt with the red pop of strawberry juice near the collar. "Count me in. Add the stop so we can reroute."

I turn back around in my seat and do as he says. Maybe it's dorky, but I'm excited. Even though it was such a long time ago, I remember pressing my nose up against the window of Dad's car, watching the attractions fade in the distance with a yearning I'd grow familiar with over the years. The yearning of being close to something—maybe something you didn't know you wanted—and never being able to reach it.

"After we stop at Confusion Hill," Sam says, glancing at our route on his phone, which I secured back into its holder after adding our detour, "we'll only have three and a half hours left. Two hundred miles, give or take."

"Two hundred miles until *Murder Me Later* live!" Kacey whoops from the back seat.

"Two hundred miles until I can hug Eleanor and Trish," I add.

"Two hundred miles until Amanda. Wink-wink, nudge-nudge," Kacey says to her brother. "Speaking of the lovely Amanda, you think she'll let us change at her dorm? Beats a Starbucks bathroom."

"Uh." Sam's gaze meets mine across the car, and I try to smile. Try to show him that I am, 100 percent, okay with this after last night's discussion about our brief romantic encounter.

"Yeah, maybe," Sam says eventually. "But her dorm isn't near the Masonic."

"We can take a rideshare," Kacey says, because apparently she's planned out this whole thing without ever mentioning it to me. "Then you can pick us up at the theater after."

I turn away, chewing on my pinky nail. Sam and Amanda felt manageable when they were an idea, but seeing them together so soon—in a matter of *hours*—is a big next step. This is starting to feel a bit masochistic.

Going to Amanda's is the worst kind of emotional torture, but I can't say no without raising Kacey's suspicions. Great. I can't wait to change my clothes in Amanda's dorm. Because after we leave, Sam will no doubt help Amanda off with her clothes, and they'll fall onto her bed together and—*what is wrong with me?* Worst mental image ever.

Before I can sink even deeper into that dangerous thought spiral from hell, Sam asks me to read him the directions for Confusion Hill.

I exhale steadily, try to ground myself. Try to get back to the good.

We pass a big yellow sign—CONFUSION HILL, IS SEEING BELIEVING?—and turn off the highway. The second we spot the tourist attraction, I smile. Because it's *so* campy. The actual definition of a quirky roadside attraction. Eight-year-old Florie would be so excited right now, and I'm pretty excited for her.

Sam parks, and we climb out of the Jeep. Like our detour at the strawberry stand, it's sweltering. We're still pretty far north up the coast, but it's *hot.* After stretching, I stand beside the Jeep and tip my head back and let the sun soak into my face.

When I open my eyes, Sam's walking my way with one hand shoved into his jean pocket, sunglasses still obscuring his face.

"What're we thinking?" he asks me. "Food or wandering first?"

"I'm all for wandering first. Kace?"

Kacey rounds the Jeep and slings her arm around my neck. "Sounds good to me."

We're parked in front of the gift shop and snack bar. Passing a gigantic totem pole, we head toward the gift shop, which is surrounded by trees. A red banner reads DOUG'S DOG HOUSE, and another yellow banner brags about something called a chipalope (chipmunk antelope?), but we head into the gift shop to buy our admission for the gravity house.

Sam trails Kacey and me as we funnel inside the one-story red building covered in yellow signage. The entire gift store is cluttered with every type of gift you can think of: T-shirts and fool's gold nuggets and wood carvings, plus bags of candy and a cooler of ice cream bars.

"Pony up." Sam slides his sunglasses onto his head, then holds out his hand. "Five bucks each."

Kacey inspects a stack of postcards before reaching for her rainbow-striped wallet and pulling out a five-dollar bill. I find some ones in the bottom of my purse and smooth them against my thigh before handing them to Sam. He chats with the cashier, all easygoing smiles and endless charm, as he pays for our admission.

Then we each get a question mark stamp on the back of our left hands.

"Let's circle back after," Kacey says. "We need mementos from California."

"For sure." I run my finger over the inked mark on my hand, heart humming happily. Everything about this place—the campiness, the quirk—is so *fun*. It's fun for the sake of being fun, nothing more and nothing less. I'm so used to everything in my life being . . . transactional. Everything has to have a purpose.

Nothing on this trip has had a purpose other than having fun, making memories.

"Let's go." Sam nods toward the exit. He leads the way out of the gift shop, past the snack bar, and our stamped hands grant us access through a small gate. As I watch him walk—tight jeans and all—I promise myself that I'll have fun this afternoon. Sure, the Amanda thing threw me a bit, but that's done with. I'm moving on.

"This place is so hokey," Sam says as we hike our way up

the hill. Trees shoot up into the sky on either side of the pathway, which is enclosed by a wooden fence painted the same shade of rust red as the gift shop. "Mom and Dad would love it."

"Oh, they totally would. And according to this pamphlet," Kacey says, brandishing a guide she picked up in the gift shop, "the founder was always very upfront that this place is basically one big confusion illusion. More weird than mystical."

We approach the slanted house, which is definitely weird and makes my brain hurt the longer I study it. Because *everything* is slanted, from the house itself, to the trees, to the fences enclosing the entrance.

"Okay, that's kind of cool." Kacey points to a trough where the water appears to be running up, rather than down. "Is anyone else dizzy?"

I step into the house and look around. There's not much inside, just an assortment of safety railings, poles, a chair, and even a ladder. A family—a mom and three young kids—wander about, the children laughing and shrieking as they almost fall over, grasping onto the poles and walking on the walls.

"Whoa," Sam says from behind me, and I step inside to make room for him and Kacey.

Kacey wanders into the big main room, stumbling and laughing. "This is so fucking cool," she says, and rolls her eyes when the nearby mother shoots her a dirty look.

Sam grabs onto a bar mounted on the ceiling that gives me flashbacks of doing pull-ups in PE and lifts himself up. Gravity pulls his feet north until his body is parallel with the floor. "We should've brought the gummies! Can you imagine coming to this place high?"

The mother—who resembles mine in both appearance and attitude way too much for comfort—gathers her kids and huffs past us. Once we're alone, we break out into laughter.

I walk over into the other room, using the various safety poles so I don't trip and fall on my face. In here the walls are splashed with graffiti and carved initials, and I find one of the hands-on demonstrations.

A small ledge runs at an angle up the graffitied wall, and I follow the instructional signs, placing one of the golf balls at the base of the ledge. When I let go, it rolls *up* the ledge, all on its own.

"Whoa, check this out!" I turn toward Kacey, but she's headed for the exit.

"I'm gonna wait outside," she says, face pale. "This place is starting to make me motion sick."

"We won't be much longer." Sam comes up beside me. He plucks the ball from my hand and rolls it up the wall again.

Kacey gives us a thumbs-up before exiting the gravity house.

Sam stops rolling the golf ball and watches Kacey disappear outside.

"Hey." He grabs my hand. "Can I talk to you really quick?"

"Aren't we talking right now?" I joke, and decidedly don't focus on the feeling of his hand on mine.

"Smart-ass. Just . . . come on." He loops his fingers around my wrist and leads me away from the door Kacey exited through, into the corner of the topsy-turvy room.

"What's up?" I hold on to one of the safety poles when we stop.

Sam's hand slides from my wrist, and he pushes his fingers through his hair, nearly knocking his sunglasses off. Flustered, he plucks them from his head, folds them, and shoves the shades into his pocket. "Okay, um. I was going to tell you this last night, but I'm chickenshit. Then at the strawberry stand, but we were having so much fun together." He pauses. Then: "Yeah. So. I'm not seeing Amanda later."

I squint up at him. "Did she bail on you? That's kind of shitty. You've driven—"

"No, you don't understand," Sam interrupts, and drags his hand across his jawline. "I haven't spoken to Amanda in a year."

My mouth goes dry. Maybe he means spoken to her on the phone or seen her in person . . . or maybe he means he was never going to see Amanda. A thousand thoughts fight for front and center in my brain, so naturally the only thing that pops out of my mouth is "No sex pilgrimage?"

"What?" Sam's eyes widen in horror.

I motion at him with my free hand, extremely aware of how close we are, how we're basically alone. "You. Driving eight hundred miles to see Amanda. Sex pilgrimage." I hold up my hands like *obviously*. Oh god, please let him say something so I stop talking.

Sam takes a half step closer, and it's like all the oxygen has left the room. "I never said I was going to see Amanda. Kacey did, and, to be honest, I hadn't thought any of this through when I volunteered to drive. When Kacey brought her up, it sounded like a better reason than why I really wanted to, so I went with it."

I think back to that moment in the Hodges' living room. A moment I've tried blocking out because hearing that Sam was seeing Amanda again hurt way, way more than it should've. "What're you talking about?"

"C'mon, you're not this clueless, are you?" The corners of Sam's eyes crinkle as he smiles. "I did it for you, Flor."

Sam's right, I *am* clueless. Embarrassingly so. And now I'm speechless, too. Because he drove all this way for me. Not Amanda. Me. I search Sam's face—half expecting this to be some huge and unintentionally devastating prank—but he's just looking at me softly. Hopefully.

No misunderstanding. No prank. This is actually happening.

Play it cool, I tell myself, which is honestly a joke, because I'm totally freaking out.

I slip out from beneath Sam. "Okay! Um. Thank you? I need some fresh air." Then I dart across the slanted floor before he can catch up with me.

Once I'm outside, I take a deep breath, which eases the nausea that kicked in real quick. Because Sam is driving us to San Francisco because of me, and I needed this information, like, yesterday.

And I'm not sure what I'm supposed to *do* with this revelation, because it doesn't fit. I've spent the last week—and the last eight months—convincing myself that winter break didn't matter. That, to Sam, I was forgettable. One girl in the line of many.

Now everything I thought I understood is complicating, fast.

"The house get to you, too?" Kacey asks, and I jump. She's leaning against the building, still pale and slightly sweaty.

"Yeah," I say, which is technically the truth. I smooth my hair back into a stubby ponytail and avoid Sam's attention when he ducks out of the gravity house a moment later. "Food time?"

I don't look at Sam—or Kacey—as we walk down the path back to the snack bar. I'm zoned out as we buy hot dogs and soda, then perch on the picnic tables surrounded by redwoods to scarf them down. But my appetite has left the building.

I'm confused and anxious, and I want to figure everything out right now. But I can't because Kacey's sitting across from me, not like I'd know what to say if I were alone with Sam. I want to hear it, hear him say how he feels about me—no room for misinterpretation. But I also want to shove my hot dog in his face for making everything so complicated.

Or was it me who complicated things originally? I really can't keep track anymore.

"We're gonna run into the gift shop," Kacey says, drawing me out of my thoughts. "You coming?"

I slurp my soda, still avoiding Sam's gaze, which keeps falling to mine like we're magnets. "Nah, go ahead. I'll wait here."

Kacey gathers up her trash, and, after hesitating for a moment, Sam follows her into the gift shop.

Alone, I set my food on the table and drop my face into my hands.

I probably shouldn't entertain my what-ifs, but I can't outrun them.

What if I pegged Sam wrong from the start? What if winter break meant something to him? What if I've been hiding behind that night, behind the Big Bad of my OCD? What if Sam wants me as bad as I want him?

That last what-if makes my heart race.

The past few months—and this past week in particular—have left me feeling stronger than ever. Strong enough to go on this road trip with Kacey and strong enough to test some of my self-made limits. The very same limits I always told myself were the reason I couldn't have something real with Sam. Not like he wanted to be with me. But now . . . now I don't know what to think.

Since I'll regret not eating later, I finish my hot dog and wash it down with some soda. Kacey and Sam are still in the shop, and I savor my last few minutes alone since I won't be getting any more for hours. I wish I could talk to Kacey about all this. After all, the best person to unload all this on would be my best friend. And the best person to ask about Sam would be his sister. But I made a mistake when I didn't tell Kacey eight months ago. I didn't see the point. I didn't want to chance it.

Since winter break, I've told myself that Sam never cared about me. That the kiss was a whim, a mistake. A boy who would kiss anyone and a girl who was desperate to be kissed. I told myself I couldn't have Sam because my OCD would get in the way. My own personal conspiracy theories.

But my OCD's already in the way. It's the reason why I've never even *tried.*

Not just with Sam, but with a lot of things.

The realization sinks into my stomach like lead.

I think back to what I told Kacey outside Voodoo Doughnut. That I want to fall, make a mess, take a chance. If not now, when?

Kacey and Sam exit the gift shop together, both of them laughing.

"Hey," I say, balling up my trash and dumping it in the nearby bins.

Sam and Kacey look over at me. Sam's spinning the Jeep keys around his finger, and Kacey's bending the bill of the baseball cap she bought in the gift shop.

Wiping my hands off, I point to the Jeep. "Can I drive?"

KACEY + FLORIE'S WILD AND ~~SUPER-COOL~~ BFF ROAD TRIP BUCKET LIST

1. Be spontaneous (yes, Florie, that means YOU)

~~2. Find bangin' outfits for the Eleanor and Trish meet and greet~~

We're going to look amazing. AMAZING!

Maybe your self-confidence is rubbing off on me because we totally will!

~~3. Be embarrassing tourists~~

SAY WEIRDOS

WEIRDOS!!!

It's official: I love Portland

And Portland loves you!

~~4. Buy a memento in each state~~

Oregon: Portland touristy T-shirts

California: Confusion Hill baseball caps

Wait. Were we supposed to get something from WA?

No we live there!

5. Kiss a random hottie

Hannah ♡ 206-555-1978

6. Break a traffic law

~~7. Say yes, no questions asked~~

Guess I should be glad it was tree houses and not matching tattoos . . . ?

FUCK missed opportunity! Can I take it back? Let's get tattoos!

~~8. Visit a roadside attraction~~

Confusion Hill! Is seeing believing? We visited and still don't know!

Who knows, but I am SO confused right now ???

~~9. Anything that makes us ask "Is this a bad idea?"~~

I'm never getting high again

Yes, yes you are

10. HAVE THE BEST TIME OF OUR LIVES

SIXTEEN

Highway 101, around Hopland, CA

FRIDAY, LATE AFTERNOON

The miles slip by—ten, twenty, thirty—and nothing bad happens.

I keep waiting for something bad to happen, but nothing ever does.

I'm gripping the wheel so tightly that my knuckles are white, but everything is surprisingly fine. I remember every little detail from driver's ed and all those behind-the-wheel driver's classes from two years ago. And while I'm constantly checking my mirrors, and my fingers are cramping as I steadily hold on to the steering wheel, dare I say it—I'm having *fun.*

And I'm not just driving. I'm driving on the freeway!

My blood whooshes in my ears, Sam's smiling, and Kacey keeps taking pictures. Even though I wasn't thinking of our list when I asked Sam for his keys, I've inadvertently checked off number six: break a traffic law. Since I don't have my license and my learner's permit is crumpled up in my junk drawer back in Washington, I definitely shouldn't be behind the wheel. But I am, and it's amazing.

I thought that, since I'd be driving, my brain would be too preoccupied and panicky to think about Sam. But it's not. I keep thinking the same three things, over and over again: *Sam's here because of you. The winter break kiss actually meant something. Stop freaking out and tell him how you feel!*

"How're you doing?" Sam asks about thirty minutes into my drive.

"Good, but I'm probably okay if you want to switch."

We pull over at the next rest stop, and as I shift the Jeep into park, I'm grinning ear to ear. Because I drove on an unfamiliar highway and didn't break down. I didn't hurt myself—or anyone else. The strange thing is, I'm not sure why I was so afraid of driving in the first place. Probably the driver's ed safety class with all those red-asphalt videos. It didn't help that my mom wasn't a fan of me driving, but despite my nerves, I kept pushing. Until that night, with the cat. After that whole fiasco, I stopped fighting. My mom was right—I wasn't ready to drive.

Driving, and proving to myself that I could, means more than I realized.

Kacey pops open the door. "I'm gonna hit up the bathroom."

"Do you need me to come with you, or are you no longer worried about getting murdered?" I shake out my hands, which are cramped from holding on to the steering wheel for dear life.

"Eh, it's busy and daytime. Not nearly as creepy. I should be okay." Kacey shuts the door and walks toward the bathrooms on the other side of the parking lot.

Sam climbs out of the passenger's seat, and I'm alone in the Jeep.

Instead of following, I take a moment.

I'm here, I'm whole, and I did it.

I did it.

Keys in hand, I step out of the Jeep and shut the door behind me. The rest stop is actually kind of pretty, with mossy green trees and pathways with picnic tables, the bathrooms in a low brick building off to our right by some vending machines.

Sam walks around the front of the car, one hand tucked into his pocket as he takes off his sunglasses. "Hey."

"Hi." Before the doubt and overthinking can creep in, I say, "I was going to walk around . . . Do you want to come with? We could, um, finish our conversation from Confusion Hill."

"Yeah, okay." He follows me onto the tree-lined pathway.

We walk down the path, past a family eating sandwiches on one of the park benches, and come across an empty, secluded picnic table. Sam sits on the bench, long legs spread out. "So," he says, drumming his hands on his thighs. "Do you hate me now? I'd understand if you did."

"I don't hate you, Sam. I'm not even mad at you for lying."

He tilts his head. "Really?"

"Really. Trust me, life would be, like, twenty times easier if I hated you."

"*Twenty* times?" Sam grins. "Huh. Who knew I made your life so difficult?"

"You have no idea." I step closer to the bench, and I'm the tiniest bit dizzy, my already-rapid heart slamming against my rib cage. Because Sam's right *there* in that white tee with the strawberry stain and a nervous smile plays on his lips and he's here because of me. I should tell him how I feel, but I'm scared, like my words are going to come out all wrong.

Since Sam's sitting down, we're nearly the same height, which makes him slightly less intimidating. I move closer until our faces are barely a foot apart, his legs on either side of me. He doesn't say a word, doesn't touch me, just looks at me with a slightly bewildered expression. Hopefully good bewildered, because I lean in and do the one thing I've wanted and told myself I could never do again: I kiss Sam.

I wrap my arms around his neck, and Sam's hands are on my hips, tugging me closer. *Definitely good bewildered,* I think, smiling against his lips. For eight months, I thought Sam was the boy who kissed me once and never wanted to kiss me again. But I was very, very wrong. Because he's kissing me, and his mouth is warm, lips parting as his tongue brushes against mine. Every little doubt that I've obsessed over for eight months is on fire, burning away. And as the kiss slows, he brings his hand to my face to cradle my jaw, and I don't know what I was so afraid of, and—

Kacey.

I press my palm to Sam's chest, and his lips leave mine. Exhaling shakily, I step back until we're no longer touching. I glance down the pathway—I can't even see the Jeep or the bathrooms from here—and I doubt Kacey saw anything, but *still.* What's wrong with me? Why am I like this?

Sam draws his hand across his jaw and then grins. "Flor—"

"I'm sorry," I blurt out. "I really shouldn't have done that."

"Don't apologize for that," he says jokingly. "Never apologize for that." When I don't smile or even respond, he pushes up from the bench, the space between his brows knitting up. "Don't worry, Kacey didn't see anything."

"Maybe not, but..." I take another step back because we're still so close. Too close. And all I ever want to be is close to Sam, to stay here all afternoon kissing him, but I *can't.* What if Kacey saw us? Even if she wasn't against her friends dating her brother, the fact I kept our first kiss from her might break us. With her leaving in two weeks, I can't have that. I can't.

"Hey, it'll be okay," Sam says with the kind of smile that makes me want to kiss him again. Because that's the magic of Samson Hodge—he thinks everything happens for a reason and that everything will be okay in the end.

Must be nice.

"I'm really sorry," I say again, because I have no idea what else to say or how to make this right. Then I turn on my heel and flee down the pathway like the cowardly, awful friend that I am.

The path loops around the back of the bathrooms and ends by the vending machines near the car. I spot Kacey by the snack machine, and when she turns, she smiles. No trace of betrayal on her face, which is a good thing, but makes me feel even guiltier.

"Hey! Want anything?" she asks, holding up a few dollar bills.

"Sure, yeah. I'm gonna use the bathroom." Then I duck into the nearby bathroom, a handicapped single stall, and lock the door behind me.

The pipes gurgle and the sink drips, but nothing is louder than the confusing steamroll of thoughts inside my head.

What was that?! Holy shit that boy can kiss. You fucked up. But the kiss, though. What were you thinking? God I still want to kiss him. Bad! This is bad! What are you doing?

I dig the heels of my hands to my eyes and take a deep, painfully tight breath.

Then another.

And another.

Until the tightness begins to fade.

I wet a handful of paper towels and press them to the back of my neck.

Okay, this isn't too terrible. Kacey didn't see us. Yes, I made out with her brother—*again*—but it was a mistake. And I don't have to figure out what it means now. I need to survive the rest of this trip. Then, when I'm home, I can untangle all this. Right now I need to focus on the trip. One last epic moment with Kacey before everything changes.

I study my reflection in the fingerprint-smudged mirror—and cringe. My ponytail is half-undone, and my lips are swollen and I smeared some of my mascara onto my cheeks during my earlier panic. I take out the ponytail holder and finger-comb my hair until it's smooth. Then I use some water and clear up the mascara. The lips I can't do anything about.

Steeling myself, I leave the bathroom.

Kacey no longer at the vending machines, so I loop back around to the Jeep. She and Sam are leaning against the side door, splitting a bag of chips. Sam sees me first, and, holding my gaze, he raises one brow, like a silent question I don't know how to answer. I *really* shouldn't have kissed him, but I also can't seem to regret the kiss either. It's confusing.

Kacey looks up from her phone, and she waves me over.

"Catch," she says, and tosses another bag of potato chips at me when I reach them.

I fumble with the bag but manage not to drop it. "Thanks." I study my best friend. But she's so oblivious that it makes me feel ten times worse.

Kacey taps at her phone then shows me the screen. "Check it out."

She posted a picture of me driving to her Instagram with a cheesy caption—*watch baby bird florie fly!*—below. My face is stretched wide in a smile, my blond hair whipping around my blotchy cheeks as it loosened out of its ponytail. I look *happy*.

"Any chance I can convince you to change that caption?"

"Never." Kacey sticks out her tongue.

"Well, thanks for memorializing the moment," I tell her, and I mean it. Driving was a big freaking deal, and I don't want to forget what it felt like to have that victory.

"Anytime, babe. I like seeing you take a risk every once in a while."

I really, really doubt she'd feel that way about the other risks I've been taking lately.

"Um, yeah." I glance around the parking lot, an antsy-anxious feeling tightening my chest. "Ready to go?"

I hand over Sam's keys and climb into the back seat, happy to have a tiny bit of distance between us after our kiss. As I click my seat belt, Kacey's phone blasts "No Scrubs" by TLC. She jokingly made it her ringtone after we heard the song on a TV show and I complained that it was the worst earworm ever.

Kacey checks the screen, then drops her phone into the cupholder. "It's Mom." The phone chirps again with a text, and she sighs, picking her phone back up. Her forefinger swipes across the screen for a moment; then, wordlessly, she passes the phone back to me.

The message is from Rosemary, and it's a screenshot from Kacey's Instagram post of me driving. The one she *just* posted when I was in the bathroom. And behind me, through the driver's-side window, is an unmistakable California highway sign that none of us noticed.

Along with the text is: CALIFORNIA?!

"Fuck," I groan, handing over the phone. Then: "Wait. Why are you Instagram friends with your mom?"

"Not the point, Flor."

Of course Kacey rebounds the fastest between the two of us. "Well," she says calmly, "we planned for this. We're too far away for them to really do anything. And we're *hours* from San Francisco. We're all technically adults—she can't stop us."

"But she can tell my mom." Suddenly all my worries about Sam have disappeared from my brain.

I have bigger issues now.

Kacey turns around to face me in the back seat, concern softening her face. "I'm sorry, Flor. I know you were trying to do this without Helene ever finding out."

Shaking my head, I say, "Don't blame yourself. We're in this together, right?"

Kacey reaches back and squeezes my fingers. "Right. But you can decide what's next. I think we should keep going, but if you want to turn around, then we'll go back. Sam can visit Amanda some other time."

I pull my phone out of my purse, but there's nothing new. If Rosemary knows we're not at the beach house, it's only a matter of time until my mom knows too. Kacey's right—we're already in trouble. Our parents will be pissed if we drive back now, or if we drive back later tonight.

The only difference would be Eleanor and Trish.

That last, epic memory with Kacey.

And that's too big of a difference for me to ignore.

Sam catches my eye in the rearview. "Where are we headed, Flor? Home or San Francisco?"

"San Francisco," I say. "We can't turn back now. Not when we're so close."

"Let's do it." Sam turns left out of the parking lot.

"No Scrubs" blasts from the cupholder again—it's going to be stuck in my head for weeks at this rate—and Kacey sighs.

"Do I answer it?" she asks, showing me the caller ID: *MOM.*

"If it were my mom calling right now," I say, "I'd throw my phone out of the window."

Kacey hits decline. "I'll text her that we're okay, and that we'll be home tomorrow."

"Yeah, I mean, there's not a lot she can do to stop you two at this point," Sam says, merging onto Highway 101.

I pull my phone from my purse and stare at the blank screen. No new notifications. Even though Rosemary can't stop us, she'll undoubtedly tell my mom, and my whole cover story will be blown.

I switch my phone to Do Not Disturb so I won't see any incoming texts from my mom. After the show, I'll read them—because she *will* text and call, that I'm sure of. After the show, I'll handle this whole mess. But not right now.

The Jeep passes beneath a big green road sign:

SAN FRANCISCO 100 MILES.

I shove my phone into my purse and try to relax. There's no turning back now.

The only thing separating me from Eleanor and Trish is a hundred measly miles.

KACEY + FLORIE'S WILD AND SUPER-COOL
BFF ROAD TRIP BUCKET LIST

1. Be spontaneous (yes, Florie, that means YOU)
~~2. Find bangin' outfits for the Eleanor and Trish meet and greet~~

We're going to look amazing. AMAZING!

Maybe your self-confidence is rubbing off on me because we totally will!

~~3. Be embarrassing tourists~~

SAY WEIRDOS

WEIRDOS!!!

It's official: I love Portland

And Portland loves you!

~~4. Buy a memento in each state~~

Oregon: Portland touristy T-shirts

California: Confusion Hill baseball caps

Wait. Were we supposed to get something from WA?

No we live there!

5. Kiss a random hottie

Hannah ♡ 206-555-1978

~~6. Break a traffic law~~

I DROVE ON THE FREEWAY AND DIDN'T DIE OR COMMIT VEHICULAR MANSLAUGHTER!

YOU'RE A BOSS! A CEO OF THE ROAD!

~~7. Say yes, no questions asked~~

Guess I should be glad it was tree houses and not matching tattoos . . . ?

FUCK missed opportunity! Can I take it back? Let's get tattoos!

~~8. Visit a roadside attraction~~

Confusion Hill! Is seeing believing? We visited and still don't know!

Who knows, but I am SO confused right now ???

~~9. Anything that makes us ask "Is this a bad idea?"~~

I'm never getting high again

Yes, yes you are

10. HAVE THE BEST TIME OF OUR LIVES

SEVENTEEN

San Francisco, CA

FRIDAY, AUGUST 12, EARLY EVENING

The traffic in San Francisco is nightmarish.

Somehow it even rivals Seattle, and by the time we cross the Golden Gate Bridge and get onto Lombard, everything slows to a bumper-to-bumper crawl.

"Rush-hour traffic." Sam cracks his neck as we slow to a stop behind a minivan. "We should be there in twenty, maybe thirty minutes."

Kacey unlatches Sam's phone. "Did you ask Amanda if we can change at her place? I can reroute us."

Sam's gaze meets mine in the rearview. I shrug at him in response. Because, over the last hundred miles, I've gained zero clarity on what to do about Sam. Rosemary finding out about our whereabouts was a decent distraction, but Sam slipped back into my thoughts as we traveled south down the 101.

I don't know what to do. I know what I *want* to do, and what I should do, but those are two very different things.

"I'm not seeing Amanda after all," he says, and the light finally changes.

Kacey shoots him a glance as we roll through the intersection. "What? Why not?"

"Just lost interest."

"O-kay," Kacey says, not at all convinced.

"Let's change somewhere near the Masonic," I tell Kacey, and really hope she drops this. "We're already almost there, anyways."

She props her bare feet up on the glove compartment. "Guess that's probably easier, huh?"

After that, there's no more Amanda talk, and we slowly make our way to the Masonic Auditorium. The parking garage beside the auditorium is marked full, but Sam offers to drop us off so we can grab our tickets while he finds parking.

"Then we'll reconvene and grab dinner?" he asks after making a third loop around the auditorium.

"Sounds good to me." Kacey points to a loading zone, and we pull over. "Meet us by the box office, okay?"

"Sure thing." Sam shifts into park while we collect our stuff.

Kacey rushes to unzip her massive hot-pink suitcase for her makeup bag, and I grab my new-to-me dress and purse, we both hop out onto the sidewalk. After Sam drives off, Kacey and I turn to face the auditorium.

"Wow," I say, and Kacey squeezes my arm.

Because between us and the box office is a sea of people crowding the sidewalk. The hype for this show is *real.* A line spills out from the entrance, *already*, and we have to wait in another line at the box office, where people are asking if anyone has extra tickets.

The girl running the box office has pretty blue box braids and drapes her upper body onto the counter, like she's too exhausted to hold herself upright. "Before you ask," she rushes to say, "no, you can't buy tickets here. The show's sold out." Then she points one finger to the sign hanging beside the window: MURDER ME LATER LIVE WITH ELEANOR DAYRIT AND TRISH WILLIAMS: SOLD OUT!

Yeah, the hype is definitely real. "I'm actually here to pick up will-call tickets."

The girl looks skeptical but taps her mouse. "Name?"

I rattle off my and Kacey's information. We each have to show our IDs—her license, my Washington state ID. Then she removes an envelope from the locked register and slides it across the counter.

"Info about the meet and greet is inside the envelope. Enjoy the show," she says, and then glances behind us with a weary sigh. "Next!"

We shuffle out of line, and I peer into the envelope. Two tickets. Two *VIP* tickets.

Kacey slams into me, and I nearly drop the envelope as she loops her arms around my neck. I laugh, staggering and trying to regain my balance. I hug Kacey tightly, fiercely, as the crowd of *Murder Me Later* fans pulses and pushes past us. Maybe I'm not as fearful about where Kace and I will stand in a few weeks, but that doesn't mean I won't miss her to my very core.

"We made it!" Kacey releases me and bounces on the balls of her feet.

I fan out the tickets in front of her and grin. "We did it."

"Hey," Sam calls, jogging over to us and weaving through the crowd. "I got lucky. Found parking on Bush."

Kacey loops her purse straps over her shoulder. "If you're not going to Amanda's, what're you gonna do while we're inside?"

Sam shrugs, buttoning up his denim jacket. "It's San Francisco. I'll figure something out."

"We have an hour until doors open," Kacey says. "Let's go find somewhere to eat."

Sam searches for restaurants on his phone while I study the snaking line of *Murder Me Later* fans, wearing their merch with the show's better-known quotes and sayings on them. I even spot one girl wearing a HOT FOR HOLES T-shirt. Paul Holes is a celebrity in the true crime community; he helped solve the Golden State Killer case through DNA evidence. He's also ruggedly good-looking for a man in his fifties, like he spends his free time hiking and backpacking.

Huh. Maybe I have a type.

We decide on Greek for dinner; a nearby food truck is a short walk from the auditorium. Despite how hot it was farther north, it's chilly in the city. The fog is cottony in the sky, the warmth of the day fading fast as the sun sets. Even if goose bumps are lining my arms and I forgot my flannel in the car, I'm too freaking excited to care.

We made it.

The Starbucks bathroom on the corner of Sutter and Powell definitely wasn't built for two people. After eating, Kacey and I funneled inside the Starbucks, received the bathroom code, and locked ourselves in with our bags and makeup. I shimmy out of my sundress, bumping into the hand dryer, and pull the shirtdress on over my head. Kacey zips me up, and once she's done swapping her shorts and crop-top combo for the jumpsuit, she opens her makeup bag.

"What do you think is up with Sam and Amanda?" She uncaps her liquid eyeliner with her teeth, holding on to my shoulder so I don't squirm.

"What do you mean?" I close my eyes, flinching as she draws a line along my lids, the felt tip tickling my skin.

Kacey runs the pen over the line again, then works on the inner corners, and I try to not sneeze. "He drove all this way and *what*? He changes his mind?" I try shrugging, but she holds me in place. "Don't move."

"I dunno." I school my voice into a calm and blasé tone, like I literally couldn't care less. "You know Sam."

"True," Kacey murmurs, then moves on to my left eye. "He has the attention span of a fruit fly. But it's still weird."

"Is it?" Sweat dampens the armpits of my dress.

Kacey doesn't say anything else, just finishes my left eye, winging out the liquid liner in the corner as a finishing touch. "Voilà!"

I turn and face the mirror. My hair is a lost cause—a shoulder-length tangle of dirty-blond strands—but between the makeup and the dress, I look kind of amazing. As Kacey does her own makeup, I finger-comb my hair (somehow we packed zero hairbrushes between the two of us) and twist it back into a bun. Then I borrow Kacey's lipstick and color my lips in a shade of red I'd normally never brave.

Dumping her pens and glosses and Q-tips back into the makeup bag, Kacey hugs one arm around my shoulder, and we grin at our reflections. "You ready?"

I'm smiling so hard, my cheeks hurt. "Ready."

Kacey squeezes me, then we duck out of the Starbucks and meet Sam outside. He's standing beneath the awning with his back to us, both hands stuffed into his jacket pockets as he surveys the hustling bustle of the outskirts of Union Square.

"Hey," Kacey calls out as we approach her brother.

Sam turns around, his gaze finding mine. A cold breeze ruffles his hair. "Wow." He clears his throat. "Who knew you two cleaned up so well."

"I know, right?" Kacey fluffs her curls with one hand. "We're very glamorous."

"Thanks." Color rushes to my cheeks, and I look anywhere that's not Sam's freakishly attractive face—a face that I kissed only a few hours ago and really want to kiss again, even though it's the worst idea. The sidewalk seems safe, so I end up staring at all the random trash and gum stuck to the cement.

Kacey pulls out her phone and unlocks it. "One sec, let me look at the directions. . . ."

Sam walks over to me as Kacey scrolls and leans his hip against the building. "Hey, have you checked your phone?"

I tear my gaze from the concrete. The breeze kicks up, and I wrap my arms around myself, little goose bumps budding to my skin. "I put it on Do Not Disturb. I'm avoiding the inevitable for as long as possible. My mom's gonna be pissed."

"Right. Smart move." He studies me for a moment before asking, "You cold?"

"I'm fine."

Sam slides his jacket off and holds it out. "Here."

"I said I'm fine." The wind gusts even harder in response, and he lifts one brow. With a sigh, I grab the jacket and slide my arms through the sleeves. "Thanks."

The jacket is much, much too big. But it's warm and smells like Sam. That mixture of earthy sawdust and pine deodorant. While I'm no longer shivering, I'm not sure if it's worth it. Because now it's kind of hard to ignore Sam and everything Sam related.

Kind of makes me forget why I want to ignore it in the first place.

"Okay, it's a ten-minute walk to the Masonic." Kacey stows her phone back in her purse. If she finds it strange that I'm wearing her brother's jacket, she doesn't comment on it. "You walking with us, Sammy? Or are you gonna hang out around here?"

"I'll walk with you." Sam tucks his hands into his jean

pockets, and when the wind blusters, I notice the goose bumps on his forearms.

Something stirs in my chest, and I tuck the jacket around myself even tighter.

The theater is even busier than it was an hour ago, and I pull the envelope from my purse when we reach the entrance. The printout inside lists the info for the meet and greet. After the show, we're supposed to come back outside and wait until 9:15 p.m., when we'll be led to a backstage greenroom where Eleanor and Trish will be waiting.

Excitement and nerves rebound within me as we reach the line.

"Okay," Sam says, surveying the crowd, "this is where I leave you."

Kacey gives her brother a quick hug. "Thanks."

Sam lets go of his sister and turns toward me. There's this awkward beat, this hesitation. My mind scrambling to figure out if I should hug him or not, when he leans down and wraps his arms around me. The hug is perfect and warm—but it sends my mind straight back to our kiss, and I really can't think about that right now. I don't know how to feel or what I'm doing, and Sam being so Sam-like is making it really hard to think rationally.

I step back and shrug off his jacket. "Thanks," I say, and the rush of blood pounding in my veins keeps me warm, even without the jacket. "For the ride and the jacket."

"Looks better on you anyway," Sam says softly.

Comments like those might be the death of me, but, yeah, I'm smiling. How can I not?

Luckily, Kacey's way too distracted by the crowd to eavesdrop on me and Sam.

"We'll text you when it's over, okay? Bye!" But Kacey doesn't wait for him to reply before hooking her arm through mine, pulling me deeper into the crowd.

I glance over my shoulder, but I can't see Sam anymore.

"You ready?" Kacey asks, tugging on my arm.

I face the Masonic. "Yeah, I can't believe we're here."

"I know," she says, breathless. Her big brown eyes are wide with excitement, and she reaches for my hand, squeezing my fingers with bone-crushing force.

The line begins to move forward as the doors open, and eventually we're let into the venue. Inside the cavernous theater, we're shown to our seats in the center of the fourth row. The crowd fades into a dull roar of excitement as I survey it all, committing it all to memory—down to the very last detail.

A mental image to remember fondly when I'm home, grounded for eternity.

"Wow," Kacey says as we take our seats.

"Wow." I stare up at the currently unoccupied stage. Our view is *perfect.*

The crowd is loud and excited, and suddenly I feel loud and excited too. My hyped-up energy is no doubt being amplified by the thousands of other *MML* fans surrounding us. I love seeing this many people with a healthy obsession for true crime and murder all gathered together.

Under ordinary circumstances, I'd be spiraling in panic right about now, but I feel perfectly okay. Like my excitement has morphed my usual anxiety into a more useful emotion and mental state. Crowds, noises, dirt—they always put me on edge. But not right now. No, right now I'm hopeful and endlessly excited.

I'm *happy*.

So happy that I barely recognize myself.

EIGHTEEN

The Masonic Auditorium, San Francisco, CA

FRIDAY NIGHT

I've seen countless photographs of Eleanor and Trish, from their social media accounts, promo, and *Rolling Stone* spreads. I've even watched a few videos—like the recent Q&A—but seeing them in person is different. There's this energy that you can't capture through a microphone and skillful editing. And that energy is electrifying, energizing.

I'm not the only one who thinks so.

Tonight, Eleanor and Trish walk out to auditorium-shaking applause.

Eleanor is sleek in black jeans and a peplum top. Trish is wearing a flowing skirt-and-top set. They wave, grinning wide, as they take their places onstage. There are two vintage-looking velvet armchairs with a small table between, like a casual living room set. A screen projects their show logo behind them.

"Hello, San Francisco!" Eleanor lowers her microphone as she gets seated.

"Hello, hello," Trish chimes in, her Texan accent charming, and crosses her ankles, showing off black booties with heels shaped like real knives. "Welcome to the last stop of our summer tour! We're *thrilled* to be here!"

Eleanor laughs. "It's always strange to be back in my hometown! How is everyone doing tonight?"

Cheers erupt and I clap, unable to wipe the grin off my face.

"We're good too, thanks for asking," Eleanor says dryly into her microphone, and the crowd laughs. Once everyone quiets, she continues. "Tonight, we're going to do something local. This murder was one of the first to ever capture my attention. Since I grew up here, it was hard to escape the Zodiac Killer: the Bay Area boogeyman. The Zodiac might've been before my time, but learning about his crimes was the first time I really felt captivated by a murder story. And we're going to share it with you, our dear murder babes, tonight!"

I nudge Kacey with my shoulder, and we share a look. Everything about tonight is overwhelming, but in a good way. A memorable way. My eyes burn with the threat of happy tears. But when Kacey turns back to the stage, a lump forms in my throat. Maybe it's because we started with *Murder Me Later* and . . . we're not ending, not really, but this chapter in our friendship is coming to a close.

Once Kacey joked that she's the Eleanor to my Trish, and she's kind of right. Just like Eleanor, Kacey is bold and confident. I'm more grounded and emotional, like Trish. And somehow, we're so much better together than apart. On paper, our friendship doesn't make a lot of sense, and beyond *MML*, we don't have much in common. But in reality?

I don't know where I'd be if it weren't for Kacey Hodge.

"So," Eleanor says as she wraps up her story, holding the microphone loosely in one hand, "the real reason why I was so captivated by the Zodiac is my parents. As I'm sure many listeners know, my mom was one of San Francisco's first female police officers. And my father worked at the *San Francisco Chronicle*—do you see where this is going? They met during the Zodiac investigation, when the killer was sending his cryptic letters to the *Chronicle*. Isn't that cute?"

The crowd laughs, and Trish coos into her microphone, "Who said true crime isn't romantic?"

Kacey whispers, "Okay, that's objectively adorable. My parents met in the ER. *Boring*."

I nod in agreement, but Eleanor's anecdote has shoved my own parents to the forefront of my mind.

Even though I know the trouble will be worth it—how can it not be?—a tiny flicker of panic ignites in my chest. Heat spreading to that space between my shoulder blades. My gaze darts to my purse, slouched by my feet on the auditorium floor. There's no doubt my mom texted, but I suddenly need to know what those texts say. And the answers to my questions are right there, in my purse.

Therapy has taught me that I should befriend the unknown, but it's easier said than done. Because if I check, then I can forget all my worries and enjoy the rest of the live show. The thought is so tempting. But it's not that simple. Checking fuels the compulsion and makes the whole thing even worse.

I tuck my hands beneath my thighs and try to breathe deep. *Be present,* I remind myself. *Focus on Eleanor and Trish.* But my breath is caught in my chest. I exhale, all shaky and weird.

"What're you sighing about?" Kacey jokes, but there's a glint of concern in her brown eyes.

I spare her a tight smile. "Nothing. I'm fine."

"No, you're not." She frowns. "You're worried about the wrath of Helene, huh?"

"Do you think she called or texted?"

Kacey hesitates, then asks, "Want me to check? I'll let you know the deal, but we won't respond. Would that help?"

"Yeah." I lean over and pull my phone from my purse, handing it to Kacey. She enters the lock code and turns off Do Not Disturb.

Onstage, Trish is chiming in with a personal anecdote about the first time she saw that old Zodiac movie with Jake Gyllenhaal, and their infectious happiness relaxes me. My worries are slipping away already. I'm embarrassed it came to this, but maybe now I can stay present and enjoy what's left of the live show.

"Okay," Kacey says quietly, humming to herself, "your mom sent *several* messages. Wow, I've never heard—or seen—Helene swear before. . . . She's upset. My mom called her after she saw the Instagram post."

I tear my gaze from the stage. "Does she know where we are?"

Kacey shrugs. "Not sure, but she's pissed. She said you guys need to have a 'big talk'."

I take this all in, trying desperately to not let my anxiety spiral out of control. "Okay, that's not terrible. I guess. Um. Did she say anything else?"

Kacey shakes her head. "Nope. She expressed her disappointment in you, that you'll be in trouble when you get home. Typical stuff."

Nothing Kacey relayed is surprising. I already knew Mom was going to be upset. But now my stomach's twisting with the reality of my decisions. I should've embraced the unknown. If I had, I could've lived in ignorant bliss for the rest of the night, but oh, no, my anxiety wasn't having any of that. It had to seek out reassurances and completely backfire in the process. Why am I even surprised? My obsessive-compulsive disorder is an asshole.

"Huh." Kacey taps at my phone's screen. "Sam texted you. I hope nothing's up with Mom and Dad. . . ."

I never knew the wind could be knocked out of you by words alone. But that's how I feel. Like that one time I fell off a hammock when I was ten, and *whoosh,* all the air left my body. My ears are ringing, and my mouth is dry. Distantly, I know I should say something, do something! Come up with a defense, smack the phone out of Kacey's hand. But I'm frozen.

Maybe the texts are innocent, about where he's parked or—

"What the fuck is this?" Kacey asks in a low, flat voice, and my stomach drops even more. She shoves the phone in front of my face and asks again, "What is this, Florie?"

When I take the phone, my hands are shaking. I scan the three messages Sam sent while we were changing for the show. Three amazing but very, very incriminating text messages.

SAM: I keep typing this out and deleting it because it's not sounding right but

SAM: I like you, Florie. I like everything about you—even your ocd and the fact you listen to creepy murder podcasts for fun and are the most confusing person ever. And that kiss? Fuck that was a good kiss. I'm not great at communicating and shit but you might be even worse. But I still want to try if you do.

SAM: maybe I misread things but I don't think I did. Can we talk when we're back home?

I reread the messages, my eyes catching on *I like you* and *can we talk*, and it's like every little thing I've ever wanted Sam to say written out in front of me. My heart soars for one pathetic beat before crashing. I drag my gaze from the phone screen to my best friend's face, which is blank. Not angry, not sad, not betrayed. Just *blank*. Which is somehow way worse.

"Listen," I whisper, reaching for Kacey, but she flinches back, her eyes narrowing. "It's not what you—"

"Are you and Sam . . . hooking up?" she asks, not bothering to lower her voice, and the people in the row directly in front of us turn in their seats, scowling. "Is this why he's not with Amanda right now? Was he *ever* seeing Amanda?"

My stomach hurts and my heart hammers and the anxiety swells.

The truth is out there. I can't lie or backtrack or do anything other than tell the truth.

"It's complicated," I tell her, and shove my phone back into my purse, even if I want to reread those messages again and again. "When he kissed me in December—"

Anger flashes across Kacey's face. "December?" she hisses. "This has been going on since *December*?"

Before I can say anything, or even open my mouth, Kacey abruptly gets up and walks down the aisle, leaving me and the *Murder Me Later* live show behind.

NINETEEN

The Masonic Auditorium, San Francisco, CA

(STILL) FRIDAY NIGHT

There's no choice: I follow Kacey. I follow Kacey even though Eleanor and Trish are still onstage. I follow Kacey even though the fight awaiting me when I find her is going to hurt. I follow Kacey because my lies might be friendship ruining and I have to try—I have to explain myself, grovel, anything!—to save our friendship.

Kacey's outside the venue, near the box office. She's standing with her hands on her thighs, leaning forward with her dark hair creating a wild, curly curtain around her face.

"Kacey," I say as I approach, "just let me explain."

Her head snaps up, and she pushes her hair off her

cheeks. "You lied, Florie! *You!* Normally, I'd be impressed, but right now, I'm just pissed off."

I walk as close as I dare, still leaving a solid three feet between us. Enough distance that she can't, you know, hit me or something. "Can I explain?"

Kacey nods. "Fine." Her cheeks are red and flushed, her eyes glassy.

I'm the worst best friend ever.

"I've liked Sam for two years," I tell her, and choose my words carefully. "Pretty much since the first day I met him. The whole crush was kind of pathetic, okay?"

"Two years?" she echoes. "You never said anything in *two years*. Why? Did you not trust me or something?"

I give her an exasperated look. "Of course I trust you! I didn't tell you because Sam was off limits. That's what you said, right? No friends dating your brother. And I wasn't going to risk my friendship with you over him."

"But you *did*, and then you hid it from me," Kacey says. "I read the texts, Flor. You can't pretend that nothing's going on with you two. It's literally in writing, on your phone."

"I'm not pretending or lying! Up until five minutes ago, I wasn't even sure if Sam liked me." I drop my hands, embarrassed they're still shaky. "Back in December, I didn't make the first move. That was all on Sam. If you want to be upset at someone, be upset at your brother. He started this. Not me."

Kacey flinches, but she steps closer. "I don't care about him. I'm upset because you're supposed to be my best friend.

You're not supposed to lie to me. I don't care if Sam lies—he's not my best friend."

I stare up at the foggy, darkening sky and try to gather myself but it doesn't work. When I shift back to Kacey, frustrated tears spill over. "I messed up. I should've told you about the kiss right after it happened. But I totally freaked out. Like, I lost my shit over a cat that ran into the road, because I thought I hit it. Then I told myself that I couldn't have Sam, that my OCD would ruin it. I felt *worthless*, and I was afraid that he wouldn't like me, once he knew me. Then he came home—"

Kacey holds up her hand. "I don't want to hear it."

"Too bad because I'm telling you," I snap, wiping at my tears, because she needs to hear this. I need to say this now, or I never will. "Sam came home, and it became clear that the kiss meant nothing to him. Part of me was relieved because I'd built it all up in my head, you know? If there was nothing there, then I hadn't lied to you. I could let myself off the hook."

Kacey sighs and stares out at the traffic along California Street before turning back to me. "Really? That's your excuse?"

I take a deep breath, try again. "Do you remember learning about confirmation bias in psych?"

"Not really."

"Okay," I say, wishing Kacey actually paid attention in class for once. "Confirmation bias is when you cherry-pick what information to believe—and you reject any information or evidence to the contrary. For people with OCD, especially

Pure-O . . . it can turn really ugly. I overvalue unwanted thoughts and beliefs about myself, constantly. Sometimes, I even seek out every negative thing to confirm every negative thought I've ever had about myself."

Kacey adjusts her weight from one foot to the other, like she's bored. "Okay, sure. But what does this have to do with Sam?"

"Kind of everything? I spend . . . um, I spend a lot of time feeling worthless, and when something happens that *could* be evidence of my worthlessness, I latch onto it. Because it makes sense, you know? It's familiar. It's like someone telling you everything you want to hear, but it's every negative, bad thing about yourself." I press my lips together for a moment as my vision goes blurry, then add, "Anything that Sam did or said that reinforced my worthlessness, I valued. And anything else . . . I ignored. Because I'm so used to feeling worthless. I cherry-picked."

Angry as she is, I swear there's a shift in Kacey's expression, and when she speaks, her voice is softer. "You've never told me that before. The worthlessness stuff."

"It's not a super-fun topic of conversation," I reply, scuffing the toe of my slip-on against the sidewalk. "I shouldn't have lied about Sam, and I'm so, so sorry. Nothing makes that okay, but I want you to know why I did it. I convinced myself that winter break was Sam being, well, *Sam*. But now . . ." I toss my hands up uselessly.

"Now he likes you, too," she says, finishing my thought.

I haven't had time to process those texts and what they could mean, but I nod. "Yeah. Maybe. I don't know."

Kacey stares at me for one long moment before easing the distance between us and hugging me. I loop my arms around her neck and squeeze back.

"Does this mean you're not still mad at me?" I ask through a face full of her curls.

"Oh, I'm fucking pissed. But I forgive you." She tries to let go, but I hang onto her for dear life.

"Really? Because I'd understand if you couldn't forgive me."

Kacey shrugs against me. "Grudges have never really been my thing."

Some of the tightness in my chest softens, and I finally let her go. "So we're good?"

"We're good." She tilts her head to one side and asks, "Does this mean you and Sam are going to date now?"

"Ugh, please don't ask me that right now," I say. "I read those texts when you did. I've had, like, zero time to process any of it, and I don't know what to do. I've been too focused on making sure I didn't explode our friendship."

Twisting her lips to one side, Kacey studies me. An ambulance races past on the street, and from inside the auditorium, I catch snippets of laughter. Then my best friend says, "You do know what to do, though. Isn't that what this has all been about?"

Kacey's not wrong, but I'm afraid. Afraid of something real. Afraid of what it all means—or could mean if I gave it a chance. Because what's scarier than getting something you've wanted for so long? "Guess I'll have to talk to him, huh?"

"Yep. And if Sam doesn't want to be with you, then he's the worthless one, not you. And I say that with complete love, as his sister."

A laugh catches in my throat. "Thanks."

"I really don't understand what you see in him. Or anyone has ever seen in him, for that matter."

"Yeah, well, it'd be weird if you did," I say, and she laughs. I'm not entirely sure if I deserve a friend as badass and loyal as Kacey Hodge, and I don't know what I'm going to do without her when she leaves for Portland in two weeks.

To break any lingering tension, I say, "So, your brother is a *really good* kisser."

Kacey hits me in the boob. "I do not need to know the details!"

"Ow!" I shield my chest with my arms, laughing. "Okay, I deserved that."

She points at me. "Yes, yes you did. And I'll get lefty if you even try to tell me more about my brother's"—she gags—"kissing skills. *Don't.*"

"I'll think about it then," I tease, and loop my arm through Kacey's, my body light with relief. "Let's go back inside."

Kacey bumps her shoulder into mine, and just like that, our friendship regains its equilibrium.

We get our tickets from our purses and hold them to the usher by the entrance.

"No re-entry," the guy says dismissively, scrolling on his phone.

My heart drops. "What?"

Kacey glances at me, then her ticket. "You've got to be

kidding me. Why didn't you say something when we came out?"

The guy shrugs. "Look, it's not my job to tell you information that's already on your ticket. Sorry."

"You're an usher," Kacey says slowly, "that's literally your job description."

The usher rolls his eyes and returns to his phone.

I step away from the entrance, disappointment flooding. "Shit."

"Sorry," Kacey says, and we wander away from the entrance. "I had no idea."

I shake my head. "It's okay. We caught most of the show. And besides, we don't have to be in the venue for the meet and greet. The instructions said to wait out here."

Kacey plops herself down on the curb and pats the cement beside her with a sigh. "Might as well get comfy."

Seated on the curb, Kacey and I talk.

We talk about the things I hid from her the past eight months. I keep my promise—and save my left boob from getting punched—and don't go into the details of kissing Sam. Not during winter break, and not a few hours earlier. But I break down everything else. The night of the holiday party. Trying to drive Sam's Jeep in the snow. A boring G-rated recap of the kiss. The cat incident.

Then I tell her about the week since Sam came home. The confusing, small moments. The crushing disappointment when he lied about Amanda. The night at Rockaway Beach and all of Sam's mixed signals. The strawberry stand

and how, as convoluted as it sounds, it's actually pretty easy being myself with Sam. But the parts I focus on the most are how badly I wanted to talk to her about it. How I should've told her that night, after he kissed me for the first time. How I should've had enough faith in our friendship to believe we could've worked it out.

"Why'd he lie about Amanda?" Kacey asks.

Our legs are stretched out into the street, shoes touching. "We haven't had a chance to talk too much, but he said he didn't think through volunteering to drive us, and when you brought up Amanda, it sounded like a better reason than the real one."

"Which was you."

My cheeks warm, and I shrug. "That or he's a secret *Murder Me Later* fan. It's fifty-fifty, really."

"Come on, it was for you. Asshole move, though."

"Maybe, maybe not." I sigh heavily. "I kind of . . . ignored his texts, back in December. He didn't know how I felt, and honestly, I don't know what I would've done if he'd told me how he felt. . . . I was so upset when he showed up out of nowhere. It felt like he was crashing the last few weeks we had together."

Kacey shifts, resting her head on my shoulder. "But they're not the last few weeks we have together," she reminds me, and I smile.

"Yeah, I know that now. It's easy to get carried away inside my head. All the bad outcomes, everything that could go wrong . . ." I stare across the street at an old, Gothic church. "Can I ask you something?"

"Always."

"The stress and anxiety over college . . . is it worth it?"

Kacey's quiet for a moment; then she says, "Definitely."

Lauren has told me, on more than one occasion, that growth doesn't come from a place of comfort. That makes sense. Because I've spent most of the last two years comfortable. And I don't have a whole lot to show for it. During my many sleepless nights, I can't help but wonder: If I'm *always* comfortable and sheltered, how will I ever become the person I want to become?

Every discomfort has been surgically removed from my life, thanks to my mom. But you can't have good without bad. I can't grow unless I push myself. Unless I act on this itchy, strange energy inside: to be vulnerable, to fall. Because I'm beginning to believe, more and more these days, that I'll be able to pick myself back up when the time comes.

"Promise me that, when we're back in Barmouth and my mom is nailing my bedroom door shut with me trapped inside, you won't let me forget what I said outside Voodoo Doughnut," I tell Kacey. "I really feel ready to . . . I don't know, push myself. Finally take a chance."

Kacey knocks her foot into mine; across the street, church bells toll nine times. "Good! And I promise," she says with a laugh. "But do you really think your mom will be that mad? She'll get over you lying. Eventually. You've been kicking OCD's ass on this trip, Flor. You've been out of your comfort zone for days and look at you."

I almost laugh but shake my head instead. "Maybe. But I'm starting to wonder if this trip went so well *because* my mom wasn't here, telling me how to feel. Every time I feel like I'm making progress with my OCD, my mom will disagree or tell me something different. And when the person who literally gave you life tells you something about yourself, why *wouldn't* you listen? Especially if it lines up with your own fears? It's the whole confirmation bias thing all over again."

Kacey wraps both arms around me and hugs me against her. "Because it's wrong."

I'm caught somewhere between wanting to laugh and wanting to cry more. The way Kacey says it makes it seem so freaking simple. All my OCD really does is make me doubt myself, and sometimes it's hard to figure out which feelings are real and true. "How do you know when it's wrong, though? What if she's right?"

"Listen to yourself. Not what anyone else tells you—that includes your mom. She might know you, but no one knows you better than you." Kacey's words are comforting. They're that little whisper I've always ignored in the back of my mind, amplified by her voice.

I study the darkening street as the sun finally slips away. "It's confusing because my mom clearly cares and wants me to be happy and safe. But sometimes I feel like she only wants those things if they're on her terms. Not mine. I really want to try. To go to college, do something *different* and hard."

Maybe my words won't make sense to Kacey—someone who never backs down, who has always been in control of her story—but they're unraveling something inside me. My eyes prickle and burn, and I shut them tight. I can't break down and sob, even though I kind of want to. Not when I'm about to meet Eleanor and Trish, and the winged eyeliner Kacey drew on my lids is so on point.

Luckily, just a few tears escape down my cheek, and I quickly brush them away.

Kacey's hand rests on my back, her palm moving in small circles. "You're going to do great—you know that, right? Even if your mom disapproves about college, I can help you through the application process. Help you visit schools. Whatever you need."

"Stop saying so many nice things, or I'm going to ruin your eyeliner," I say, only partially kidding. "I probably already look like a raccoon."

"Kind of, yeah." Kacey laughs, then pulls a mini pack of tissues from her purse and presses one into my palm. "But don't worry. I can fix your eyeliner."

"I don't deserve you," I mutter, blowing my nose.

"Yeah, you do." Kacey throws her arm around my shoulders and adds, "You deserve way more than you think you do."

"Thanks, Kace." I lean into my best friend, and it's like my entire body sighs. After a beat of silence, I ask, "Can you hand me my phone?"

Kacey grabs my phone from our pile of bags beside her and passes it to me.

Before I lose the teeny-tiny flare of courage, I open my email. Find my homeschooling guidance counselor's email and type out a quick message. Because once I put this out in the universe, it's going to be harder to backtrack, to retreat. If I don't do this now, my gap year could turn into gap *years.*

"What're you doing?" She peers over at the screen.

"Emailing my guidance counselor and telling him I want to talk about my options. Before my mom grounds me forever and I forget how to use technology." I finish the short message and, after a wavering moment of hesitation, hit send.

An action I can't take back. Even if the counselor can't help me, I've taken one tiny step forward. And it feels so good. The church bells toll again across the street, and I palm my phone, staring out at the stained glass illuminated from within. Despite everything, I'm hopeful. For the first time in a long time, I'm hopeful about my future.

The kind of hopeful that isn't followed by dread or superstition or magical thinking. All that's left is pure hope. A feeling I want to hold in my palm and wrap my fingers around, pressing it into my heart, where it can flourish and make me stronger.

TWENTY

The Masonic Auditorium, San Francisco, CA

FRIDAY, LATE EVENING

Luckily, Kacey and I don't have to wait for much longer. From our seats on the curb, we can hear snippets of the live show, and they're winding down. We only really missed the last twenty minutes. A bummer, but I'm actually not all that disappointed. After that conversation, I'm too busy feeling lucky and hopeful to be disappointed.

While we wait out the rest of the show, Kacey fixes my eyeliner, and then I read the texts from my mom. They're bad in that super-vague way that leaves way too much to the imagination. As for Sam's texts . . . I don't know what to say. Maybe when I'm standing in front of him, it'll all fall together. Yes, I drove, and maybe I'm ready to apply to college. But I have no idea if I'm ready for something real with Sam.

Sam says he likes me, OCD included. But there's so much he hasn't seen or experienced. The only person who's seen it all is Lauren, but that doesn't count. She's paid to deal with my mental illness. Being with Sam would mean opening up—completely—with him. And how do I explain that OCD isn't like what you see on TV or in the movies—it's a thousand tiny traumas I have to deal with in therapy and with the help of medication?

And what if it all falls apart or goes up in flames? I wouldn't be able to avoid him or never see him again. Not if I stay friends with Kacey. It'd be like when I saw him in the Hodges' kitchen a week ago—only eight million times worse and more painful. But the worst part is, I don't know how to be around Sam and *not* want him.

"What do you think they're like in real life?" Kacey asks, and yanks me out of my Sam spiral. "Eleanor and Trish?"

Thankful for some non-Sam thoughts, I say, "Fearless. Funny. Down to earth." Then I shrug. "Honestly, I don't even mind if they're assholes. Not like I think they will be, but you know, just covering my bases here."

Kacey chuckles. "They won't be assholes. Even though I doubt they'll be *exactly* what we imagine them to be. You nervous?"

I'm actually not nearly as nervous as I thought I'd be. For a week, there's been this pressure as we got closer to tonight. And while this trip was initially all about Eleanor and Trish, they now feel like the cherry on top of this weird, wild adventure.

Kacey and I have already gotten what we wanted. This trip is already utterly unforgettable.

Eleanor and Trish helped me get here, but it's up to me to figure out what's next.

And I hope that, when I'm standing in front of them, they'll know how much my thank-you means.

"More excited than nervous," I tell her, pleasantly surprised by how right that sounds.

Vaguely, in the distance, Kacey and I hear:

"Good night, San Francisco! Murder me later, because I have shit to do!"

A few minutes pass, then the crowd begins to funnel out of the Masonic.

We shuffle to the side of the entrance, where we're supposed to wait for the meet and greet. The crowd swarms all around us as people make their way to the street and parking garage. I'm practically bouncing on my toes in excitement.

An official-looking guy wearing an old, classic *MML* shirt paired with dress pants comes out of a door marked PRIVATE. It takes me a second to recognize Antoni, Trish's husband, who manages their tours. "If you have tickets for the meet and greet, please line up beside this column here."

Kacey and I exchange grins before filing into line behind maybe a dozen other fans. Nervously, I trace the crease of the envelope, over and over again, with my thumbnail. The crowd is so loud, full of this tangible and frenetic energy, that when I hear my name called, I don't turn around, figuring I misheard.

When I hear my name again, I turn to Kacey, who's also

searching the crowd of exiting fans. For a split second, I think it's Sam, but the voice is distinctly female. And familiar. I push onto my tiptoes to see over the crowd, and my stomach drops.

"Mom?" My brain struggling to figure out what the hell is going on. Because my mom is here. In San Francisco. Among an excited sea of *Murder Me Later* fans. She couldn't be more out of place if she tried.

"What?" Kacey snaps to attention and follows my line of sight. "Oh shit," she murmurs beneath her breath.

My mom stands near the curb. Her usual pristine outfit—a matching sweater set and a low chignon—has been replaced by travel jeans and a wrinkled dress shirt, her blond hair pulled into a harried bun. For a second, I stand and stare. Because even my anxious, obsessive mind didn't prepare for this outcome. I rely on my brain to prep me for these types of moments—but I didn't see this coming.

Thanks, anxiety. Literally the *one* time I needed you.

"All right," Antoni says, "we're letting groups in one at a time. Each group gets a few minutes. Let's get this meet and greet rolling! Feel free to hand me your phones for pictures. Eleanor and Trish are so excited to meet y'all . . ."

I shift my attention from Antoni to my mom. She pushes her way through the crowd, not tearing her gaze from mine.

"Hi, Mrs. Cordray," Kacey murmurs weakly, all her badass bravado draining.

"Kacey," Mom says stiffly, then rounds on me. Her lips are pressed into a colorless and tight line. "Florie, we're leaving. Now. Come on."

I step back, bumping into the people surrounding us. "Are you kidding me? I'm not going anywhere except through those doors." I intend for my words to be forceful and strong, but my voice wavers and fades. I don't have a lot of practice pushing back against my mom, and it shows.

"We're going back to my hotel, okay? We'll talk more there." That vein in Mom's forehead bulges, the only visible sign of her anger.

"Next!" Antoni calls, and the group in front of us enters the hallway to the greenroom.

Maybe I wasn't nervous earlier, but now I am. An anxiety infused with anger that's building every second. I can't believe my mom tracked me down, like some wayward kid. "We're next, okay? It'll be, like, five minutes. Then I'll go with you."

Mom massages her brows. "I flew all the way here and I'm exhausted. I'm sorry, but you don't get the luxury of five more minutes. Come on." She beckons me with her hand.

"This is ridiculous," I say with a flat laugh, and Kacey grabs my hand in support.

"*Now*, Florie." Mom pulls a set of keys from her pocket and raises her brows expectantly.

Lowering my voice, I change tactics. "Mom. Please. This is really important."

"Too bad. Let's go. Unless you want to lose the rest of your privileges? Your phone? Your laptop?"

"Next!" Antoni motions at us "C'mon, ladies."

A sinking feeling weighs down my gut. If I try to follow Antoni, I'm afraid Mom will drag me by the wrist from the

Masonic, even if it means making a scene. If we'd gotten in line a minute sooner, stepped into the building before Mom showed up, then we could've avoided this. But I was doomed the moment Mom emerged from the crowd.

Resigned, I turn to Kacey. "Take pictures, okay?" She opens her mouth to argue, to fight for me, but I shake my head and press the envelope with our tickets into her hand.

Kacey nods. "Of course," she says, then follows Antoni down the hall. She glances back once before the doors shut, her face etched with concern.

"How'd you know where we were?" I ask flatly as Mom guides me from the crowd, her hand firm on the small of my back, all the way to the rental car parked in a three-minute loading zone.

"After Rosemary mentioned you were in California and I realized you'd lied to me, I went through your room." Mom unlocks the car; the lights flash. "I found your binder. Maybe next time you lie to me, don't leave a literal map to your location behind."

The laugh that escapes me isn't a humorous one. Because of course. Of course I left that binder in my closet! Kacey tossed it aside when she came over, and I totally forgot about it.

I duck into the sedan that smells like Febreze and bleach. Right now I should be meeting Eleanor and Trish. Instead, I'm sitting in a sticky rental car as my mom loads directions to her hotel.

While Mom studies Google Maps, I pull out my phone, but she reaches over and snatches it from my hands before I can unlock it. She tosses the phone into her purse in the back seat. I'm not sure what I was going to do with it—Kacey knows what's happening, she'll tell Sam—but it's like my life-line has been ripped from my grasp.

"Make a U-turn," the robotic Google Maps lady says, and my mom starts the sedan. As she pulls from the curb, I wait for her to yell at me, say something, but she doesn't say a thing. It's almost like my mom knows I'd find this lack of explanation upsetting. I want to speak, just to break up the unknown of the situation—to figure out where I stand—but I don't give in.

I'm sure I'll get plenty of explanation when we're at the hotel.

My mom has taken so much from me. Maybe not intentionally, or as a punishment. But the fact is, she has. And I'm desperate to hold on to how I've felt the past two days. Hold on to the blurry outline of the girl I know I can become. Because I'm desperate to fill myself in and see the whole picture.

I lean my temple to the window and shut my eyes.

This can't be over, not yet.

Not when I can still feel Sam's mouth on mine. And remember the roar of energy and happiness in that fourth row at the Masonic. Or the comfort of Kacey pressing a tissue into my palm. This can't be over when I still have so much more to prove. Because something changed inside me, on a molecular level, during this trip.

If Mom loves me, she'll understand.

At least, I hope so.

TWENTY-ONE

San Francisco, CA

FRIDAY, NIGHT

Mom parks in the garage of a nondescript hotel outside the San Francisco International Airport and grabs her bag from the back seat. “Come on,” she says shortly.

I follow and, as I shut the car door, remember that my duffel is still in Sam’s Jeep. Along with my pajamas, a change of clothes, medication, and toothbrush. All I have in my purse is my Portland rainbow T-shirt, my wrinkled sundress, my makeup bag, and some used gum wrappers.

In silence, I follow her up the steps of the hotel. Inside, an enthusiastic concierge greets us as Mom checks in. Since it’s late, the lobby is pin-drop quiet and still. But as I lean against the wall beside the check-in counter, I can hear the rumble of airplanes above. Once Mom has her room key, we trudge into the elevator and get off on the top floor. I'm achy and exhausted by the time Mom swipes the room key into the reader and pushes open the door.

"There's only one bed," I say as we enter our room.

Mom wheels her suitcase in and sets it up on a luggage rack. "This was their cheapest room; they had a deal. We can share." Then she nods her head to the side. "Or there's a couch."

I sink onto said couch and kick off my slip-ons. In most of the books I've read and movies I've watched about road trips, there's "only one bed." But having to share a bed with my *mother*? No thanks.

Mom sits on the bed, and her arms hang limp in her lap, all those lines deepen into grooves on her face.

I want to be mad at her, but guilt worms its way into my chest. "I'm sorry," I tell her, but keep my voice even and strong.

Mom's tired gaze finds mine. "Honey, I had to find out from Mrs. Hodge that you lied to them. That my daughter wasn't where I thought she was. I had no idea if you were safe or lying in a ditch somewhere."

"You knew I was safe, though. Kacey replied to Rosemary's text; she knew we weren't in a ditch," I explain, and that even strength in my voice is already fading fast. "I shouldn't have lied, but can you blame me?"

"I can blame you all I want because you *lied*, Florie. This isn't like you," Mom says, and rather than mad, she sounds

tired. "Was this Kacey's idea? I always knew she was a bad influence."

"Kacey isn't a bad influence," I say quietly. "She's my best friend."

Mom tugs the ponytail holder from her bun and massages her scalp. "Two years ago, before you met Kacey?" She turns to me. "You would've never done something like this."

"But that's not because of Kacey. That's because of *me*, Mom. I'm allowed to change, aren't I?" I dig my toes into the carpet and stare directly at my mom even though I want to turn away. I need her to understand. "I drove. Earlier today."

"Florie, you don't have your license!" Mom presses the heels of her hands to her eyes for a moment before dropping them. "What's gotten into you?"

Sweat slicks my palms. This isn't going the way I need it to go. All my words aren't coming out right. "But isn't that great? I did fine! I drove!"

"No, you know what that was? Illegal. You could've gotten into a crash or been pulled over," she says frantically. "You could've been arrested, Florie. And for what? To prove a point?"

Something delicate inside me snaps. "Driving isn't a *point*. That was a huge deal to me."

How does she not understand? Driving was a good thing, wasn't it? I try to recall those thirty minutes behind the wheel. The excitement and freedom and accomplishment. But they're watered down now, harder to grasp.

"This conversation isn't going anywhere. Let's talk more when we're home with your father."

"It's not going anywhere because you don't want to listen to what I'm trying to say." Frustration builds inside me. "I'm eighteen. And yeah, I made a mistake. I shouldn't have lied. But I'm allowed to make mistakes, aren't I?"

"You keep saying you're eighteen, but eighteen is a number, not some magical indicator of maturity, as you've shown tonight." Mom stares at me. "And if you're expecting me to be impressed, stop right now. If you'd gone through the proper steps—lessons and logging your hours behind the wheel and passing your test—then I'd be proud of you. But I'm not. No, I'm deeply disappointed in you, Florence."

My eyes are hot. *Don't cry, don't cry, don't cry.* I'm overwhelmed, but I can't cry. "How do you do that?"

"Do what?"

"You take something I'm proud of or happy about, and you squish it like a bug." My throat tightens up, and the tears fall. Sliding precariously down my cheeks. *Shit.* But what if Mom's right? What if she's been right this whole time? No. No, I did all those things. I did them and I was happy.

"You've always been so dramatic. You get that from your father, you know." Mom shakes her head, exhaustion shadowing her eyes. Her gaze doesn't land on mine for more than a few seconds, as if my tears make her uncomfortable. "You need to calm down and stop crying. How do you expect me to take you seriously like this?"

This isn't fair. I'm allowed to cry and be upset; it doesn't make me weak. But try telling my mom that, the woman who I've never seen cry, not even when my grandfather—her dad—died. I'm tired of being made to feel like I'm bro-

ken just because I process the world differently. Because it doesn't mean I'm broken . . . does it?

"I'm allowed to cry." I say the words out loud, hoping that'll make them true. "I'm upset. People cry when they're upset. It's normal."

"But you're always upset." Mom makes no move to comfort me, to even hand me a tissue. "You're always crying or anxious or depressed. Always. You need to learn how to control yourself."

"Control myself?" I lean over to the side table for a tissue. "So I can be more like you?"

"Don't talk to me that way." Mom's jaw hardens.

Stay strong, I remind myself. But all that confidence is dwindling, and I'm scrambling. The doubt is seeping in. "I've proved a lot to myself this trip, things I've been scared to face or talk about. I thought I might break if I faced them, but I'm still whole. And I want to see what else I'm capable of . . . like college."

"We've talked about this. College is off the table for now."

"I know, but what if I changed my mind? What if I'm ready?"

"You're not ready, Florie. College is hard, and I'm very worried that you'd crumble under the pressure," Mom says firmly but calmly. "I have no interest in wasting tens of thousands of dollars so you can have an expensive mental breakdown and drop out."

I wait for her to take it back and admit she's gone too far, but she says nothing. Does nothing. Silence fills the room. I never knew silence could be so loud, but here I am, losing my hearing from all this noise.

Before Mom can say anything else, I push up from the couch and run into the bathroom. Lock the door behind me. Tears stream down my cheeks, and I want to scream at myself for being *so stupid.* Mom's right. Of course she's right. I wish she wasn't, but my mom knows me. Maybe better than anyone else on the planet. More than Lauren and more than Kacey—and way more than Sam. Mom only wants what's best for me.

I pace around the tiny bathroom before collapsing onto the closed toilet. Pulling my feet onto the lid, I wrap my arms around my shins and bury my face against my knees. Mom's words are the bright light shining on all my deepest, darkest insecurities. I should've never listened to those deceptive what-ifs. The lies inside my brain, tricking me into thinking I'm somehow better and more capable than I really am.

I'm nothing. Absolutely nothing.

In the bedroom, I can hear Mom moving around, but she doesn't knock. Doesn't ask if I'm okay.

After a moment, I lift my head. There's a mirror on the back of the bathroom door, and, even though the overhead light is off, the nightlight plugged in beside the sink glows. Just enough to illuminate me.

My blond hair is messy and tangled. My eyes are bloodshot, the winged eyeliner Kacey lovingly drew across my lids smeared like matching black eyes. I'm every bit the failure my mom accused me of being. All that strength and confidence really was a lie. Because this, right here, is me. The real me. That girl, the one who faced her fears time and time again over the past few days, doesn't stare back.

I'm starting to doubt she ever existed in the first place.

TWENTY-TWO

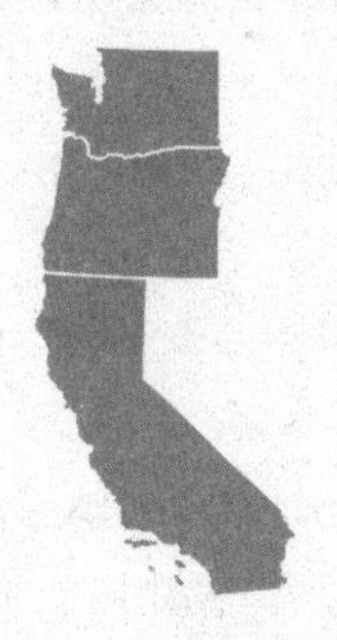

California to Washington

SATURDAY, AUGUST 13

Mom let me have the window seat, like some peace offering after last night. I slump my shoulder against the side of the plane and stare down through the small oval window. The city is barely visible beneath all the fog. If Kacey and Sam stuck to the original plan, they left last night after the show. They should be in Oregon by now. Maybe in some parallel universe, I'd be there in the passenger's seat of Sam's Jeep, finishing what we started.

"Here." Mom places my phone on my lap and then passes me a pair of tangled earbuds.

"Thanks," I mutter, the first word I've spoken since we returned her rental car at SFO.

Mom glances at me from her seat beside me. It's a small plane, two seats per row. "I love you, you know that, right?"

I blink at her, my fingers fussing over a knot in the earbuds.

"Florie," she says, my name like a sigh. "I'm sorry about what I said—"

"Don't be." I finally undo the knot in the cord. "You were right."

Then I plug the earbuds into my phone and shift as far away from my mom as possible.

I'm both thrilled to be out of the airplane and back on solid ground and dreading my crash landing back into reality. Last week, I'd tricked myself into thinking I wouldn't be coming back to this. That, when I returned from our road trip, I'd be different. And if I were different, maybe my life could be too. But Mom popped that bubble last night, and I'm a fool for thinking things might change.

We land at Sea-Tac, the closest commercial airport to Barmouth, and since we didn't check any luggage, we go straight outside and wait for my dad to pick us up. It's raining, which isn't surprising. The sky is thick and gray, the rain a constant drizzle. All around us, people hail rideshares and climb onto buses, or flag down loved ones circling the terminals.

I don't know what to expect when Dad arrives. Dad's always been the neutral, more hands-off parent. But I've never exactly been in trouble before. Actually, this might be my very first infraction. I've lived so, so carefully up to this point, and I don't know what's going to happen. If my dad will take my side, or if he'll take Mom's and slowly whittle away the last flecks of my self-esteem.

Mom and I wait in the sheltered pickup area until Dad's SUV pulls alongside the yellow-painted curb. The right-hand blinker is still flashing as he climbs out of the driver's seat and walks around the car. He says something to Mom, then heads over to me.

"You okay, sweetheart?" Dad asks quietly, holding me by the shoulders so he can study me. As if the hurt Mom inflicted last night is something he can see.

I nod, and then collapse into him. My dad wraps his arms around me and gives me a bear hug. As I hug him back, it hits me how badly I needed to be hugged. So I hug him even tighter.

"Let's get you home," Dad says, and we join Mom in the car.

I fall asleep during the drive. It's two hours from Sea-Tac to Barmouth, and I sleep through almost all of it. But when we enter our neighborhood, I wake up. Rain sloshes against the car windows as Dad slows down, turning onto our street. We park in the garage and funnel into the house.

"I've taken your laptop from your room." Mom slides her shoes off beside the door into the garage. It's the first thing she's said to me since she handed me the headphones. "And I've made you an appointment with Lauren Monday afternoon, one p.m. You aren't to speak to or see Kacey. No phone, computer, or TV privileges until I say so. Got it?"

"Yep." I'm too detached to care much about anything at this point. Yawning, I walk upstairs to my bedroom. The door is open, and I stop in my tracks when I reach the threshold.

Mom admitted that she went through my room, but this is a complete mess. She didn't even bother to clean up after herself. My bed's unmade, the pillows out of their cases. My drawers pulled out or overturned. My carefully organized bookshelf and collectibles—a mess.

On my bare mattress is that purple binder. My sad attempt at controlling the last three days, coming back to bite me in the ass. Lauren always told me that my over-preparedness and hypervigilance would be detrimental to my life. I had no idea how much. It's almost funny.

What Mom's done, it's an invasion of my privacy. Distantly, I know I should be more upset than I am. That my mom not only went through all my stuff but trashed my room in the process. That my mom clearly doesn't trust me, not one bit. But it's like I've run out of the energy to be upset. I can't deal with this right now.

With a sigh, I walk into my bedroom and join the disaster on the floor because this is where I belong. I stretch my legs out and rest my head against my bedframe. Normally, I'd be unable to stand the mess and clean it up, but I don't have that fire inside me anymore.

I sit among it. Counting my heartbeats.

How did things go so terribly wrong?

TWENTY-THREE

Barmouth, WA

MONDAY, AUGUST 15, AFTERNOON

On Sunday, Dad helped me clean my room.

Together, we put my pillows back in clean pillowcases and remade my bed. He organized my bookshelf for me while I arranged my collectibles and clothes. All day, I kept waiting for Dad to get upset with me. To accuse Kacey of being a *bad influence.* To ask me what had gotten into me. But he never did.

Mom doesn't bring it up again either. I wonder if she's embarrassed by what she said about college. If she feels bad. Or maybe she's just done with me. Doesn't want to deal with me and all my messy emotions. She doesn't ignore me, but she barely talks to me either. Like we're existing in the same space, but she can't be bothered to interact with me. Like a bad roommate. The weekend passes pretty quietly, though. Surprisingly uneventful considering last week.

When Monday rolls around, I'm not sure how I feel about therapy. Part of me is eager to unload onto another human being all the angry, depressed, and anxious feelings that have been slowly building up inside me since Mom showed up at the Masonic Friday night. But another part of me doesn't want to talk about it.

I'm not sure if I can deal with one more person confirming all my worst beliefs about myself.

Dad left for the city really early this morning, but he's supposed to be back tonight for dinner. He rarely takes day trips due to the long commute; Mom probably asked him to stick around more this week after what happened. Like she can't handle me on her own or something. Not like I'm complaining; I like having Dad around. He's a buffer, our peacemaker.

And without Dad around this afternoon, my communication with Mom is nonexistent before therapy. Wordlessly, she serves me lunch and tidies the kitchen while I pick at my sad excuse for a salad, all wilted lettuce and too many tomatoes.

When the doorbell rings, Mom pulls back the curtains over the sidelights. Then she sighs and opens the front door. Leaning back in my chair, I can just barely see through a gap in the curtains. And on the porch is Kacey clutching my duffel bag, and behind her is Sam.

"Hi, Mrs. Cordray," Kacey says, hesitant but polite.

A thousand emotions hit me at once. Longing. Pain. Happiness. Depression. Anger. Shame. Embarrassment. A lot of embarrassment. They roll over me as I sit there with my fork in hand, staring out at my best friend and . . . whatever Sam is to me; I don't even know anymore. Since I don't have a phone or laptop, I haven't spoken to either of them since San Francisco.

Part of me is sad. I almost want to get up and walk over there. But what's the point? All I'm going to say to them will be a disappointment. And I'm tired of disappointing people. I already disappointed myself. And my parents. I don't want to witness disappointing Kacey or Sam. I don't want to talk about the scene outside the Masonic. I don't want to talk about that kiss with Sam or the texts I never had a chance to answer. I don't want to face Kacey and have her witness me curled up in defeat.

I don't want them here, but that doesn't mean some small part of me isn't happy to see them.

"Kacey. Sam." Mom nods, her voice cold. "Can I help you?

"We wanted to bring Florie's bag." Kacey holds the duffel out. "Is she home?" She shifts on her feet, peering past my mom, but she can't see me from this angle. If she looked through the gap in the curtains, she might be able to see me. But she doesn't.

Mom takes the bag. "Florie's not allowed to have visitors right now. She's grounded."

"We'll only be a second, Mrs. C." Sam's voice is smooth, no doubt flashing her a grin meant to be charming.

"Thank you for bringing Florence's bag," Mom says, then shuts the door.

As Mom turns, she catches my eye but says nothing. Just

walks upstairs with my duffel bag. I hear a thunk as she tosses it on the floor outside my room. A moment later, she returns, sliding a light cardigan over her linen top.

"Ready?" she asks.

If my count is correct, this is the third time she's spoken to me since this morning.

I shove the last of the wilted salad into my mouth. "Yep," I say, and follow Mom into the garage. I slide into the passenger's seat of her crossover and stare out the window as she backs out into the driveway.

The journey downtown is quick, and Mom parks in the small lot behind the two-story brick building.

Mom turns toward me. "I'll wait here until your session is over, okay?"

I nod and slide out of the car without a word. I duck into the back door of the building and take the stairs, my feet cement blocks. The second floor is home to several businesses—a dentist, a law office, and Lauren Thomas, PhD. The inside of the small waiting room is soft yet sterile, an attempt at calm with a stone fountain on a glass-topped coffee table and whale songs instead of music.

I perch on the loveseat, and stare at my shoes until the frosted-glass door opens and Lauren leans out. Her black hair is naturally curly, and she gives me a warm smile. "Come on in, Florie," she says, opening the door wider. She's wearing a green maxi dress that's about ten times too fashionable for Barmouth.

I push up and shuffle into her office, taking my usual seat in the armchair across from my therapist's.

"How are you?" Lauren sits on her chair and sets a yellow legal pad onto her lap.

My mouth goes dry. How much did my mom tell her?

The space between Lauren's brows narrows in concern the longer I go without speaking. Then it all comes pouring out. Like once I turn the faucet on, I can't stop it. She already knows all about *Murder Me Later* and my confusing history with Samson Hodge, but I fill her in on everything that happened the last two weeks.

Lauren listens, jotting down notes. Then I get to the part about my mom showing up.

"Hold on," she says, pen paused on the pad, "your mom flew to San Francisco to take you home?"

"Yeah. Showed up right in front of the Masonic. I tried talking to her . . ." I shrug as my words fade. "But she didn't listen. I knew I could either stand there and fight with my mom in front of a hundred strangers or go with her. So I went with her."

"You missed the meet and greet? After all of that?"

"After all of that. Eight hundred miles and I missed it." I tug at a loose thread on the cushion, ignoring the tightening in my throat. "The live show was cool, though."

Lauren scribbles some notes. "And then what happened?"

"Um. I tried to apologize and explain. But she was so upset that I'd lied in the first place that she wouldn't listen to me." My voice cracks a tiny bit. "She even blamed Kacey, said she was a bad influence."

"Kacey's an influence," Lauren says with a small smile, "but not a bad one."

I huff a laugh. "Yeah. So then I told her that I'd driven earlier. I wanted her to understand that . . . that I'd accomplished something big, you know? But my mom flipped out. And I guess she's right. I shouldn't have done that. I could've been pulled over or—"

"Florie," Lauren interrupts, "you drove. Maybe the circumstances weren't . . . ideal, but that doesn't take away from your accomplishments. Whatever your mom says, that was big, okay?"

"Okay." I swallow hard and sniff. "Things fell apart after that. I started crying. She told me to cut it out, called me dramatic. Every time I tried to stand up for myself, she knocked me back down. So I stopped trying to stand up."

"Oh, Florie," Lauren says gently, sadly.

I grab a tissue from the box on the coffee table and dab my eyes. "That wasn't the worst part. I told her that I felt like I was doing well and that, maybe, we could revisit the idea of college. And she said no." The more I talk, the more confused I feel. Because the way Lauren is treating me is like Mom's in the wrong, not me.

Who am I supposed to believe?

"You told your mom you wanted to go to college?"

"Yeah." Sniffling, I crumple the tissue in my hand. "And she said she didn't want to pay college tuition just for me to have a breakdown and drop out."

Lauren massages the space between her brows before saying, "I hope you know that isn't true. That the image your mom is painting isn't you. *Maybe* a year ago that was you, but not now. You've grown and challenged yourself. College would be a healthy next step. Just because your mom or your guidance counselor suggested that you wait a year doesn't mean you have to."

I'm crying again and don't bother holding back. Mom isn't here to turn my tears into a weakness. Lauren hands me a few more tissues and leans back in her seat. She's quiet as I cry. I cry until my chest feels lighter, my head clearer.

"I was so proud of myself during the trip," I say eventually. "The entire time, I was like, 'This is how I'm supposed to feel,' and it felt *good.* But when my mom said those things . . ."

"You believed her because it was safer than fighting back," Lauren fills in. "You've spent so many years under her care, listening to her, and trusting her—which isn't bad, your mom is so caring and loving. But you've grown, and I don't think your mom knows how to deal with that."

I ball up the damp tissues in my hand and stare across the office at Lauren. "Yeah?"

Lauren nods. "Yeah." She clicks and unclicks her pen a few times. "What you did on that trip? That was a huge accomplishment. You shouldn't have lied, but I hope you're as proud of you as I am."

"You really think so?"

"I do. And I'm sorry your mom's comments made you doubt yourself," she says carefully. "No one likes change, and I'm sure your mom is struggling in her own way. She loves you, but as we've talked about, she enables some of your behaviors. For years, she's known what's best for you, and I'm sure that's hard to let go of. We become so used to living one way that adapting—changing—can feel dangerous or wrong. But in reality, it's just different."

I sit quietly, shredding the tissues in my hand, and process Lauren's words.

Is it possible that my mom was wrong? That this is on her, not me? That maybe I'm as competent as I felt on that road trip? Lauren's words feel right, like a puzzle piece snapped into place. Mom's words felt like they were ripping me apart from the inside out.

Maybe it doesn't matter what Mom thinks of me.

Maybe it only matters what I think of me.

Lauren gives me a sympathetic smile. "This has been hard on you, huh?"

I laugh-cry into my ball of tissues. "You have no idea."

"I think the best next step is to have a family meeting." She opens her planner. "Is your dad home tomorrow evening?"

"He should be."

"Would five work?"

"Yeah, I think so."

Lauren pencils us in for tomorrow. "Hopefully, we'll figure things out between the four of us." She sets her planner aside. "College is such an important step. A big step, and if that's what you want, I don't see why you can't do it. We'll talk it out, okay?"

"Okay." I exhale for what feels like the first time since I heard my name outside the Masonic and sink back in my chair. "I emailed my old guidance counselor. Maybe he can help."

"I'm sure he'll be able to. You have a lot of people on your side."

I turned to my mom for help and advice on, well, everything. My mental health was always so scary, so *big*. And it was nice when my mom had all the answers, when she made all my decisions. Mom was my mirror, and no matter how distorted the image was, I accepted it. But I need that dynamic to end. I can't keep doing this.

"Well, we only have five minutes left," Lauren says after checking her special fifty-minute hourglass on the mantel. "Anything else you want to talk about? You really glossed over what happened with Sam."

I sink even farther into my chair, as if it can swallow me whole. "There's not a whole lot else to talk about. The kiss . . . I shouldn't have kissed him," I say quietly, my brain spinning with all the regret I've collected over the last few days. "I realized that, if I hadn't kissed him, he would've never texted, and if he hadn't texted, Kacey and I wouldn't have left the venue—"

"Let's keep the Florie train on the tracks," Lauren interrupts with a soft laugh. "You can't know any of those things. Maybe things would've ended up differently, but maybe not. Now why don't you tell me what you're really worried about? Because there's more, isn't there?"

With my head leaned back against the cushion, I stare at a painting hanging on the wall behind Lauren. "Sam's great. And that entire trip, I kept . . . falling more and more for him, even if I didn't realize it. Usually, the more you get to know someone, the bigger their flaws become, right? The shine comes off. But that didn't happen with Sam. And I'm really, really afraid that's going to happen with me."

"That the shine will come off?"

I drop my gaze from the painting to my therapist. "Yeah. Like the more he'll get to know me, the bigger all my flaws will become. Eventually, he'll see it all, and I'm kind of a mess."

Lauren closes her notebook and sets her pen on the side table. "We're all messes, Florie. Some people are better at hiding it than others."

For some reason, that makes me think of my mom. After swallowing hard, I shrug. "I don't know. Every book, every movie, the girl with the mental illness doesn't get the guy, right? Either she's this manic pixie dream girl who teaches another character a lesson, or she's a hurricane of hurt, taking everyone down with her. I can't picture *it*. Even if it's what I've wanted for years."

"Picture what?"

"Having a love story. Or a happy ending." Tears line my lids, and I try to sniff back some of the hurt, but it's unraveling inside me. "It's not like I've dated a ton, but . . . they all lost interest once they realized that I'm kind of weird, that I can't be spontaneous and fun twenty-four-seven. That sometimes my brain stops me in my tracks and, no matter how hard I try, I can't let the most insignificant of shit go. I'm either too much or I'm not enough."

Lauren exhales, the sound sharp in the quiet office. "You're right," she says, and I lift my brows in surprise. "The media shows a very narrow experience when it comes to mental illness, and most of it is tragic. But that doesn't mean there's no alternative. If you want a love story, you can have one."

The tissue in my palm is shredded and damp, but I don't move for a fresh one. "You really think so?"

"I do. And I think you're closer to your love story than you realize."

TWENTY-FOUR

Barmouth, WA

MONDAY, AUGUST 15, EVENING

Can I use my phone really quick?" I ask my dad after another stilted and polite family dinner. Mom's out on the back deck with her post-dinner tea and a book, and we're tidying up the kitchen.

Dad slides a Tupperware of spaghetti into the fridge, frowning over his shoulder at me. "Oh, I don't know, sweetheart. Your mom said no laptop or phone . . ." He trails off uncomfortably. It dawns on me that he probably has no idea where my mom even hid my electronics, let alone feels like he has the authority to hand them over.

I rinse off a plate before setting it into the dishwasher's bottom rack. "Can I use your laptop then? I'll be quick . . .

Kacey still has my bag from the trip and my meds and stuff are in there," I say, mentally crossing my fingers that Dad didn't notice the duffel in the hallway or doesn't know that I have a full prescription bottle in my bathroom. "I won't talk with her or anything, just send her an email so they can drop it off."

If I asked my mom this—even though it's a total lie—she would call Rosemary. But my dad shuts the fridge and studies me, his brow puckered. "Yeah, I guess that'd be okay. But only to email Kacey."

I run the dishwasher and kiss my dad on the cheek. "Thanks, Dad."

He nods, his gaze straying toward the sliding glass doors to the deck. "Just be quick," he says, which is clearly code for *I'm not telling your mom.*

After wiping my hands off on a rag, I duck into the hallway and head for Dad's office. It's the door closest to the garage—a converted spare bedroom—and the one area of the house my mom rarely touches. I flick on the light, illuminating his desk, laptop, and piles of papers, and slide into the desk chair.

Sam is still a big panicky question mark inside my head, and tomorrow's family session will help me work out everything with my parents. But to deal with both, I'm going to need my best friend.

I log into my email and open a new message. But as I'm debating what to say to Kacey—ask for a jailbreak? Reassure her I'm still alive and my mom did not, in fact, bury me in the backyard?—I notice an unread email from earlier today.

The guidance counselor, Dennis, emailed me back.

Even though I told Dad I'd be quick, I click on the email.

To: Florie Cordray <florencedcordray@gmail.com>

From: Dennis Feldstein <dfeldstein@wahomeschoolorg.edu>

Subject: Re: College Application Questions

Dear Florence,

I'm so happy to hear from you. And yes, I'd be glad to help to go over the application process for homeschooled students and answer any questions. I'm thrilled to hear you and your mom changed your minds about you taking a full gap year. Many colleges are eager for spring semester applicants; I can put together a list for you . . .

The message continues, but I reread the first few lines. Snag on the third sentence. *I'm thrilled to hear you and your mom changed your minds about you taking a full gap year.* Last year, Mom told me that *Dennis* was the one who'd suggested the gap year. Not her, and most definitely not me. It was never my idea, even if I agreed to it.

I push back in the desk chair and leave Dad's office—lights on, laptop pulled open to my email—behind. Dad's still in the kitchen when I march past and make a beeline for the sliding glass doors. I push the slider open and step outside.

Mom glances up from her book. "Hi, honey—"

"Dennis," I say, "the guidance counselor. Did he suggest I postpone college, or did you?" I'm weirdly breathless as I wait for her answer.

Mom shuts the book, sliding it onto the side table beside her tea, tendrils of steam coiling into the sky. Her lips pull with a tight smile. "Florie, I'm tired, and I really don't want to have another talk about college right now."

"Answer me." I stare down at my mom, all relaxed in the Adirondack chair, a throw blanket draped over her angular frame. "Was that your idea, or Dennis's?"

With a sigh, Mom sits up and swings her legs over the edge of the chair. "We made a collaborative decision."

That's not an answer. All she has to say is the truth—unless she knows it's the exact opposite of what I want to hear. Unless she lied to me. Honestly, it makes so much sense. My grades were good, despite my mental health dip in junior year. I volunteered at the Barmouth animal shelter for all of sophomore year. My test results were pretty decent, all things considered. Even though I hadn't been seeing Lauren for long last year, she noted to my mom about how much progress I was making.

"What's going on?" Dad hovers behind me with one hand on the doorframe.

"Mom lied to me about college," I say, and take a gamble. "Did she tell you it was her idea for me to postpone college, or did she blame the guidance counselor?"

Dad slips out onto the deck, a forgotten dishrag held in one hand. His gaze darts between me and my mom. "Helene, what is she talking about?"

"I didn't lie," Mom says after a beat, and stands up. She looks down as she folds the blanket. "Dennis asked to speak with me, and I told him about my concerns. We had a chat, and in the end, he came around to my point of view. You're making me out to be a villain—"

"You lied, Mom! You went off on me in San Francisco about lying, and here you've been lying to me for over a year." My hands are shaking, and I cross my arms to hide them. "I wanted to go to college! I could be getting ready like Kacey right now!"

Mom tosses the folded blanket on the chair and turns to me. Shakes her head sadly, like she pities me. "Florie, you couldn't even finish junior year at a traditional high school. Do you really think you're ready for college?"

"I couldn't finish because you pulled me out—"

"Because you wanted me to," Mom interrupts, and her cheeks flush red. "You hated it there. You were having panic attacks every day at that school. What was I supposed to do, when I had to pick you up, in tears, from the front office?"

Shame washes over me. "You should've made me go back," I tell her. "You should've told me I was strong, that I could do it. And when I was nervous about college, you should've helped me feel confident, not weak."

"Oh, is *that* what I should've done?" she snaps, her tone sliding fully into fury. "You aren't a parent, Florie. You don't know how difficult it is. I was trying my best. I'm still trying my best!"

"Well, your best isn't good enough." My eyes are hot, and I will myself not to cry. I'm not sad—not really, anyway—but overwhelmed and angry. "You're overbearing, Mom. You have no life, so you've made taking care of me and my OCD your *job.* I've spent over two years thinking my OCD was the biggest barrier in my life. But it turns out, it was you."

Dad takes a step forward. "Florie, don't talk to your mom like that."

I shift my weight onto my other foot, holding myself tight. "Did she tell you what she said to me? In San Francisco?"

"No," he says slowly. "No, she didn't."

"When I told her I felt ready for college, she told me I wasn't. That she didn't want to pay tens of thousands of dollars for me to have an expensive breakdown and then drop out."

Dad's face pales, and he turns to Mom. "Helene, tell me you didn't say that to our daughter."

"I shouldn't have," Mom admits, "but Florie was trying to conflate her going behind our backs with being mature enough for college. It was ridiculous. She's not ready."

"College is my decision. Mine. Not yours."

Mom stares across the deck at me. "One day, you'll stop throwing fits when you don't get what you want, and you'll see what I see: a spoiled brat."

"Helene!" Dad's painfully out of his element, glancing between us like we're some sports match gone rogue. Always neutral, never involved. "Let's talk this out tomorrow, with Lauren, yeah? Family therapy seems like a good place to talk all this out."

Mom and I ignore him.

"This isn't throwing a fit," I tell Mom as my eyes well, "this is me pushing back against you for the first time in *eighteen* years. The first time I haven't listened to you without question. If anyone is throwing a fit, it's you. Maybe if you weren't such a terrible mom, *you'd* calm down and listen to what I'm saying."

Then I turn on my heel and run inside. Up the stairs and

to my bedroom. I slam my door shut—hard—before locking it and sliding onto the floor. I pull my knees to my chest and bury my face into my kneecaps.

After ten minutes, Mom comes up the stairs—her footsteps light on the carpet—but she doesn't come to my door or knock. She continues down the hallway until she reaches her bedroom, and the door shuts quietly behind her.

Maybe another fifteen minutes go by, and my dad's footsteps mount the stairs.

"Florie?" Dad knocks gently. He doesn't sound mad. Just tired.

I consider answering. But I don't want to know if he finally chose a side, so I stay quiet. He knocks a few more times and says my name again before retreating to their bedroom.

Sometime later, I'm not sure how long, I lift my face and wipe my eyes. That definitely didn't go well. I should've kept my mouth shut until we were all in Lauren's office. But finding out Mom lied about college . . . there's no way I was keeping that inside me until tomorrow. Not like it matters. It's too late now.

I push to my feet and grab some tissues from my bedside table and blow my nose. We ate dinner late because of Dad's meeting in the city, and it's almost eight. Less than twenty-four hours until the family therapy meeting and—

Something pings my window.

I turn around, but nothing's there.

But a moment later—*ping*—as a rock hits the glass.

I walk around my bed and peer out my window. Today was cloudy and gloomy, and the sun hasn't fully set, hidden behind clouds. But there's enough light for me to see Kacey and Sam standing in my backyard.

Turns out, I didn't need to email Kacey to have her come to my rescue.

I lift my hand in a wave.

Kacey waves enthusiastically, motioning for me to come down. Sam stands beside her with his hands shoved into his pockets, shifting his weight from one foot to the other in the damp grass, head tilted back as he stares up at me.

Stepping away from the window, I grab my jacket, and, after shutting my bedroom door behind me, I tiptoe downstairs. Even if my parents find out that I've snuck out, what can they do that they haven't already done?

The alarm sensors are broken in the garage, and I slip out into our backyard that way. I walk past the trash cans in our side yard and unlock the gate. It creaks open, and Kacey and Sam look over.

I button up my jacket and walk their way. "Hey—"

Kacey runs over and tosses her arms around me. "You're alive!"

Unexpected laughter bubbles in my chest, and I squeeze her back. "Were you expecting something different?"

"Dunno," she says, and releases me from her tight grip. "I know to never underestimate Helene."

"Yeah, well. She didn't kill me, but it wasn't pretty. I have a lot to tell you." I turn from Kacey to Sam. "Hi."

The corner of Sam's mouth twitches with a smile. "Hey." He makes this half move like he's going to hug me, then stops. Like he's not quite sure how to approach me after I made out with him, ran away, never replied to his texts, and then disappeared for three days. Fair.

Whatever confidence I had on our road trip—specifically at that rest stop—is long gone. How did I ever walk up to him and just kiss him? Yikes, it's like three days of absence somehow made Sam ten times hotter, or me ten times more insecure. Maybe both.

Panic tightens my chest, and I try to remember what Lauren said at the end of our session. *If you want a love story, you can have one. . . .* And I want that. I want Sam. I want to chase that dizzying, all-consuming feeling I have when I'm near him. Despite the doubt the world has constantly drilled into me, I owe it to myself to be happy. My OCD is a speed bump, not a barrier, to happiness.

I walk past Kacey and wrap my arms around Sam. He hesitates, his hands hovering above my waist for one long second that fills me up with doubt. Then he pulls me close, hugs me tight. Instead of the flurry of anxious feelings I normally have around him, right now there's only comfort. Being near Sam reminds me of the trip, of the girl I know I can be—the girl who is me, even if she's afraid and maybe totally not there yet.

"You good?" Sam asks, his voice low and gravelly.

"Yeah." But I hold on to him even tighter, bury my face against his chest.

Kacey clears her throat behind us. "This is cute and all, but Florie was mine first, and I'm *dying* to find out what happened after her mom showed up."

Sam gives me one more squeeze before letting go. "For

the record," he says, "I'm also glad that you're alive. Probably more than Kacey. Not like it's a competition or anything."

I laugh—almost giddy—and smile at him. Then I turn to Kacey. "Long story, but a lot has happened since San Francisco, and I'm grounded. I'm not even supposed to see or talk to you. But we have family therapy tomorrow, so hopefully things will be better after."

"Come stay at our house," Kacey says with a shrug. "Until it all blows over."

Considering my parents can't take anything else away from me at this point, why not? "Okay, yeah. Give me a few minutes." Then I turn and retrace my steps into the house.

In the kitchen, I grab a notepad and write:

Staying with the Hodges. See you at Lauren's.

-Florie

I creep up the stairs. Mom left my duffel bag outside my room, and I grab it. There are enough meds in there for a few days, plus some clean underwear. Slinging the bag over my shoulder, I hurry back downstairs and make my escape.

Back at the Hodges', Sam disappears to run an errand—mysterious, but okay—and takes the Jeep, so Kacey and I curl up on her bed. I rehash everything that happened after I left the Masonic—Kacey laughs when she hears about the purple binder, hugs me when I tell her about how my mom acted at the hotel, and is righteously upset when she hears about the guidance counselor lie.

Once that's all unpacked, I say, "Tell me about the meet and greet! It's got to be way more interesting than my family drama."

"It was amazing," Kacey says, eyes shining. "They're really fucking cool. I told them about you and tried to explain how much we'd gone through to see them. They were touched and thought you were a badass."

I snort at the absurdity. "Badass. Right, that's me."

"Hey, Eleanor and Trish are wise. Maybe you should listen to them." After a beat, she says softly, "I'm sorry you missed it."

I shake my head. "It wasn't your fault, Kace. Not even close. But it's okay. I mean, meeting Eleanor and Trish was the cherry on the sundae, right? We got what we wanted. I don't think we're ever going to forget this summer."

"Oh yeah, this summer's going down in history." Kacey laughs. "But I still took some pictures. Check 'em out." She passes me her phone, and I stare at the screen.

An ecstatic, smiling Kacey is squished between Eleanor and Trish. I'm not jealous, not in the least. I love how happy Kacey is in these photos, because that makes me happy too.

"You were right about that jumpsuit." I flick through the rest of the album before passing her phone back. "We should definitely frame these."

"They were really nice. Super chill and down to earth. Maybe we can catch them next time? Splurge on meet and greet tickets?"

"Yeah, maybe." I pull my knees to my chest and chew on my bottom lip. "Or maybe I should save up some money for college?"

"Stop being so responsible," Kacey says, but she's smiling.

Before Kacey and I can keep talking about college, Sam

knocks on her doorframe. He's dressed in all black—turtleneck, jeans, beanie—with a backpack slung over one shoulder.

Glancing between us, he says, "We need a morale boost. Who wants to go prank Mrs. Miranda?"

Kacey snorts. "I'm in. She's gotten way too comfortable with her lawn gnomes since you left. I swear, they're multiplying."

"Florie?" he asks with a raised brow.

"Let's do it," I say, and he tosses me an extra black hoodie. It's way too big for me, hanging near my knees, but it disguises my yellow sundress.

Rosemary and Alec are working tonight—they took on extra shifts, since they returned earlier than expected from Bainbridge Island—so we don't have to sneak out of the house. Once we're outside, Sam clicks on his flashlight, and we hurry down the driveway, turning left along the cul-de-sac. Mrs. Miranda lives three houses down from the Hodges, and we creep up on the house, trying not to laugh.

Kacey's right—the lawn gnomes *are* multiplying. And Mrs. Miranda doesn't have funny, novelty lawn gnomes. Nope, all her gnomes are dancing with birds, sitting on mushrooms, holding trowels or lanterns, and they all have these big, creepy smiles.

One or two lawn gnomes is cute. Twenty is serial killer status.

We might feel the tiniest bit bad about pranking Mrs. Miranda if she weren't a grump who turns off her porch light on Halloween and who used to make noise complaints to the non-emergency police line whenever Sam used his carpentry tools after 8:00 p.m. on weekends. She's the worst.

"Are we sure they don't come alive at night and murder people?" Kacey whispers, and we huddle behind a hedge bordering the side of Mrs. Miranda's yard.

"If so, wouldn't they have gotten revenge on Sam by now?"

"True." Kacey peers thoughtfully through the hedge. "Still creepy as fuck, though."

"Agreed." I crouch on my heels. "What's the plan?"

Sam kneels beside me, and the side of his thigh presses into mine. The closeness, the feel of his jeans against my bare skin, almost makes me forget what we're doing out here in the first place.

Right, a morale boost.

I glance at the boy beside me and grin. Consider my morale *very* boosted. But then Kacey settles across from us, Sam dumps his backpack on the grass, and I focus on the prank.

"Thought I'd mix it up tonight." Sam removes a lawn gnome from his backpack. This lawn gnome is definitely of the novelty variety—his pants are down, revealing his big white gnome ass. "We're going to replace one gnome with Moonie Loonie. Found him at the hardware store downtown. Perfect, right?"

"Ooh, she's going to hate this," Kacey says in delight.

Laughing, I point to Moonie Loonie. "Did you seriously run out and buy a garden gnome?"

"Anything to make you laugh," Sam says, and winks.

I might perish on this lawn outside of Mrs. Miranda's because of that wink. And you know what? I'm really okay with that. There are worse ways to go.

Kacey mutters, "Oh god," beneath her breath, but we both ignore her.

I'm smiling so wide, my cheeks are already hurting. "Which one do you think is her favorite?" I whisper, and Sam scans the lawn with the flashlight. The beam lands on a gnome that looks suspiciously like Jesus.

"Bingo." Sam flicks off the flashlight and turns to us. "Who wants to do the honors?"

"I volunteer Florie," Kacey says, and before I know what's happening, Sam's passing Moonie Loonie to me and Kacey's shoving me out from behind the hedge.

Trying—and failing—to muffle my laughter, I dash across the darkened lawn with the gnome tucked beneath my arm like a football. The wet grass dampens my socks—I didn't bother with shoes and also, no shoe prints (fun fact: shoe prints were the downfall of Richard Ramirez, the Night Stalker)—and I find Jesus Gnome beside the porch steps. I carefully arrange Moonie Loonie in Jesus Gnome's spot before scurrying back to the hedge.

I hold Jesus Gnome up like a trophy and plop onto the grass. "Ta-da!"

Kacey pumps her fist in victory, and Sam nods his approval.

"What're we doing with this guy?" I ask, breathless.

Sam takes Jesus Gnome and glances around the front yard. "Be right back." He slinks off toward the garage. Kacey and I—still giggling—watch as Sam hoists himself onto Mrs. Miranda's trash cans and situates Jesus Gnome in the rain gutter above the garage door. Then he jumps down and runs across the lawn.

We're all laughing—not bothering to keep quiet—as we sprint from Mrs. Miranda's house. Sam's leading, Kacey jogging beside me with her wild curls escaping from her bun. My damp socks smack the concrete. That feeling from the road trip is back, and I feel *good.* Amazing, even.

When we reach the Hodges' porch, we slow down, panting and laughing. Kacey hops up the porch steps, and I grab Sam's hand, tugging him backward.

"Hey, hang on a sec," I tell Sam, and weave my fingers with his.

Kacey makes a face—a funny one—and slips through the front door. Leaving us alone.

The Hodges' lovingly messy porch is lit only by the bug zapper hanging off the side awning and the streetlamps. I lower myself onto the top step and Sam settles beside me, squeezing my fingers before letting go. He tugs off his stealthy beanie and runs his hand through his hair; his foot taps against the wood.

Wait a second. Is Samson Hodge *nervous*?

I pull the length of the borrowed hoodie down around my knees to keep warm. "Hey."

"Hey," Sam says with a smile. Not for the first time, I'm wondering if it's possible for this boy to *not* look good. It's practically midnight, and he's kind of sweaty from running, dressed in a ridiculous all-black ensemble. But he's perfect.

"My mom took my phone away when she showed up in San Francisco," I explain, my palms already moist. "And my laptop. So that's why I haven't replied to your texts."

Sam glances sideways at me, and I swear he seems relieved.

"Kacey told me what happened at the live show. I'm really sorry, Flor."

I shrug both shoulders. "It's okay. You had no way of knowing she'd see the texts."

"Sure, but you two are joined at the hip." He drags his hand through his wavy curls again. "I didn't think. Kind of a common theme, huh? I swear, I'm normally not such a . . ." He trails off and shrugs, then twists the beanie between his hands.

"Not such a what?"

"Dumbass? I don't know," he says with a quiet laugh. "I meant what I said, though. In the texts."

"Which part?"

"All the parts." Sam stops fidgeting with the beanie. "None of that's changed. I like you. A lot."

Okay, hearing those words out loud is ten times better than reading them. "I like you too. Obviously."

"Yeah, you're not as obvious as you think."

My cheeks ache from all the smiling. "Maybe you're not very observant."

"So all our miscommunications are my fault?"

"Basically, yeah." I grin, and he reaches out to tuck my hair behind my ear, his palm hot against my skin.

Part of me wants to keep talking and figure everything out. But all I've done today is talk. And Sam likes me. Despite everything, Samson Hodge likes me, and this still doesn't feel real.

I lean closer and rest my forehead against Sam's. His hand slides from my cheek to the back of my neck, fingers tangling in my hair.

"If I kiss you right now," he whispers, "are you going to run away or not speak to me for eight months?"

"Nope," I whisper back. "Not going anywhere."

Sam smiles wide, and his glasses scrunch up his nose. Then he leans in a little closer until his lips brush mine. Unlike the two kisses before it, this kiss is slow, so slow, and so sweet. His fingers weave deeper through my hair as his lips part mine, and I slide my arms around his neck, trying to keep him as close as possible.

Sam and I might be terrible at other forms of communication, but we kind of have this one down.

TWENTY-FIVE

Barmouth, WA

TUESDAY, AUGUST 16, LATE AFTERNOON

Sam and I kissed on the porch for a while last night, but when the headlights of Rosemary and Alec's car flashed through the darkness as they returned from their night shift, we broke apart. I crawled into Kacey's bed and slept in until ten, which almost never happens. Maybe it was so easy to fall asleep because I was happy. Or maybe all the exhaustion of the last week has finally caught up with me.

I had breakfast with Rosemary and Alec—vegan french toast, which is actually better than it sounds—and apologized for betraying their trust. They were too kind and accepted my apology, but they also said it really wasn't necessary. Kacey had probably explained the lengths of my grounding to them while I was in the shower, and they knew I was suffering enough already.

All day, I kept my family therapy appointment in the very back of my mind, but now that it's four thirty, I can't stop sweating. It's like our fight last night broke something open between me and my mom, and I have no idea how to repair it. And worst of all, I'm not sure if I even want to repair it, to go back to normal. But I also don't know how to love my mom any other way.

Unspooling some toilet paper, I dab at my underarms before tossing the damp tissue away and checking my hair. Kacey plaited it into twin french braids. I fix a few loose strands and dab on my SPF lip balm before deeming myself acceptable. Inside, I'm an anxious mess, but at least I'm pretty put-together on the outside.

I flick off the bathroom light and knock on Kacey's doorframe. "Good to go?"

She slides her sunglasses on. "Let's do this. Is Sammy ready?"

I glance down the hallway, where Sam is already walking toward us. Kacey and Sam offered to drop me off at therapy and are going to hang around downtown until my session is over.

"Ready." He hugs me from behind, resting his chin on my head.

Sam and I didn't talk much last night. Or really at all. And we definitely didn't figure anything out, but I'm surprisingly okay with that. Right now I have to deal with my parents. One thing at a time.

The three of us head downstairs and walk into the August warmth. A sticky breeze blows, and the air smells like evergreen trees and fresh dirt. This summer is, without a doubt, the most unforgettable summer of my life, but I itch for normalcy. I don't want to go back to how things were. I want Normal 2.0. A better kind of normal.

We pile into the Jeep, and, as we drive out of the cul-de-sac, we spot Mrs. Miranda in her front yard. Standing by the garage, she's trying—and failing—to use the handle end of a broomstick to dislodge Jesus Gnome from her gutter. Moonie Loonie's pale gnome ass is sticking out of her trash bin.

Kacey cackles. "Oh my god. Priceless."

"Stop staring!" Sam says, and we all train our focus forward. After we exit the neighborhood, we break into side-splitting laughter.

Sam took the soft top off the Jeep, and we drive to downtown with warm summer air whipping our hair into tangles. As we make the short journey, I hold on to this summer feeling. Hold on to the good I felt on the road trip. Because this meeting is going to be hard. I let Mom break me down once this past week, and I'm not about to let it happen a second time.

We pull in front of Lauren's building, and Sam shifts the Jeep into park.

"Good luck." Kacey twists around in the passenger's seat. She pushes her sunglasses into her curls. "You've got this."

Sam catches my eye in the rearview. "We'll be here after, okay?"

"Thanks." I pop open the back door and hop out, my

nerves rushing to the surface. No amount of deodorant can tame my anxiety sweats. "See you two in an hour."

I wave, then take the back entrance into the building and head upstairs. Per usual, Lauren's waiting room is its strange brand of sterile and spiritual; the whale noises are oddly soothing today. I plop down on the couch, crossing my legs. My flip-flop dangles from my foot.

Not a minute passes before the door opens—and my parents walk in.

"Hey, Flor." Dad stalls in the doorway, like he's unsure what to do. "You beat us here."

I press my palms between my knees. "Kacey and Sam dropped me off."

Mom nods, so stiff, I'm amazed her neck even allowed for the range of motion, and sits on the other loveseat opposite me. When she crosses her legs, I quickly uncross mine.

Dad paces around the small waiting room, grabbing an old magazine off the coffee table and flipping it open. Then he puts it down again, walks over to me, and squeezes my shoulder. "You doing okay, kiddo?"

I shrug and say quietly, "Yeah," like I don't want Mom to overhear.

"The Hodges good? Don't mind you staying over?"

"They're good." I appreciate that Dad's trying, but the small talk is making me more nervous.

Luckily, Lauren opens her office door and puts us out of our awkward misery.

"Hi, Cordray family," she says cheerfully. "Come on in."

We file into her small office. Me on the armchair like

usual, but the cushions don't feel nearly as soft and comforting. My parents take the small couch. Four people is about two people too many for Lauren's office.

Lauren settles in her chair and flips open my file. "Well." She beams, resting her hands on the papers. "Florie caught me up yesterday, but it's great that we're all together to talk things over. Thank you both for making time in your schedules today. Florie, you want to start us off?"

I glance at my parents, my hands fidgeting and knotting in my lap. Even though I had planned on easing into things, the words burst out of me. "Last night, after our session, I found out that my mom told my guidance counselor I wanted to take a gap year. She lied."

Lauren—the consummate professional—doesn't betray a single emotion. She taps her pen to the pad of paper. "I see. Helene, do you want to take this time to talk about that decision?"

"Not particularly. I made the decision I felt was best for my daughter—"

"Then why didn't you even tell Dad?" I interrupt. "You knew what you were doing was shitty, otherwise you would've told him."

Dad rubs his brow in response, and I'd bet ten dollars he wishes he was anywhere else in the world right now.

"I don't know what they want from me," I tell Lauren. "I lied, but so did my mom. And from where I'm standing, her lie is ten times worse than mine. At least I apologized."

Mom smooths back a rare loose piece of hair hanging against her cheek. "You apologized, but I doubt you're sorry."

"Why do you say that?" asks Lauren.

"What Florie isn't telling you," Mom says, "is how she said some very hurtful things to me last night."

Lauren turns toward me. "Oh?"

"We got into a fight," I mutter, and stare straight ahead at the abstract wall art above Lauren's head. "When I found out about the guidance counselor, I confronted her. We talked about junior year and college, and the entire time she acted like she was doing me some favor. I told her . . . I told her that she's been the biggest barrier in my life, not my OCD. She's enabled me, right? Isn't that what you said?"

Mom makes a noise, like she's mad that I've spoken to my therapist about her behind her back. "Florie blamed me for everything that she's unhappy with in her life. She told me my best wasn't good enough and called me a bad mom."

"I'm sensing a lot of hurt," Lauren says calmly. As if we're not all inches away from a trip wire of emotion. "Florie, do you blame your mom?"

"Kind of," I admit, and drop my gaze to my hands. "She's trying to help, but sometimes too much help is . . . hurtful."

"That's absurd." In my peripheral vision, I watch as Mom crosses her arms tight over her chest. "All I've tried to do is take care of her! When she was younger, it wasn't like this—we didn't clash—and she needed me. Now, everything is so *hard* with her. It's exhausting, if I'm being honest."

"If I'm that much of a burden, you should let me go to college. Then I won't be your problem anymore."

"We would love for you to go to college—" Mom begins to say, but I cut her off.

"Really? Then why lie? You could've gotten rid of me this year, but you chose to go behind my back."

"I don't want to get rid of you, Florie," my mom says. "Last year, I didn't see the harm in you taking some time before leaving home. I thought you'd like that option."

"Mom, it's not an option when you make the decision for me. Even if it's the one you think is best for me."

Mom massages her temples like this conversation is giving her a migraine. The room falls silent until my dad clears his throat and leans forward, elbows on his knees.

"Everything that happened last year aside," Dad says to Lauren. "Do you think Florie's ready to apply to college?"

"I do," Lauren says. "Honestly, she was probably ready last year. But I can say with complete confidence that she's ready to take that step."

Mom sinks farther in the loveseat, her arms still crossed tight. "I don't know."

"And that's okay," Lauren adds. "I just want to open the doors on the conversation. Trust has been abused, and there have been many . . . miscommunications. But that's why I'm here. To assure you she's ready. Holding her back now would only come as a detriment to Florie's emotional growth."

I watch my parents' faces as Lauren talks. Dad's brows are pinched, like he's thinking hard, considering Lauren's words. Mom's still staring at the carpet with her arms crossed—unreadable, as always.

"Last week, I did a lot of things I never thought I could do," I say, knowing that I'll never say this if I don't say it now. "Maybe that isn't impressive or important to you. But

I pushed myself and tried new things. For the first time in a long time—maybe ever—I felt *capable.* I know you're trying to protect me, Mom, but when you're afraid, or doubt my abilities, then I doubt myself too. So yeah, I shouldn't have lied . . . but if I hadn't, would you be proud?"

"But you did lie," Mom says, "and that makes it hard for me to be proud of you."

"Just . . . humor me." I stare at my mom until she lifts her gaze from the carpet.

"What you did on that trip," she says, slowly and unsurely, "might look like growth to you. But to me, it's you acting irresponsibly."

I turn to Lauren. "What am I supposed to say to that?"

"Helene, Mark." She addresses my parents. "Do you have any questions for me? I don't support Florie lying, but I want to stress that she's made leaps and bounds with her mental health. What she's saying might be difficult, but listen. She wants to take the excellent foundation you've helped her build and *grow.* Any parent would be thrilled with that. Florie's worked extremely hard to get to where she is today, and we should all celebrate her progress."

Dad rubs Mom's back in soothing circles, and the gesture makes my chest ache. I know that's his wife, but I want Dad on my side. I *need* him there, especially if Mom will never be. "College could be good for Florie. Right, Helene?"

Okay, maybe Dad's on my side after all, but I don't dare smile. I cautiously look over at Mom.

"Lauren isn't Florie's mother," she says, and I sigh. "But I am. I get a say in her life, don't I?"

"All you've ever had is a say in my life!" Lauren shoots me a warning glance that I ignore. "*You* made the decision to pull me out of school. *You* decided college was off the table and lied about it. *You* decide *everything*!" Angry tears spring to my eyes.

"I'm trying to help."

I wipe at my tears before my mom comments on them. "I don't want your help anymore."

"Florie," Dad says, shaking his head.

Mom's mouth pinches up tight. "I see." She picks up her purse from the floor. "Well, if that's the case, I don't think I have anything else to say. I'll be in the car."

When the door shuts behind her, my dad says, "I'm sorry." He drags both hands over his face and sighs. "Last year, I was so busy with work and never really paid attention to the college stuff, and I should've. But your mom's heart is in the right place. We both love you so much."

"I know," I say through a cracked voice.

Dad stands up and motions me closer. "I had no idea things were so tense between you two," he says, and hugs me when I reach him.

"They weren't," I admit. "Not until recently." Because it took that trip for me to realize that the walls Mom lovingly built around me were no longer keeping the bad out. They were only keeping me in.

"I'll talk to your mom," he says, "and we'll figure all this out, okay?"

I nod into his shoulder. "I'm going to stay at the Hodges' another night."

Dad kisses my forehead before stepping back. "Sounds good." He gives me an unsure smile that I return. "Okay, I need to go find your mom. . . . We'll touch base tomorrow, okay? I'm going to take the week off work."

"Yeah, okay."

Dad thanks Lauren and apologizes again before ducking out of the small office.

I sigh heavily, my arms falling limply to my sides. "So, that went well."

TWENTY-SIX

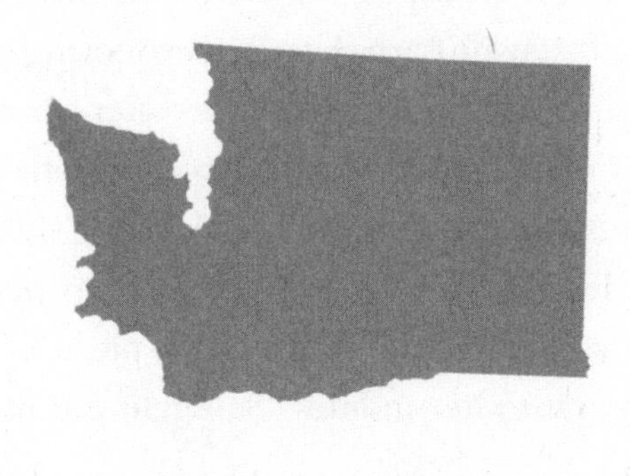

Barmouth, WA

TUESDAY, LATER THAT NIGHT

I'm spread out on the floor of the Hodges' game room with Kacey and an extra-large pizza. After recapping the disaster of my family therapy session, we all went back to their house, ordered the biggest pizza we could afford, and put on *I'll Be Gone in the Dark,* the amazing true crime documentary based on a book about the Golden State Killer, written by the armchair detective and author Michelle McNamara, who helped bring him to justice.

"I could get used to this," Kacey says from her spot up on the couch. "You living here."

"Me too, but you're leaving next week." I'm surprised that my chest doesn't fully cave in with sadness at those words.

Maybe because I don't feel trapped in Barmouth anymore. It's like the lock on my future has been unlatched. The ache is still there, sure, but Kacey wouldn't be Kacey if she decided to stay in Barmouth. Kacey moving to Portland is one reason why I love her—she goes after what she wants, even if she's afraid, and never doubts that she'll succeed. This is the next step for her, and just because she'll be living in Portland doesn't mean she'll stop being my person.

"I'll take you with me." She pops a piece of pineapple from the pizza into her mouth. "Smuggle you in one of my suitcases."

I snort. "What am I? A pet cat or something?"

"You'll keep Portland in mind when you make your enviable college plans?"

"Of course." Even if my parents haven't agreed to anything, I'm doing this. With or without them.

The only problem? I don't know what I'm doing with my life. What to study or major in, or even what kind of job I want. Since I wasn't on campus for senior year, I missed all the hype. The prep and college fairs. But all my options don't feel as overwhelming as I thought they would. They feel . . . hopeful.

Later, when we go to sleep, I crawl into Kacey's bed and burrow beneath the covers, oddly at peace despite how today was a total and complete disaster.

"Good night," Kacey says in a singsong voice, tucking in beside me. She has a queen-sized bed, and even sharing with her is roomier than alone in my twin back at home. As she gets comfy, she accidentally kicks me in the shins, and I smile.

"Night," I whisper, pressing my eyes shut.

Not soon after, Kacey's fast asleep beside me.

I toss and turn for an hour before scooting quietly off the bed and padding to the bathroom. Well, I *mean* to make it to the bathroom, which is across the hall from Sam's room. But I stop, staring at his closed door.

Bad idea, I think, but I knock quietly.

"Yeah?" Sam calls, and I inch the door open. He's awake in bed, his laptop on the comforter. "Hey there."

I lean against the doorframe. "I can't sleep."

"Maybe lay off the murder podcasts." He shuts his laptop, setting it aside.

"You're hilarious."

Sam motions me inside, and I shut the bedroom door behind me.

After a brief hesitation, I sit on the edge of the bed. I'm not sure if I've ever been in Sam's room before, and even though he invited me in, I feel like I shouldn't be here. Like I'm still way, way too uncool to be hanging out with Samson Hodge.

Sam puts his laptop on his bedside table and sits with his back to the wall. "So. Do you ever sleep?" He grabs his glasses and slides them up the bridge of his nose.

I shift on the bed to face him. "I'll have you know I slept in until ten this morning."

"Ooh, impressive," he teases, and the way he's looking at me makes it impossible to forget that I'm wearing a tank top and pajama shorts, sitting on his bed.

Heat warms my cheeks, and I glance away. The only light

comes from the lamp on his bedside table, and I study the bookshelves crammed with unreturned library books and old school texts. The duffel dumped unceremoniously in the center of the room, clothes spilling out and onto the hardwood. Today's heat gave way to light rain smattering the big window overlooking the Hodges' backyard.

The Cheeky Monkey bag—more wrinkled and worse for wear than it was days ago—sits beside his car keys and sunglasses on his desk.

"What'd you end up buying?" I'm suddenly super nervous. Because, you know, I'm on Sam's bed in my pajamas.

Sam's brows draw together as he follows my line of sight. Then he laughs. "Shit, I totally forgot." He reaches across his bed and snags the bag off his desk. Settling back against his pillows, he holds it out. "Here."

I take the bag. "You bought me something?"

"What? Don't look so surprised." Sam grins. "Consider it a late birthday-slash-graduation-slash-I-felt-awful-for-accidentally-lying-to-you gift."

I peer into the bag, not sure what to expect, considering the random assortment of crap we saw inside Cheeky Monkey; the options are endless. But in the bottom of the bag is a book. The black paperback is clearly old, but in good condition. *Green River, Running Red: The Real Story of the Green River Killer* by Ann Rule.

"Have you heard about this guy?" Sam asks, scooting over to sit beside me.

"Gary Ridgway?" I laugh. Not *at* Sam exactly, but he is

pretty cute with his lack of true crime knowledge. "Yeah, but I haven't read this one yet."

Sam rests his weight onto one hand and leans across me to open the cover. "What's up with the Pacific Northwest and serial killers, anyway?"

I flip through the book with my thumb, pages and pages of words flashing by. Sam bought me an Ann Rule book. *Sam.* Samson Hodge bought me a book on the Green River Killer, and my brain doesn't know how to handle this information.

"Do you like it?" he asks, and a rare slice of uncertainty crosses his face.

I drop the book onto the comforter, and when I kiss Sam, he makes this surprised noise in the back of his throat, pulling me closer. I adjust until I'm in his lap, without even really thinking about it or making a conscious decision. My body just moves against his, and when Sam shifts onto his back, I shift with him. His hands slide along my hips, fingers brushing my bare skin where my tank top rides up. The longer we kiss, the quieter my brain becomes.

The only thought to cross my mind is how much I like this, how I don't want it to stop.

Sam pushes me onto my back, his body covering mine, and his hand glides down my stomach, presses against my hip bones. Before his fingers slip beneath the waistband of my pajama shorts, he asks, "This okay?"

"Yes," I say, shifting until he can reach me easier.

My muscles tense up with nerves, and the second he starts touching me, I don't relax, but the nerves disappear. Sam and I keep kissing, and my own hand strays beneath the fabric of his pajama pants. His breath quickens against my ear, and it's empowering. Like he's as weak to my touch as I am to his.

I silently thank Rosemary for being the one who talked to me about birth control and drove me to Planned Parenthood last summer, even if it was slightly weird getting sex advice from the mom of the guy I wanted to sleep with. Given my mom isn't exactly sex positive, I was so grateful to her. Especially right now, because the only thing on my mind is how much I want Sam.

I don't believe in virginity, but I've never done this before. Not like it was some conscious decision *not* to have sex up until this point. It just never happened. But now, here's Sam—kissing me in his bed, *touching* me in his bed, our legs tangling together, and the only thought on my mind is *why not?* Sam's leaving soon, and I want this. I want him.

"Hey." I pull away and look at Sam, who's propped over me on his elbow. "Do you have a condom?"

He stops touching me and shifts back, studying me in the faint glow from his bedside lamp. "Is that what you want?"

"Yeah." I nod, trying to appear calm when I feel anything but. Now that the kissing and touching has stopped, my brain is kicking back into gear. I sit upright with my back to the wall. "But, um, only if you want to."

Sam smooths back my hair, cradling my cheek with one palm. "This isn't how I expected my night to turn out, but I'm really, really okay with it," he says. "I should have some condoms in my dresser."

I take a deep breath, hoping what I'm about to say doesn't ruin this moment. "Just so you know, um, I've never had sex before."

His expression doesn't change. "Okay. We'll take it slow. If you want to stop, say so. You can change your mind beforehand. Or during, whenever. I don't want you to do something you don't want, or you're not ready for."

"Okay," I say, embarrassed by how my voice shakes. "I want to, and I'm ready as I'll ever be. But I'm kind of nervous." I wish I were confident right now—in control and *sexy.* But I've never been this nervous in my life. Which is really saying something.

I'm about to have sex. With Sam.

"Good, because so am I," Sam admits, and kisses me hard before sliding off the bed.

I lie back down and stare up at his ceiling, trying to breathe, as I hear the click of his bedroom lock. But knowing I'm not the only nervous one calms me. I purposefully don't think about how much more experienced Sam is than me—Kacey's been making man-whore jokes about her brother for as long as I've known her. But it doesn't matter.

Maybe this is my first time, but this is also Sam's first time with *me.* And that has to count for something.

Sam pulls out the drawers of his dresser, tossing clothes into the air as he searches, finally unearthing a crumpled box of Trojans. He sets the small foil-wrapped condom onto the bedside table; then he climbs onto the bed and folds the comforter back. I slide beneath the sheets—*Sam's* sheets—which are flannel and soft against my skin.

I reach for the hem of his shirt and help him pull it off. Then Sam does the same for me, cautiously removing my tank top. I've never been naked in front of a guy before—or anyone, really—and I've never felt so vulnerable. Not just physically, but emotionally, too.

Sam's hands rest on my hips for a moment, then he slides my pajama shorts down my legs. He stares, and all I can think about is my flat chest and narrow hips. But then he shakes his head and says, "You're so beautiful." I don't have time to respond, because he kicks off his pajama pants, and I'm lying beside a fully naked Sam.

And here I thought the well-fitting jeans and tight T-shirts were distracting.

He leans over and grabs the condom, ripping open the wrapper.

"Say the word and we stop," he says, rolling on the condom. "Or if something doesn't feel good, let me know. I want you to feel good, okay? That's all I want."

Anticipatory anxiety hits me in the chest, but I'm more excited for this moment than anything else. I'm nervous, but that's natural. "Yeah, okay. C'mere." I draw his mouth on mine. We kiss until I'm pretty sure I can't take it anymore, and I'm tugging him closer and closer. Until our skin touches and our breath catches. I expect pain, but there's only a quick pang of pressure.

I try not to think—just experience—but all I keep thinking is, *I'm having sex with Sam! Samson Hodge! Holy shit, holy shit, holy shit.*

We're awkward at first, repositioning until we figure out

what feels good. Which we eventually do, and it feels kind of amazing. Sam pauses frequently to kiss and ask me if I'm okay. Surprisingly, I am okay. *Very* okay. The sex isn't perfect, but when it's over, I can't wait until we try again. I like how our bodies fit together.

Sam throws the condom away and cleans up, neither of us saying much. Not in a bad way—more like, what else could we possibly say to each other? We had sex for the first time, and it's scary and new and amazing and overwhelming. I slide my shorts and top back on, and Sam pulls on his pajama pants. Then he climbs back into bed and wraps himself around me, my back held against his chest.

"Are you okay?" he whispers against my ear.

"Very okay," I press my face against the warm skin of his forearm. "Surprisingly okay."

"Surprisingly? Why are you surprised?"

"What?" I laugh, my cheeks burning. "I didn't know what to expect! I'm *pleasantly* surprised, okay?"

Sam nuzzles his face against my shoulder, tightening his hold on me. The rain splatters against the window, and I shut my eyes, breathing him in. No anxiety, no doubt, no regret. Just . . . calm. Just me and Sam, together. Finally.

After a moment, he says, "That really happened, huh?"

Now it's my turn to ask, "Why are *you* so surprised?"

Sam laughs, and the noise rumbles against my body. "Seriously? I kiss you, you don't speak to me for eight months. I come back to town, and you ignore me. You kiss me—plot twist—but then you literally run away from me."

"I didn't think you liked me," I point out, and shift in his arms until I face him. "And I had a lot of supporting evidence."

"Oh, c'mon." He presses his forehead to mine. "What evidence?"

"Amanda, which I know it was a misunderstanding, but *still.* And then the beach—"

"What about the beach?"

"You asked if we were good, and you were so relieved when I said yes!"

"What? I wasn't relieved," he says. "I was bummed out, but I wasn't going to tell you that. Not after I offered to take you and Kacey on this trip. That'd be messed up."

"Oh." It all makes so much sense that I want to pull Sam's comforter over my face in shame. "We really are bad at communicating, huh?"

Sam's mouth catches on mine for one sweet, short kiss. "We're the worst." His eyes search mine; then he says, "But I'm okay being the worst if I can be with you."

"You want to be with me?"

"What'd you think we're doing right now?" he teases, tugging playfully on one of my braids. "Hey, can I ask you something?"

I squint at him but nod. "Yeah."

"When Kacey explained what happened outside the Masonic, she made some comment about how you hid liking me from her for your entire friendship. Was she being dramatic or . . . ?" He grins, words trailing off as he waits for me to fill in the blanks. The embarrassing blanks.

"I've liked you for a while, okay? We don't have to get into it."

"What's a while? Because you and Kacey have been friends for, what, two years?"

Here I thought my crush was the most painfully obvious thing in the world. I spent two years secretly pining for Samson Hodge, and it turns out I did an excellent job. Maybe *too* good of a job. How did Sam not know?

"Um." I shift my gaze around his room, debating if I should lie or not. But I mumble the truth: "Yeah. Pretty much since the day I met you. Happy?"

The smile that breaks across Sam's face almost eases my embarrassment. "Extremely. Two years, huh? Wow. You're, like, really into me, aren't you?"

I worm out of his arms and pull the comforter over my face. Nope, this is still embarrassing. "Shut up."

Sam's laughing now and tugs the comforter back. "Admit it," he says. "You really like me. I'm all you *ever* think about."

"No, you're the worst," I fire back, but now I'm laughing too. "And your ego is big enough. I'm not feeding it with compliments."

Sam's fingers trail my ticklish ribs, and I yelp, shoving him back. But he pulls me closer and rests his forehead to mine again. My chest rises and falls, breathless from laughing. We lie there, all tangled up together beneath the flannel sheets, the only noise in the room our breathing and the rain on the windowpane.

"For what it's worth, I really like you," he says in this teasing tone that somehow both stops and restarts my heart all at once. "You're all I ever think about."

Oh yeah, I'm so far gone.

"Is it my turn to ask you something?"

"Look at us," Sam says cheerfully, "communicating."

I roll my eyes and adjust so I'm lying on my side, head propped up with my fist. "Why'd you kiss me during winter break? Was it because . . . I was there?"

Sam mirrors my position and tucks the comforter up around us. "I kissed you because I liked you. Because I've always noticed you—even if I didn't want to because of Kacey—and that night, you were flirting with me."

My brain's stuck on that phrase—*I've always noticed you*—but all I can say is, "I wasn't flirting with you."

"You were, one hundred percent, flirting with me at that holiday party."

It amazes me how differently Sam views our situation. Just how wrong I had, well, everything. Before we can continue arguing about the night that changed everything between us, the garage rumbles open beneath us.

I sit up, smoothing my flyaway hairs back. "I should probably go back to Kacey's room."

Sam tugs me back down onto the mattress, and his kisses are soft, sleepy, intoxicating. "You sure you don't want to stay? I like you here."

"I like being here," I say, and inch away from him, "but I'd also like it if your parents didn't see me sneaking out of your bedroom." While they probably wouldn't care, I'm too mortified of that ever happening to consider staying.

"I'll sneak you out early, before breakfast," he offers.

I force myself off his bed and grab my book from the floor

where it fell. I hold it to my chest and say, “Tempting, but I’ll see you in the morning, okay?”

Sam tucks his arm behind his head. “Sweet dreams, Florence Nightingale.”

I sneak out of his bedroom and quickly use the bathroom before slipping back into Kacey’s room.

“Did you hook up with my brother?” Kacey asks sleepily, and scares the *ever-loving shit* out of me.

I jump, my heart rate pounding. “Yes?”

“Hmmh.” She sits up to fluff her pillow. “Was he, like, decent with you?”

I snort, trying to quiet my laugh, and climb into bed beside her. “*Extremely* decent.”

“Ew. Pretend I didn’t ask,” Kacey mutters, and lies back down.

I roll onto my side, escaping into an effortless sleep with a smile still on my lips.

TWENTY-SEVEN

Barmouth, WA

WEDNESDAY, AUGUST 17, MORNING

I'm awake for less than ten seconds before I remember last night. The rain on the windowpane and Sam's super-soft flannel sheets and the warmth of his skin against mine. Any early-morning sleepiness vanishes in an instant because holy shit, *I had sex last night.*

I swing my legs off the bed and get up, pulling on the black hoodie Sam lent me the other night. I don't expect to feel different or anything, but it's still weird. I smooth back any flyaways escaping from my braids, mind reeling.

Sam. I had *sex* with *Sam.*

I lean against the wall, resisting my urge to do a happy dance.

That. Happened.

"Hey." Kacey yawns, pushing herself upright. She has a serious case of bedhead, curls everywhere. "What time is it?"

"Nine," I tell her as I pull on a pair of socks over my bare feet. "Wanna get breakfast?"

Nodding, she scoots off the bed. "Did I dream you sneaking back into my room last night?"

"Nope."

Kacey twists her lips to one side as she scoops her hair into a ponytail. "Spare me the details, *but* what exactly happened?"

I glance to the closed door, then back at my best friend, and lower my voice: "We had sex."

"And here I thought I was the slut in our friendship," she teases.

"Oh shut up. I've liked your brother for two years. All things considered, I moved incredibly slow."

Kacey laughs. "I'm just giving you a hard time."

"Your brother gave me a hard time last night." I dissolve into a fit of laughter as Kacey shrieks and tosses her pillow at my head.

Once our laughter dies down, Kacey says, "I seriously can't believe you slept with my brother."

"Well, what did you expect would happen?"

Kacey shrugs, stretching both arms over her head. "I didn't want to think about it. Still don't."

I've been awake for five minutes, the fog of sleep has lifted, but even I'm struggling to believe it. Not the sex part—which I refrain from telling Kacey was actually good, which I didn't think was a thing for first times—but everything after. How comfortable I felt, despite being so incredibly vulnerable with Sam. The conversation that followed, the way he kept pulling me closer like any distance was too much . . . Usually I overthink and overanalyze and doubt. But I'm pleasantly surprised to find I don't want to do that. That I don't *need* to do that.

"So." Kacey tugs on a sweatshirt. "Are you guys like an official thing now?"

"We didn't really put a label on it, but yeah, I think so."

"Good. I want you to be happy—you of all people deserve some good. And if you find that in my brother . . ." She trails off and wrinkles her nose. "But we already have enough change with me leaving next week, and I want to make sure this doesn't change us too much, you know?"

"What can I do to help?"

"Don't ever bring up anything related to what you two do behind closed doors, please and thank you," she says, then bites her lip in thought. "You can still talk to me about stuff, obviously, but I'm staying out of any drama. I'm not risking my relationship with either of you by getting myself involved."

I wrap my arms around her neck and hug her tight. "Fair enough."

Kacey returns my hug, even tighter. "Let's head downstairs. I could use, like, ten cups of coffee."

I'm surprised to find Sam in the kitchen making pancakes. My heart does a little spasm at the sight of him. He's in the same pajama pants as last night and a T-shirt. I take a moment to appreciate how his muscles strain against the fabric, and, as if he can sense me checking him out, he turns around.

When Sam sees me, his entire face lights up—which makes my entire face light up.

"Hey," I say as I find a clean mug from the rack to fill with coffee.

"Morning." Sam wedges the spatula beneath a pancake and flips it. "Pancakes?"

"Yes please." I lean against the counter with my mug warming my fingers as Kacey sits at the kitchen table.

"I can't remember the last time you made breakfast," Kacey muses, head propped up on her fist. Then she says to me, "Flor, you should sleep with my brother every night if it means blueberry pancakes."

The pancake Sam was in the process of flipping lands on the counter as he turns around. "How?" he asks with a laugh. "How does she already know?"

"To be fair," Kacey interjects, "I kind of guessed. Florie stumbled back into my room at two last night."

"Sorry." I shrug, and sip my coffee.

Sam shakes his head, then gives me this look. Like he's asking—without words—if I'm actually sorry, if I have any regrets about last night. I smile into my coffee cup, because I'm not sorry, and I don't regret a single moment. *Huh.* Maybe having someone else read my thoughts isn't the worst thing in the world. Because he grins in response before turning back to the stove.

Sam uses the spatula to flip the rogue pancake in the trash, then he divvies up the rest onto three plates. I sit across from Kacey, and Sam slides into the seat beside me. Beneath the table, Sam holds my hand.

I don't even get my first bite of pancake in before the doorbell rings.

"Shit." Kacey winces. "I thought everyone knew not to use the doorbell! We put a sign out and everything."

My stomach aches. Because there's definitely one person who never comes over to the Hodges' house. And who would totally disregard a handwritten sign asking people *not* to use their doorbell. "I think it's my mom."

I get up and walk down the hall, then peer through the peephole when I reach the entry.

Sure enough, my mom stands opposite the door. Even at nine thirty in the morning, she's impeccably dressed and painfully out of place on the Hodges' cluttered porch. Before she can ring the doorbell again and wake up Kacey's parents, I unlatch the door and open it.

"Florie, hello," Mom says.

I slip outside, shutting the door behind me. "What're you doing here?"

"Can we go have breakfast and talk?" she asks, the words rushing out of her like she's unsure, worried she might change her mind and take them back.

I shift my weight on my heels, playing over my options inside my head. I really want to turn around, close the door in her face, and go eat my pancakes with my best friend and my . . . Sam. But my mom and I need to talk if I'm ever going to come home. Whether I like it or not, I can't live at the Hodges' forever.

"Let me go change," I say, guilted by the surprise on my mom's face. It's time we hashed it all out. I'm not ready, not even close, but this is the closest I'll ever be.

The W Diner, circa 1974, is my family's usual haunt in the off season. The diner is kitschy and lake adjacent, making it the perfect lure for seasonal tourists, so we usually avoid it during the summer and winter months. But my mom still pulls into its packed parking lot. As if the promise of omelets, french toast, and house potatoes might make this awkward mother-daughter conversation more bearable.

As we're led to a small table by the windows facing the lake across the street, I'm struck with the desire to turn and run in the opposite direction. Because Mom and I don't do this. We don't have *talks.* Mom talks at me. Rarely are our conversations two-sided. We can't even do it in therapy, with Lauren as our neutral third party. What makes Mom think we can do it here, at the W Diner?

I settle into the wooden chair. All the furniture looks like it belongs in twenty different kitchens, all mismatched. Our table is a two-seater pushed up against the window, and someone recently wiped down the top. It's slightly damp with a mixture of disinfectant and wood polish.

Mom opens her menu, but she'll order an egg-white Mexican omelet, a glass of orange juice, and a coffee. It's the exact same thing she orders every time we're here. I always order the french toast, but I open my menu and stare at it. Not really reading. Just worrying.

"So." Mom smiles tersely after we've each placed our orders. "How're the Hodges?"

Ugh. We're doing small talk. I sip my coffee and say, "They're . . . good."

"It's very kind of them, letting you stay." Mom pours a splash of creamer into her coffee and stirs in some sugar. "I'll have to write them a thank-you card."

I fight the urge to roll my eyes. The Hodges aren't thank-you-card people. They're huggers and talkers and gift givers. They pull you in close and make you one of their own, rarely bothering with the niceties and social norms my mom rigidly lives by.

"You were right," Mom says after a moment. "I lied about the guidance counselor. I told him all about what I felt comfortable with, but I didn't stop to consider your comfort. You seemed so . . . stressed by it all, and I didn't consider if that was normal, or even good stress."

In eighteen years, I can't remember my mom *ever* admitting that she might've been wrong. "You're not a terrible mom," I say, somewhat ashamed of myself. "I shouldn't have said that."

"Thank you." Mom palms her mug, staring down at the steaming liquid. "But there was some truth in what you said. I have made taking care of you my full-time job—which made sense. I'm a stay-at-home mom. When you started having . . . *problems*, I wanted to help. I thought I could. I never liked seeing you suffer, and you suffered so much. But helping you gave me some purpose."

I grab a sugar packet from the lazy-Susan condiment holder so I have something to do with my hands. Something to focus on other than my mom being emotionally vulnerable in front of me for the first time, well, *ever.* I feel like I should say something, but I don't know what.

"I hope you know how much I've loved being your mom," she continues, and when her gaze flits to mine, I ache at her glassy eyes. "You've been my purpose for so long, and I never realized how badly I've needed that purpose until I felt like I was losing it. Losing you."

"You're not losing me." I roll the edge of the sugar packet between my thumb and index finger. "But you also can't make me feel broken so you feel whole."

"I never meant to make you feel broken, honey."

"I know, but you don't get to tell me who I am anymore. *I* need to figure that out on my own."

"It's funny," she says. "I don't know who I am if I'm not taking care of you. I haven't been in the workforce in . . . well, in eighteen years. I was supposed to go back to work once you were in school. I never intended to stay home full-time, you know."

I meet her gaze. I've never heard my mom talk about this. About her life before she was a mom. All I know is she used to work for a successful PR firm. "Really?"

Mom's lips twitch, and she shifts her attention out the window. The two-lane road separating the diner's parking lot from the lake is busy with traffic, early lake-goers jaywalking down to the docks.

"At first, I stayed home because your dad and I thought it was best. We were new parents—*nervous* new parents—and we didn't want to leave you alone with a babysitter. But as you got older, I considered it. Another income would've been nice, especially after your dad joined the start-up. But the longer I stayed away, the harder it became to consider going back. When you began struggling, I thought I'd made the right choice by never going back to work." Mom turns back toward me, her fingers fretting around the mug of her coffee. "You needed me. How could I go back when you needed me?"

My mom has never made sense to me. She has too many layers and walls around her. But this helps me understand her more than I ever have before. Maybe it was selfish, but I never, ever considered that my mom didn't want to be a stay-at-home mom. That raising me hadn't been her plan—mostly because my mom loves plans. Everything she does is so *intentional.* Except this. She never got the chance to be more than a mom for almost two decades.

"Just because—" I hesitate, struggling to find the right words to express the confusing swirl of emotions inside me. "Mom, I might need you *less,* but that doesn't mean I don't need you."

"Thank you. And I know, logically, that that's true. But it's hard. Not being *your* mom, but being a mom in general. I've been . . . afraid for you, for so long. I thought I was big enough, strong enough, to keep you safe."

"What are you afraid of?"

Mom shrugs one shoulder. "Everything. You leaving and

never coming back. Car crashes and murderers and rapists. Losing you—either by driving you away or someone else taking you from me. I thought . . . I thought that if I kept you close, kept you safe, we could avoid any pain. Pain from the outside world, pain from your disorder. But that wasn't right, was it?"

"Probably not." I avert my gaze and look out the window, my stomach twisting itself up. "Lauren always says growth doesn't come from a place of comfort."

"That's why you want to go to college," she says, but it's not a question, "to keep growing."

I shift my attention back to her. "I can't stay here, Mom. Even if I want to sometimes. It's safer—it's less stressful, easier—but it won't be good for me."

Something shifts in my mom's expression. A softening. "I understand." She smooths back her hair even though a strand isn't loose from its bun. "I want to apologize again, for what I said in San Francisco. You're a lot stronger than I've given you credit for."

My mom has never called me strong. "Even if I cry a lot?" I say, only half kidding.

"Especially because you cry a lot." Her lips tug with a small smile. "I was raised to view crying as a weakness. It's . . . *messy.* And we've never been a messy family. I used to take a lot of pride in that."

"Crying isn't messy. It's healthy."

"I know," she says. "The fact it makes me uncomfortable is my problem, not yours. We could all use a little messy sometimes."

This is probably the first real conversation I've had with

my mom—ever. There's no yelling or panic or walls keeping each other out.

After a moment, I say, "I know I have OCD and things are harder for me than most people. But I also know that I've done a lot the past year to do better. My mental illness will always be there, but that's for me to manage. And I'm starting to feel like I can manage it on my own. That's kind of the whole point, isn't it?"

"Yes, yes, it is." Mom sips her coffee. "And I'm proud of you."

I bite my lip and stare at the table, eyes hot. "Thanks, Mom."

Our food arrives shortly after, and I inhale the sweet aroma of the french toast. Mom takes a bite of her omelet. We smile across the table at each other as we eat, and I'm hit with a heavy load of relief. But I can't help feeling the tiniest bit sad, too. I always knew I was a focal point for my mom, but I never really thought how I'm the only thing in her life. She doesn't have a career or friends. She barely has hobbies.

Mom poured herself into me, and it's no wonder she's struggling to let go. But my mom—and my dad—are only human. They're flawed and trying their best. The fact that I'm here and thriving and wanting to push my boundaries means they actually did an okay job.

After we've had our breakfast, she surprises me by saying, "I listened to that podcast. The murder one."

My brows shoot up. "Really?" Then: *"Why?"*

"Because you care about it." She shrugs, placing her paper napkin on her cleared plate. "I was curious."

"And?" I prompt, genuinely interested in her reaction.

"I don't get it?" Mom says. "Those girls are awfully loud. And why do they have to swear so much?"

I laugh. Hey, at least she tried. "Give it another try. It's part of their charm."

As people, as humans, we constantly make mistakes. But we're allowed to grow, to change. There's beauty in that. At the very least, I owe my mom the chance to truly change, if that's what she wants. Just as long as she supports my growth too.

I'll never be the little five-year-old girl who clung to her leg like a safety blanket ever again.

But I hope she'll love the current me all the same.

TWENTY-EIGHT

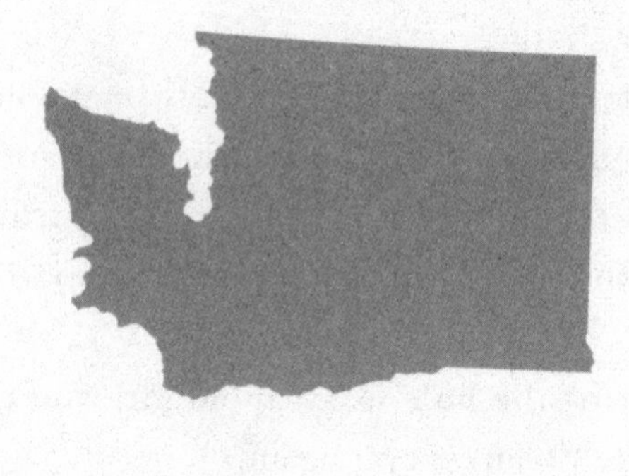

Barmouth, WA

WEDNESDAY, LATE MORNING

During the car ride back to the Hodges', Mom and I iron out the smaller details.

When I come home, I'll get my laptop and phone back—and my mom promised to never invade my privacy and go through my belongings again, so I consider that a major win. I'll still have a curfew, but, rather than 10:00 p.m., it's midnight on weekdays and 2:00 a.m. on weekends. And if I want to stay somewhere overnight, all I have to do is let them know beforehand. I'll get a part-time job, and we're going to have family therapy meetings every two months with Lauren.

"Thanks again." I turn in my seat to face Mom, my hand

lingering on the door handle. "For breakfast and everything. It was . . . really nice."

Mom leans across the car and wraps her arms around me tight. "Of course. If you need an extra day—and the Hodges don't mind—I understand. But your father and I will be happy to have you home."

I hold on to her for one long moment before slipping out of the car and walking up the path to the Hodges' house. I let myself in, but the kitchen is empty, so I head upstairs.

"Hey!" Kacey waves from the couch in the game room. "How'd it go?"

I plop onto the couch and fill her in. "My expectations were pretty low but, honestly? I feel like we made some serious progress."

"You're going back tonight then?" She crosses her legs into what looks like an uncomfortable yoga position.

"Yeah, probably. No offense, but you snore, and I kind of miss my bed."

"You'll sleep over again before I leave, though, right?" Kacey picks at her toenail polish, peering up at me.

"For sure. But I think it'll mean a lot to my mom if I stay at home for a few nights."

She bobs her head. "Okay, cool. Because I'm going to miss you like hell, and I don't want my memories of our last sleepover to include you having sex with my brother."

Heat flushes my chest and neck. It's not like I forgot about last night, but I was so focused on my mom at breakfast that it hasn't been at the forefront of my mind. "Where is Sam, anyways?" I glance down the hallway.

"Nope! You're hanging out with me right now, not Sam." Kacey gestures up and down at me. "I called dibs."

"I'm a person. You can't call dibs on a person."

"Agree to disagree. Besides, he's not even here. He went to the grocery store for our mom."

"I wasn't going to ditch you for him." It's the truth, but I don't admit that I'm the tiniest bit disappointed he's not around.

"Good," Kacey says with a self-satisfied smirk. "Because it's Wednesday."

I've kind of lost my concept of time since returning from San Francisco. And I totally forgot that today was Wednesday, aka new *Murder Me Later* episode day. "Cue it up! I can hang around for a bit before heading home."

Kacey opens the podcast app on her phone and loads the new episode. Turning up the volume, she positions the phone on the cushion between us, and we listen. It's kind of weird, listening after seeing them live, but weird in a good way. Like I can envision Eleanor and Trish even clearer inside my head. A few minutes in, they start talking about the San Francisco show.

"Y'all," Trish says, drawing the word out, "you rock. The San Francisco show was *amazing*."

"Seriously," Eleanor adds. "What a great crowd; you all are so fucking awesome! And we heard some great true crime stories during our meet and greet. We love meeting our li'l murder babes in person. It's the best."

While I'm still bummed that I missed the meet and greet, it doesn't sting that much. Meeting Eleanor and Trish would've been awesome. But missing out isn't the end of the world. And I'm so glad Kacey went, even if I couldn't.

"Do you want to share or should I?" Trish asks.

"Go ahead!"

"So." Trish clears her throat theatrically. "During our meet and greets, this teenaged girl—this young woman—came up to us—"

"She was precious," Eleanor adds.

"Very, very precious. Anyway. She went on to tell us how she and her brother helped their friend—who won VIP tickets from *Cold Cases, Cold Bitches*—drive over eight hundred miles to come to our show! Eight hundred miles."

I glance at Kacey with my brows raised. "Holy shit, are they talking about you?"

Kacey shakes her head. "Nope. They're talking about *us*."

"But in order to come to our live show, her friend lied to her parents; her mom found out and took her home before the meet and greet! So much drama. I really don't miss being a teenager. Anyway! She told us all about her friend and what our podcast meant to them. It was touching, y'all."

"I . . . might've teared up," Eleanor admits with a sniff. "We won't give away any names or too many details, but this girl has a serious anxiety disorder and found *MML* to really help her through therapy. It just—my heart, you guys. My heart."

"We were so bummed that the girl—this badass—couldn't make the meet and greet. Can you imagine? She drove eight hundred miles and didn't even get to meet us," Trish says. "Not to sound incredibly self-involved or anything."

Eleanor laughs and adds, "We're very humble, aren't we? To the young woman and her badass friend—you know who you are—email us! We want to meet you! If we ever do a show in your city or somewhere closer to where you live, we'll hook you up with some tickets."

"And I hope everyone else enjoyed the show!" Trish continues. "These live shows are such a thrill for us, and we're lucky to have fans who are such awesome people. Seriously."

I reach out and pause the podcast.

"Holy shit." I bug my eyes out at Kacey.

"Holy shit," Kacey agrees. "They talked about us! About you! And they're going to get us free tickets!"

I laugh in disbelief. Kacey did this. Kacey spent her meet and greet time talking about *me.* I've never doubted how amazing of a best friend she is, but this proves that there's no one else in the world like her.

"You're the best best friend, you know that, right?"

"I'm well aware." Kacey nudges my foot with hers. "You're the best best friend too."

When I walk into my bedroom later that day, it takes a moment for me to realize what's different. The rug is vacuumed, and a pile of clean laundry rests on my freshly made bed. The shelves are tidied after Dad helped me clean, and the house is as quiet and calm as I remember. All the windows are open, but the air still smells like paint, potent and new.

Because the walls. Those ugly yellow walls are gone. Instead, they've been covered up with a soft shade of lavender. Even though I'm pretty sure my dad was the one who actually did the painting, I have no doubt that this was my mom's idea, and it warms me up from the inside.

I drop my duffel bag on the floor by my closet, then fall backward onto my bed and press my eyes shut.

Home. This is what home feels like.

The exhaustion washing over me feels good. Like I'm only tired because I've accomplished *something*. But I didn't accomplish just one thing.

I survived an eight-hundred-mile road trip and stretches of unknown and sleeping in a tree house. I drove—on the *freeway*. I survived confronting my feelings for Sam—and admitting said feelings to Kacey. I did it *all*.

My obsessive-compulsive disorder will always be an asshole. But it's not in control anymore. I let it be in control—I let fear be in control—for most of my life. I made all my decisions based off my anxiety, bending to its will. I let myself become small. I let my mom instill her wants, and fears, into me until they became my wants and fears too.

I lost myself in the process of trying to protect myself.

"What do you think?" Mom asks, knocking her knuckles to my doorframe. "It's a nice shade of purple, isn't it?"

I blink my eyes open, inhale a deep breath, and exhale slowly. I sit upright and cross my legs. "Yeah, it's perfect. Thank you, Mom."

Mom smiles warmly. "Your dad helped too," she says, then turns around and disappears down the hall.

Part of me wants to ask her to come back, to talk to her about *everything*—like missing Kacey and falling for Sam and all the unknowns unfurling in front of me—but I let her go.

My mom will never be a best friend or a confidant or a Rosemary Hodge. But she loves me. I have no idea what our relationship will be like in the future, but with enough time and family therapy, we'll figure it out.

For now, though, we all still need space. Space to calm down. Space to come to terms with our improved situation and agreements. Space to figure out who we are when we're not tethered to each other.

But I'm glad my space is here, in this house.

I smooth my hands along the comforter and smile.

Home.

KACEY + FLORIE'S WILD AND SUPER-COOL BFF ROAD TRIP BUCKET LIST

~~1. Be spontaneous (yes, Florie, that means YOU)~~

What did I do that WASN'T spontaneous?!

You're the Queen of Spontaneity!

~~2. Find bangin' outfits for the Eleanor and Trish meet and greet~~

We're going to look amazing. AMAZING!

Maybe your self-confidence is rubbing off on me because we totally will!

~~3. Be embarrassing tourists~~

SAY WEIRDOS

WEIRDOS!!!

It's official: I love Portland

And Portland loves you!

~~4. Buy a memento in each state~~

Oregon: Portland touristy T-shirts

California: Confusion Hill baseball caps

Wait. Were we supposed to get something from WA?

No we live there!

~~5. Kiss a random hottie~~

Hanna ♡ 206-555-1978

Does a non-random hottie count?

~~6. Break a traffic law~~

I DROVE ON THE FREEWAY AND DIDN'T DIE OR COMMIT VEHICULAR MANSLAUGHTER!

YOU'RE A BOSS! A CEO OF THE ROAD!

~~7. Say yes, no questions asked~~

Guess I should be glad it was tree houses and not matching tattoos . . . ?

FUCK missed opportunity! Can I take it back? Let's get tattoos!

~~8. Visit a roadside attraction~~

Confusion Hill! Is seeing believing? We visited and still don't know!

Who knows, but I am SO confused right now???

~~9. Anything that makes us ask "Is this a bad idea?"~~

I'm never getting high again

Yes, yes you are

~~10. HAVE THE BEST TIME OF OUR LIVES~~

Unforgettable

Epic

Romantic

So. Much. Fun.

Life changing!

What do you say to making this an annual thing? Florie and Kacey's Summertime Extravaganza?

Wait, no Sam?

Ugh. Why?

The Jeep? Plus, your brother is hot, and I like having him around.

I HATE YOU ☺

EPILOGUE

Barmouth, WA

FRIDAY, AUGUST 26, AND SATURDAY, AUGUST 27
ONE WEEK LATER

Tomorrow, Kacey's leaving for Portland, and tonight is her going-away party.

Rosemary and Alec are throwing the shindig in their backyard, and since they didn't need our help with the setup, the three of us head to the lake. Summer might be winding down, but the lake and its beaches are crowded with late-season tourists. The heat's still hanging on and brought everyone out in droves to the small body of water, smack-dab in the center of Barmouth.

Despite the busyness, we nab one of the floating docks at the public beach.

Kacey unloads a tote and a stack of towels onto one of the damp dock planks, while Sam drops a mini cooler beside us.

"Snacks and drinks," he says, pointing to the cooler. "But Mom packed them, so proceed at your own risk."

Kacey snorts. "I have real snacks in the tote."

"You're my favorite sister." He pulls out a bag of sea salt and vinegar chips.

I slide off my slip-ons and sit on the edge of the dock, hanging my legs over the edge. My toes brush the surface of the water. Sam lowers himself beside me; he smells like sunscreen and pine deodorant. The side of his body—hips and waist and arm and shoulder—presses solidly into mine.

Kacey kicks off her sandals, then tugs off her cover-up and leaps off the dock, cannonballing into the water. When she surfaces, she shrieks at the water. "Fuck, it's cold!"

Sam chuckles and pops open his bag of chips. "Want one?" he offers, tilting the bag toward me.

I wrinkle my nose. "Satan's chips, remember?"

Laughing, he shakes his head, then pops a chip into his mouth. "You're weird." After swallowing, he adds, "But I'm into it."

In the water, Kacey disappears beneath the surface. When she resurfaces, she calls over, "Are you two coming in? It's actually not too bad once you get used to it. That or I'm going numb."

"Maybe later," Sam calls back, then sets his nasty chips aside. He brushes his hands off, then wraps his arm around me. I lean my head onto his shoulder and shut my eyes, the warmth of the sun and the body beside me calming and comforting.

"You two are nauseating," Kacey says, and when I open my eyes, she's swimming toward the rock past the buoys.

After a moment, Sam says, "I double-checked my school schedule. I don't have to be back in Idaho until the second week of September. I'll probably leave the ninth."

Over the last week, Sam and I have spent *a lot* of time together. Whenever I wasn't with Kacey, I was with Sam. And even if no list was involved, Sam and I have been pretty intent on making sure our limited time together is memorable.

Last weekend, we parked the Jeep on the back road outside of town and folded the seats back, kissing and laughing and breathing each other in. After therapy last week, we went to the two-screen movie theater downtown and teased each other over our candy preferences. Yesterday he convinced me to go on a really ill-advised hike, where I almost broke my ankle; he let me use him as a human crutch on our walk back to the Jeep.

But like my best friend, Sam's moving on too.

"Two weeks," I say, and keep my tone light. Shifting to face him on the dock, I smile. "Luckily for you, I have absolutely no plans between now and then. I'm all yours."

Sam's in swim trunks and a plain white T-shirt. His hair is messy, the sides growing out into soft, dark waves curling against his scalp. He's traded his glasses for prescription sunglasses, and whenever he smiles at me, they scrunch up the bridge of his nose.

"Yeah?" he says. "Do you have plans for that weekend? The ninth?"

"Doubtful. Why?"

"You could come with me, if you want." Sam drags his fingers through his hair. "I could show you around, and we could hang out all weekend. And I could take you back Monday. Or if you wanted to stay until the following weekend, I could drive you back then."

"Really?" I grin, and my heart lifts in my chest. "Isn't that like an eight-hour drive?"

"Yeah, but that means eight hours with you, Florence Nightingale."

"If I agree, will you stop calling me Florence Nightingale?"

"Nah, sorry." Sam bumps his shoulder against mine. "The nickname fits you perfectly. I remember the first day Kacey brought you over to the house. I'd cut myself working out back and you pulled a Band-Aid out of your bag and handed it to me. The similarities are uncanny."

I laugh, my face flushing with embarrassment. "You remember that? I barely even remember that."

"What? Were you too blown away by my good looks to remember?" he says, and I resist the urge to push him into the lake. Because he's not entirely wrong. "So. Idaho. You in?"

"Definitely." I reach for Sam's hand—which is braced on the dock between us, and he laces his fingers with mine. "But are you sure you won't get sick of me?" I joke, except maybe I'm worried the tiniest bit that he might. If not between now and then, when we're in Idaho.

He gives me an amused smile. "You really think I could get sick of you?"

I shrug one shoulder. "I get sick of me."

Sam falls silent for a moment and glances out at the water. Kacey's currently sitting on the rock beyond the buoys, wringing out her curls. "Do you want to know what I think?" he asks, taking off his sunglasses and setting them on the dock.

"Um, sure?" I say uneasily, because the way he's staring at me is *very* weird.

"I won't get sick of you." Sam brushes his thumb over my knuckles. "But if we spend more time together, I might fall more in love with you."

My heart slams into my rib cage, stealing my breath and any chance at a response. Because Sam just said he loves me. *Me.* I almost look over my shoulder to make sure he's not talking to someone else. But before I can, Sam bridges the very narrow gap between us to kiss me. A light brush of his lips—since we promised minimal displays of affection around Kacey and she's technically still within sight.

When he pulls back, Sam says, "I love you, Flor. But you don't have to say anything. You hate the unknown, so I wanted you to know where I'm at. One less unknown, okay?"

One less unknown.

I fall even more in love with Sam, hearing those three words. He understands me—more than I've given him credit for—and he still loves me. And it's the best feeling in the world.

I shift closer and rest my forehead to his. "I love you too, Sam."

Sam's mouth is on mine the second his name leaves my lips. And it's not a Kacey-sanctioned kiss. Oh no, this kiss is a full-on and graphic display of affection. It's messy and earnest and somehow says all the things I haven't gotten to say yet: that I've loved Sam for so long I can barely remember what it's like *not* loving him, that I want him—not only for the rest of summer, but even after he's back in Idaho, and that, despite our messiness and miscommunications, I believe in us.

Cold water splashes across my face, and I shriek, pulling back from Sam.

In the lake by our feet is Kacey, who scowls at us as she treads water. "All I asked was that you two don't go totally horndog in front of me!" She splashes us with more water, and I hold up my hands, as if that does anything. "Was that so difficult?"

Sam's laughing, his cheeks rosy red, and his smile is the most endearing thing. He takes off his shirt—that's never going to get old—then slides off the dock and into the water. He splashes Kacey in the face, and she sputters.

I tug off my cover-up and brace myself as I lower myself into the icy water to help Sam gang up on Kacey. And even though my best friend will be leaving for college in less than twenty-four hours, I don't lean into the sadness, or obsess over what this will mean for our friendship.

For once, I stay present.

The following morning, Kacey wakes up before me. Which I can say, with complete certainty, has never ever happened before in our two years of friendship. But I'd be excited too if I were leaving for college today.

"How many cups of coffee have you had?" I ask from the

edge of Kacey's bed as I help throw all the last-minute stuff that she forgot to pack into a reusable shopping bag.

"Two." Kacey drops to her knees to peer beneath her bed to check for any orphaned shoes. She pops back up empty-handed. "Wait, three."

I toss an eye shadow palette into the bag. "You sure that's a good idea?" I think back to the frequent bathroom breaks we had to make on our road trip.

"Mom won't care," she says. "Besides, we're in no rush. Orientation is on Monday. I'm taking the weekend to get settled."

Rosemary's driving Kacey and an entire minivan full of her stuff down to Portland in about a half hour. And maybe if I keep distracting myself with packing and logistics and checking Google Maps traffic updates, I won't have to focus on how much I hate this.

Because I really hate this.

Yesterday, at the lake, and afterward, at Kacey's going-away party, I was able to stay present. But now Kacey leaving *is* the present, and there's no outrunning this, no matter how much I wish there were.

"I think we got everything." Kacey stands beside the bed and surveys her empty bedroom. The only items left behind are the furniture and a few boxes of childhood memorabilia Rosemary's planning on storing in the attic.

I hold out the tote. "Probably. I don't think I've ever seen your room this clean."

"Me either," she admits, and takes the tote. "Be right back!"

With way, way too much energy for nine in the morning, Kacey skips out of her bedroom, and I lie flat on my back on her bed, staring up at the ceiling. I knew this moment was coming—Kacey wasn't meant for a small town like Barmouth—but it still stings. After all the good that's happened over the last few weeks, I'm still lying here, on the verge of tears.

I'm happy for Kacey, but I'm also sad for me.

"Okay." Kacey walks back into her bedroom, and the mattress sinks as she sits down beside me. Poking me in the ribs, she says, "Sit up. I have something for you."

I haul myself upright and blink back any tears. "You're not going to try giving me your thigh-highs again, are you?" Kacey owned two pairs of these ridiculous thigh-high boots and tried convincing me to take the second pair so she wouldn't have to give them away.

"Nah, my mom already took them to Goodwill. RIP." Kacey shakes her head mournfully, then shoves a wrapped package into my hands. "Here. Definitely more your style."

I rotate the package in my hands, my heart somewhere in my throat. At this point, even if she tried gifting me those thigh-highs, I'd probably start crying. I take a deep, shaky breath, and unwrap it. Beneath the floral wrapping paper is a picture frame.

Kacey leans over. "It actually folds out," she says, and shows me. The frame is a trifold, each with its own photo. The first is our framed list, messy and wrinkled with our notes and doodles all over it; we checked off everything. The second is one of Kacey's meet-and-greet photos with Eleanor and Trish.

And the third is what looks like a letter. "We can replace the meet-and-greet photo with one of the both of us later."

I sink into Kacey, and she wraps her arm around me. "This is amazing, thank you." My throat tightens, and I stare at the three frames. "What's this last one?"

"My journal entry from the day we met, after you came over to my house," Kacey says. "I thought you'd maybe want to read it. But wait until after I leave, okay? I'm already emotional enough as is."

I set the frames down and hug Kacey. "Thank you."

"Thank *you*," she says, holding me close, "for being the very best friend I could ever ask for."

That does it, and the tears roll down my cheeks. "You're the best."

"I know." Kacey sniffs loudly, and when we part, she grabs a tissue box off her bedside table. She laughs, her mascara bleeding onto her cheeks. "We're such messy bitches, huh?"

I blow my nose and laugh a tiny bit too. "Seriously."

"Knock knock." Rosemary pokes her head into Kacey's room. Her face crumples at the sight of us, and if she starts crying too, I'm done for. But she keeps it together and says, "Sorry to interrupt, but are you ready to go?"

Kacey glances over at me, and I want to beg her to stay longer. Remind her that they're not on a strict schedule and what's a few more hours? But instead, I nod. Almost like I'm giving her permission to leave me behind, that I'll be okay.

"Yeah, I'll be right down," Kacey tells Rosemary, who watches us sadly for a moment before retreating down the hallway.

I grab another tissue and wipe away my tears, even though the waterworks aren't close to being over. "Text me when you get there?"

"Duh. You're not getting rid of me that easily."

"It's going to be great, you know," I tell her. "College. You're going to rule that school in no time."

A laugh catches in Kacey's throat. "I really hope so." She stands and tugs me to my feet. "Guess this is it."

"Guess so." I hug Kacey as tightly as possible, and she hugs me back, and we both start crying again.

If I had my way, I'd keep dragging this moment out, but eventually Kacey lets me go. She wipes her tears back with her hand. "Wanna walk out to the car with me?"

"Nah." I motion to the photo frame. "I think I'd rather do all my crying in solitude."

Kacey slings her purse over her shoulder and smiles, her eyes glassy. "Bye, babe."

"Bye." The word comes out choked, but I return her smile and give Kacey permission to go. After hesitating, she hugs me again and steps out into the hallway.

I sink back onto Kacey's bed with the box of tissues and her gift.

The journal entry is one page, dated two years ago almost to the day, and once I stop crying long enough to see clearly, I begin reading.

Dear journal,

Okay, junior year isn't off to a bad start. Today I met the coolest girl named Florie and guess what?! She ALSO loves MML and lives like a ten minute walk away. It's friendship fate, I'm telling you. She came over after school and we talked about all our favorite episodes, and she ate Mom's nastyass vegan cauliflower wings without complaining once. Even Sam seems to like her. I don't know, we totally clicked, and I've never had a friend like her before. Is that weird? We barely know each other but I know that we're meant to be friends. I even told her about my crush on Veronica and she said they had bio together and she'd put in a good word for me.

Anyways! I am so excited to have like a friend-friend at Barmouth High. Ever since Madison moved and Sam got way too cool to hang out with his little sister, it's been so lonely. But maybe Florie can be my person. That one best friend who sticks by me no matter what, from high school all the way until we're terrorizing the nursing staff at some retirement home. The Trish to my Eleanor. I kind of feel like she can. - K

Footsteps pound up the stairs, and I swipe at my tears with a fresh tissue.

"Hey." I try—and fail—to smile as Sam steps into Kacey's bedroom.

"She's off," he says, and drums his hands on his thighs. "You doing okay?"

"Yeah. No." I shrug, my hands full of tear-dampened tissues. "I mean, it's terrible, but I'll be okay."

He motions to the bed. "Want some company?"

I grab Sam's hand and pull him down beside me.

"Less terrible now," I admit as I lie against his chest, even though I'm crying again. Sam kisses my hair and wipes away my tears with the sleeve of his flannel. Through the fabric of his shirt, I can hear the slow, steady thump of his heart. And I breathe.

Everything *is* terrible, but here's the difference: I'll be okay. The terribleness will pass, my tears will dry, and I'll be okay. Because I'm exactly where I need to be. Not here, in Kacey's bedroom with Samson Hodge to lean on—although that part is really, really nice—but in a moment where the only direction I can move is forward.

Not just with Sam, but with a part-time job and college.

My future is open-ended, full of more possibilities than I can imagine.

And instead of fear, I can't wait to discover what's next.

ACKNOWLEDGMENTS

All the thanks in the world to my fierce and lovely agent, Melanie Figueroa. After every email and phone call, I'm reminded of how lucky I am to have you in my corner. You are simply, undeniably, the best. Additional thanks to everyone at Root Literary, for being so supportive and welcoming me into the fold. And thank you to Heather Baror-Shapiro at Baror International, Mary Pender at UTA, and Kathleen Carter at KCC. Thank you all, so very much, for being on my team.

Thank you to my editor, Jessi Smith. Not only were you empathetic and compassionate toward our anxious-stressed-true-crime-obsessed girl Florie, but you helped turn that introspective draft into an actual book with an actual plot! (Thinky girls forever!) Thank you to Simon Pulse, the imprint that originally acquired this book, and Books for Young Readers for carrying it across the finish line. Endless gratitude to Katrina Groover, and to cover designer Krista Vossen and artist Jeff Östberg for bringing Florie and Sam to life. This is the loveliest cover that I have *ever* seen.

Thank you to Britney Brouwer and Rachel Simon, this book's very first readers. You both loved Florie, Sam, and Kacey, and gave me the boost to see this story to completion. Much love to Erin Cotter, Elora Ditton, Sabrina Lotfi, Jenna Miller, Emily Miner, Page Powars, Kylie Schachte, and the Mel's Belles for the friendship and support! And thank you to my adventuring friends, Cooper, Phil, and Trent, for reminding me a world outside of publishing does indeed exist.

Many thanks to Karen Kilgariff, Georgia Hardstark, and the entire *My Favorite Murder* community—SSDGM.

Thank you to Heather, who shared with me one life-changing sentence, *"The feelings are real, the thoughts are not."* My OCD will never be gone but, because of you, it's only a speed bump, not a barrier. Thank you to Eve, for always listening.

As always, thank you to my amazing family, who have supported me and my bookish dreams every step of the way. Chin scrubs to Sofiya, the best emotional support cat an anxious girl could ever ask for; the allergies are worth it. And a thousand million thank-yous to Steve for accompanying me to rest stop bathrooms on road trips so I won't get kidnapped and/or murdered. Jokes aside, thank you for understanding me in all the ways that matter most, and keeping the Amelia Train on its tracks. I love you.

AUTHOR'S NOTE

Dearest reader,

Maybe you're a true crime addict like I am, maybe you randomly plucked this book off a shelf, or maybe you wanted to read about OCD. No matter the reason, thank you so much for picking up this book—you're my new favorite person!

Exactly Where You Need to Be is the book of my heart and my soul for many reasons. I was diagnosed with obsessive-compulsive disorder in high school, but unlike Florie, I didn't seek help until a decade later. As I began treatment, I knew I wanted to write a story with a character who shared my disorder. And five years later, I'm lucky enough to share that book with readers.

I intentionally began Florie's story as she's finding happiness and independence while coping with her mental illness, rather than the throes of untreated obsessive-compulsive disorder. While those stories are important, I believe it's equally important to show how much you can thrive *with* a mental illness. The journey is never easy, and Florie is privileged to have access to a support system, therapies, and medications to help her cope. At the end of this letter, you'll find several fantastic resources for OCD, as well as general mental health support.

Florie's mental health journey shares many similarities with my own, but it's entirely a work of fiction. No mental health journey is the same and obsessive-compulsive disorder can display an array of symptoms not mentioned in this book. If you're at all concerned that you might be suffering from OCD, know that you are not alone, and please reach out for help.

The International OCD Foundation:
https://iocdf.org/

The National Alliance on Mental Illness (NAMI):
https://www.nami.org/

Beyond OCD: http://beyondocd.org/

Anxiety and Depression Association of America:
https://adaa.org/